AF407622

SANDOVER BEACH FOREVER

A SANDOVER ISLAND BOOK

EMMA ST. CLAIR

For the Rob
It was anything but instalove but thankfully, I wore you down
over time

And to Ginny & Fiona-
If we hadn't gotten stuck in that elevator, this series wouldn't be
the same

CHAPTER ONE

Amber never thought of God as cruel. Not when the guy of her dreams, Jimmy, broke up with her (publicly, no less) for his childhood sweetheart, a literal supermodel. Not when she lost her group of friends because it was too awkward to hang around Jimmy and Emily.

Not even when her mom died in a car accident a few months ago. That was the hardest pill to swallow, both for Amber and for her dad. But still … no bitterness.

Pain? yes. Questions about how this fit into God's plan? You bet! But Amber didn't feel like he was smiting her or something.

Why start thinking God is cruel now? Amber wondered, reaching across the big desk to shake the doctor's hand.

He stared at her for a moment, which is when she realized that it was probably weird to shake your doctor's hand after he told you that you have ovarian cancer at age twenty-six. In the same hospital where your mother died a few months earlier.

Still, he shook it, his blue eyes sympathetic. His hand was

firm and dry, just what a doctor's hand should be. Secure. Stable. Trustworthy.

"For what it's worth, women survive this kind of cancer all the time," he said.

Amber couldn't help asking the next question, or keep the bitter edge from her voice. "And go on to have children?"

His mouth tightened, his sympathy turning to something more like pity.

"Only in the most unlikely of cases. I'm very sorry, Amber."

She nodded and smiled, excusing herself before she said or did something more awkward and embarrassing. Like wail or cry or throw his bowl of hard candy at the wall. Dr. Espana had probably gotten used to strong reactions, but Amber would be better than that. She would be ...

She would be ...

The words hovered at the edge of her mind like fog. She would be *what*?

"Fine," she said, not meaning to say the word out loud. Dr. Espana gave her a look. She cleared her throat. "I'll be fine."

"I have no doubt. We've got your first treatment scheduled for next week. As soon as we see how things are progressing we can schedule surgery. If you need to talk to someone, we have—"

"I've got the pamphlet," Amber said, waving it in the air before shoving it into the dark recesses of her purse. It held the basics of ovarian cancer, all reduced into a trifold color printout. The last thing she wanted to do was talk to anyone else about it.

Amber forced herself to walk through the lobby staring straight ahead, not making eye contact with anyone, not running for the door, not standing and shaking her fist at the sky.

I'm not bitter, she told herself. *God is still good.*

I'll be fine.

But she really, really wished her mom was there to hold her hand.

CHAPTER TWO

A glass and a half of wine later, she felt only more confident of her fineness. *Wine is wonderful! Wine is fine —and that rhymes! Why don't I do this more?*

The *this* was sitting at a bar, drinking moscato alone. Neither of which were very like Amber. A pleasant warmth seeped through her chest, and she felt a lightness, a happiness that had eluded her, not just today, but for months. Years, maybe.

She had decided as she walked out of Dr. Espana's office, blinking in the almost-summer sun that seemed far too cheerful, that it was high time to start doing things outside of the box.

It was *not* a bucket list. Definitely not. Dr. Espana had said many women survived. Amber would be one of them, even if her dream of having biological children had died in that office. No, this was more of a ... *living* list.

"And I haven't really lived. Not really," she said, leaning closer to the gleaming wooden bar. The bartender nodded.

She was an hour early to dinner with her father, and the

bar was almost empty. Which left the bartender, who had become a captive audience to her occasional attempts at conversation. He was close to her dad's age, with a decent bit of gray around his temples. Which made him feel decidedly safe.

The few other patrons ignored her, all of them with another friend or significant other. No younger, single guy in sight.

Not that Amber needed to be thinking about dating right now. If she hadn't found anyone she liked since Jimmy dumped her over a year ago, how likely was it now? She could imagine the small talk on a first date.

"I'm Amber! I'm an event planner, I like dogs, and I'm about to start an aggressive cancer treatment that may or may not work but will prevent me from having biological children."

Yep. Dating right now would be *swell*.

"Did you go to Catholic school or something?" the bartender asked, drying a glass with a rag. "Homeschool?"

"Me?" Amber giggled, then threw a hand over her mouth.

"You, uh, said that you haven't really lived."

Right. She had said that out loud. "Nope. Just … a good girl, I guess."

"I like good girls."

The bartender grinned, and it made something twist a little in her stomach. Until now, he had seemed like the kind of man her father would call a *nice fellow*.

But now, his smile was not nice at all. It made her think of an alley cat who had just spotted a whole bag of fish scraps.

Does that make me the fish scraps in this scenario?

She hiccupped. And *this* was why she didn't do this kind of thing, drinking alone in a bar. Amber shook her head, trying to clear it. She wasn't too wine-addled, and there weren't two of anything in her vision. That was good. She had never been drunk but knew the signs to watch out for. So far, she was a little tipsy, but not in her cups, as her father would say. She needed to *stay* out of her cups considering her father would be here soon.

Her eyes flicked away from the bartender, who stood so close on the other side of the bar that his cologne drifted to her nose, making her want to sneeze it away. She looked behind her, scanning the restaurant. The restaurant was starting to fill, the noise picking up, and when Amber turned back to the bar, she was thankful that a few other people had settled onto stools, drawing the bartender and his feral-cat smile away.

"Saved by the bell," she muttered, taking another sip of wine.

"I didn't hear a bell."

The voice was so close to her ear that the man's breath tickled Amber's cheek and made the small hairs rise on the back of her neck. He smelled of leather and masculine spice.

Her nerves had started to fray, which explained why she dropped her wineglass. It would have shattered on the floor had the man now sitting on the stool next to her not grabbed it. A little wine sloshed out, making a damp circle on her black pants.

Thanks, favorite black pants, she thought to herself. *You're always here for me when handsome strangers make me spill my wine.*

Handsome might not have been an adequate enough word, she realized, looking fully in his face. The man who held out her glass to her was *art*. He could grace magazine covers or calendars. He could sell the ugliest sweaters on QVC or the slowest cars with the worst gas mileage and no airbags. Amber would buy anything he was selling.

"Whoa," he said, still holding out her glass. "I'm sorry. Didn't mean to startle you."

"I'm easily startled. Like a baby deer," she babbled. "It's not you; it's me."

He grinned, and Amber wanted to drop through the floor. But he seemed amused in a good way, and she didn't want to stop looking at him. His golden brown hair glinted under the lights, and he had eyes the pale blue of the sky at the horizon's edge.

Art, she thought again with a little thump of her heart.

"It's a little soon for the *it's not you, it's me* talk, isn't it?" he asked. "We haven't even had a proper date, or a first kiss."

A date? A *kiss?*

Now, Amber laughed, feeling heat climb up her neck. She'd gone a year and a half without so much as a guy looking at her twice. Now that she had been diagnosed with cancer, a bartender was hitting on her and a handsome stranger was flirting. God might not be cruel, but it seemed he had a sense of humor. And maybe, just maybe, this man was a gift, delivered at the end of a rotten day.

He was close to her age, maybe late twenties, and his comment didn't make her feel squirmy and uncomfortable the way the bartender had. This guy was definitely flirting, but it was friendly, not smarmy.

He hardly took his eyes off her as he ordered a beer, and thankfully, the bartender seemed too busy now to care that Amber had company.

"I'm Nick," he said, turning back to her, beer in hand.

"Amber."

"It's good to meet you." That winning smile appeared again, and he sipped his beer. "If I ask if you come here often, will you promise not to think it's a terrible pick-up line? I'm new to Sandover, and I really don't know where I should be spending my time."

With me, she thought.

Out loud, she said something almost as scandalous. "What if I want it to be a pick-up line?"

Amber wanted to die of mortification. She really wasn't drunk! But the wine had loosened her honesty, or loosened the guards she usually kept over her tongue.

Nick blinked in surprise, his eyes bright with amusement. That slow grin returned, making her heart do a little skip.

"I like a woman who says what she thinks."

Amber bit her lip. "I usually don't." She stared down at the damp spot on her pants from the spilled wine. It was starting to dry, as though it had never happened at all.

Nick's voice dropped, the rough edge of it softening. "Hey, that's okay too. But I happen to like honesty."

His fingertips brushed her bare arm, making her shiver. *Embarrassing!* Amber glanced at Nick from under her lashes, but his face was open and warm. Taking a breath, she met his gaze again.

"I don't usually come here often. Just twice a month with my dad for dinner."

"I'm meeting my mom." Then, in a teasing tone and with another smile that made her heart shimmy, he exclaimed, "We have so much in common!"

She laughed. Nick chuckled and took a sip of his beer, twisting the bottle in his hands when he finished, still studying her with an intensity that made her feel excited and nervous at the same time.

"Just visiting? Or are you here for a while?"

Amber was fishing, but Nick didn't seem to mind.

"Permanently. Or, at least, for a while. My mom finally convinced me that I was missing out on island living. I'm a little concerned it's a mistake, that she's going to be trying to fix me up or just micromanage my life."

Fix me up. So, he was single? Hopefully so—otherwise, his flirting would make him the absolute worst.

"My dad is the same way. Not as bad as—"

Amber stopped herself just before she mentioned her mother. Swallowing, she took a quick sip of wine. Mentioning your dead mother was how light conversation got heavy *fast*. Remembering her mom also totally mellowed her out, and Amber didn't want to lose the unfamiliar happiness coursing through her.

"Anyway, if you're new, this probably isn't where you'll be hanging out a lot. Mostly the older crowd, and some of the *On Islanders*." She lowered her voice. "That's what the locals who have lived here forever call themselves. You're Off Island."

The corner of Nick's mouth lifted, and he gestured between them. "Does that make this a Romeo and Juliet story?"

She didn't want to read too much into the fact that he was referencing one of the greatest love stories—never mind the tragedy part—except she also really *did* want to read into it. Amber wanted to latch on to that idea and run with it.

"You're not exactly a guy from the wrong side of the tracks," she said.

"Just the wrong side of the ocean?"

"The sound." She pointed toward the sound side of the island. "That body of water is the Currituck Sound. Technically, I guess you're a guy from the wrong side of the sound. Aka, a landlubber."

Nick laughed. "Answer me this, On Island girl—is dancing outlawed here too? Is there a controlling preacher who tells everyone how to behave?"

"Dancing is totally fine. And there's actually a really great church here. Not controlling at all. If you're looking for a church, that is."

Another stupid comment Amber wanted to kick herself for. *That's one way to crash and burn a conversation,* Amber thought. There's a reason people say to avoid politics and religion over dinner. It probably holds doubly true at a bar.

"I'd like that, actually." Nick shifted in his seat. "If you have a recommendation, I'd love that."

Hot, funny, friendly, and wants to go to church. If Amber had a list for the perfect guy, which she certainly had not created in a Google doc, this guy ticked all the boxes. What's more, he made her *feel* something. For months, she had been feeling either nothing or a deep, dark sadness. Nick made her heart feel light again, as though it had emerged from some dark basement into the bright sun. Even before her mother's death, the last guy who made her pulse quicken was Jimmy.

That's when the other shoe dropped, which didn't surprise Amber at all. Because who was cozied up in a booth tucked away on the other side of the bar? Jimmy and his gorgeous wife, Emily.

As Amber watched, Jimmy nuzzled her neck, and Emily laughed—right before her eyes met Amber's. Emily's eyes widened for a moment, and then she glanced away, saying something to Jimmy. He also looked her way, then pulled away from Emily as they studied their menus with forced casualness.

It didn't hurt to see them together. Amber got over Jimmy not long after he broke up with her. But the awkwardness was painful whenever she ran into them, which was about as often as you'd think on a small island.

"Hey, you still with me? I thought I lost you for a second," Nick said.

Amber forced a smile, trying to ignore Emily and Jimmy in the background. Though, honestly, if it appeared like she was on a date, that couldn't hurt.

"Sorry. I'm here. Just … got caught up in my head. It happens sometimes."

"It's a pretty head to be caught up in."

Whoo, boy! This man was a sweet talker. Or was sweet. Maybe both? Amber finished her wine in a quick swallow. The bartender appeared, and Nick nodded for another beer.

Nick tapped her hand, which was still loosely holding the empty wineglass. The light touch made her shiver.

"So, Amber. Would you like to take on the role of my official tour guide?"

She would take on about any role he asked for right now. "I'd be happy to show you around in whatever capacity you'd like. Dancing is also optional. I do like dancing."

His broad shoulders relaxed, and he gave her a brilliant smile. "I'd like that. Though I'll warn you—I have four left feet, not just two. But only if we can call it a date."

A date.

A *date*!?

Would she even know how to behave? Had all the rules changed since she dated Jimmy a year and a half ago? Amber felt panic like a fist squeezing her throat. She hazarded a glance over to the booth and both Jimmy and Emily jerked their heads away, like they'd been watching.

Good! Let them watch.

The momentary distraction kept Nick's words from sinking in fully. When they did, Amber almost fell off her stool.

"A d-date?" She never stuttered. Never. So, of course this would be the inaugural moment.

Nick's eyes softened, and he dropped the flirtation. "Was

I presumptuous in thinking you might be single? Or … interested? You said your father was the same as my mother with the, uh, matchmaking. I thought—"

"I'm single."

He smiled, then stared down at his beer for a moment before meeting her eyes again. It was adorable the way he fumbled with his words, just a hair's breadth from stuttering himself. He had confidence, but humility too. Not a shred of cockiness in sight.

This guy was the kind of guy she could really fall for. Or, was already starting to fall for? Not that you could know someone that well in ten minutes. Amber tried to tell herself that, because it already felt like a big piece of her heart had let Nick stake a very real claim. She had never believed in instalove, but this felt like insta-really-really-really-like.

"I haven't dated anyone in a year and a half," Amber blurted. "I'm rusty."

That certainly didn't need to be said. Amber fanned her face. In the future experiments with living, one glass of wine would do, at least on an empty stomach. There was also the very real sense that Jimmy and Emily were watching her.

"That's not a problem." Nick's grin touched her, like a fingertip trailing up her spine slowly, leaving heat in its wake. "I'd prefer not to imagine you with anyone else."

Ooooh, hello, touch of alpha male. That made for a combination Amber liked even more. Sweet, but possessive. Wait—was he already feeling possessive about her? Did he hate thinking about her dating other people?

Nick continued, oblivious to the way her thoughts were carrying her away. "Is the island so hard up for eligible gentlemen?"

"What?"

"I only meant to say that there must be a shortage of men

if you are still single." He grimaced, setting the bottle on the bar and wiping his hands over his dark jeans. "But, I realize that also sounds like a line. I'm sorry."

His smile appeared, then faded as he peeled the label from his beer with clean, short nails. Strong fingers. They would feel good wrapped around her waist. Strong, and firm. Secure and warm.

The flush from earlier returned, creeping from the center of Amber's chest to her cheeks. She shouldn't be considering the way his hands would feel wrapped around her, not when she'd known him less time than it would take to watch an episode of *The Office*.

Nick's eyes, like a cut piece of crystal hiding sapphire underneath, drew hers.

"Don't be sorry. As I said before, I wouldn't mind you using lines on me."

Amber knew she shouldn't answer so quickly, sound so desperate for his affection, which had hardly been earned. She hadn't been at top form. Stuttering, saying stupid things, and getting defensive didn't usually get you the guy. Did he see something else in her? Hard to imagine.

Amber knew she had a pretty enough face and a body that, while it wasn't in the *wouldn't quit* category, at least fell into the realm of *wouldn't look too terrible in a bathing suit*. Still, she wasn't the kind of woman who commanded attention. Made only more obvious by the fact that Emily sat with Jimmy *right over there*, looking all beautiful and modelesque with her legs for days and long, blonde hair.

Amber decided she didn't care why Nick was interested in going on a date with her. He was attractive, seemed like a decent guy, and wanted to go out with her. She wanted to go out with him, like now. If it came down to skipping dinner with her father, she'd do it in a heartbeat.

With a sinking feeling, Amber remembered her appointment with Dr. Espana just a few hours ago. There was an ovarian cancer pamphlet at the bottom of her purse, probably next to a few gum wrappers and a receipt from CVS.

She had *cancer*. Maybe she would survive, a woman with a permanently useless womb. And maybe she wouldn't.

In front of her was a handsome, charming man who made her feel things she hadn't ever felt. He was *interested in her*. And he was having dinner with his mom, further proof that he was a good, trustworthy guy.

I want to live, Amber thought. If not for long, at least for now. It was time to do brave things. The kinds of things she normally wouldn't ever do. Her living list, not her bucket list.

And that thought made Amber lean closer, resting her hand on Nick's shoulder, whispering, "Would you think less of me if I asked you to kiss me?"

Had she planned this out, the way Amber did most things, she might have made a contingency plan. It would have come in handy right at that moment. Nick's eyes widened, and his smile turned nervous. He chuckled, rubbing a hand up the back of his neck.

And THAT'S why I don't go outside the box. The box is safe and warm and doesn't result in total humiliation.

Amber was on her feet, muttering an apology before she had even taken a breath, hoping Jimmy and Emily weren't watching *this* part. But those same strong fingers she'd been admiring grasped her elbow gently, holding her in place.

"Amber—"

"I'm sorry." She couldn't face him again. She couldn't. But she did let him stop her, let herself soak up his quiet touch, the affection she had been so starved for. A tiny indulgence.

"No, I'm the one who's sorry. You just surprised me."

"I surprised myself," she said. "I got some news today. Unexpected. Disappointing. I've got an uncomfortable conversation coming up with my dad. And I think I hit the wine on an empty stomach."

Nick's fingers traced up the inside of her elbow. "So, you only asked to kiss me because of the wine and a bad day? No other reason?"

He was teasing her, lessening the awkwardness of the moment.

"Maybe another reason. Or two."

Amber resisted leaning into his touch, but barely. Her self-control was held by a thread. When Nick's fingers tightened, spinning her gently toward him, that thread snapped.

Their eyes met, his blue chips of ice and her own boring brown. What did he see when he looked at her? What caused the intensity of his gaze now?

He pulled her closer until she stood between his knees, his hands warm anchors on her waist. Those strong fingers felt just as she had imagined they would. The scent of him, aged leather and spice, rose up stronger than it had when he first sat down.

"Could I try to answer that question again?" Nick asked.

"W-what?"

The caress of his gaze fell to her lips. What was happening? She felt his eyes on her mouth, as warmly as though his fingertips rested there instead. An invisible touch.

"You asked me something a moment ago and I ..." He swallowed, licking his lips before continuing. "I didn't respond as I should have."

"Oh?"

Her mind hardly registered his words. Something about a response. Who could follow conversation when a man who looked like Nick stood so close? And how did such a strong face come to have such soft lips?

Lips that were coming closer …

"I definitely don't think less of you for asking me to kiss you. May I?"

The question had hardly left his lips when Amber realized he actually meant to kiss her. Even though she had been the one to ask him, somehow the reality of it hadn't registered. Not until now.

And then, as her gaze shot up to his eyes, he did kiss her.

It was the lightest, softest, most perfect kiss Amber had ever known. His strong hands tugged at her waist as his mouth met hers. It ignited something in Amber. A desire for more—and not just more kisses. More of him. *All* of him. She felt slightly feral, and had to hold back something like a growl when he pulled back.

Nick brushed one fingertip over her cheek as he pulled away, ripping a bit of her heart with him as he went.

There weren't words for how deeply that brief, sweet kiss rattled her soul. Nick's hands dropped away, his lips parted, he blinked, looking every bit as overcome as she felt. Could he possibly feel as much as she did? It seemed impossible, considering the fact that Amber felt far more than she should after this brief conversation and even briefer kiss.

Amber stepped back, needing distance before she did something stupid, like kissing him again or climbing into his lap. She searched for words, but there were none. What do you say after that kind of kiss? Nothing. Words would only take away from the moment they just shared.

She took one more step back, noting with a tiny bit of satisfaction that Jimmy and Emily were watching.

That's when she heard her father's voice behind her. "Amber! There you are."

Could he have had worse timing?

Actually, yes. He could have walked in while we were kissing. That would have been terrible.

When she turned, Nick stood, moving beside her, still keeping what seemed like a safe distance between them.

Amber lifted a hand when her father did, only then noticing the woman beside him. Not just beside him, but clutching his arm in a familiar way. Looking nervous, yet ecstatic. She waved, and Amber froze when Nick raised his hand to wave back.

Half turning, Amber exchanged a confused glance with Nick. Understanding passed over his features first, and he squeezed his eyes shut, saying only one word. "Unbelievable."

The realization slid into place only a moment before it was confirmed by her father. And *unbelievable* was right.

"We meant to tell you both the happy news over dinner, and it looks like you're a step ahead of us."

Her father smiled, a familiar grin, one that usually could cheer up Amber's darkest mood. Today that smile was like the sound of a slamming door.

"Amber, meet Linda, my fiancée." He grinned again, his eyes sliding to the woman beside him. The affection there made Amber feel the wine sloshing around in her stomach. "And you've clearly met Nick, soon to be your stepbrother."

CHAPTER THREE

Of all the women in the world to kiss, especially after vowing to avoid women altogether, Nick had kissed his future *stepsister*. That felt like two degrees away from kissing your cousin. He was lucky to be able to keep down his dinner.

Especially when Amber was seated across from him and he had to keep seeing her beautiful eyes. And the lips he had kissed not an hour before. Her twin dimples, which made every smile that much more, were nowhere to be seen.

Stepsister. Stepsister. STEP. SISTER.

Chanting this in his head only gave him a headache. Which served to make Nick's dark mood more bleak.

He was angry, no, *furious.* How could his mom spring this on him? He had just moved to Sandover—out of concern for *her,* so she wouldn't be so alone after his father's death almost a year ago. As the youngest brother, Nick got the short straw. And after his relationship with Kim went down in flames, Charlotte felt claustrophobic to him. Nick wanted as many miles between his ex and himself that he could manage. It seemed like a win for both of them. Now that he knew she was not only in a relationship, but getting *married* —he felt cheated.

His mother obviously didn't need Nick here, and he didn't know if he wanted to have a front-row seat to this.

Maybe she wouldn't want to get married, if only I tell her—

He shook *that* thought off, turning to Amber's father. Nick was just as furious with her mother's *fiancé*. It was hard to even think of that word. Tom kept looking at Nick's mom with totally besotted eyes. It appeared genuine. But then, his father had appeared genuine as well, and fooled them all the same way.

Did his mother and Tom not think about how awkward and awful it would be to announce their relationship and engagement at a public place with two of their children??

Then, there was Amber. He wasn't angry with her, but he had no idea what to do with the things he *did* feel. Looking at her gorgeous face set his blood to boiling.

Amber seemed as shocked as he had been. But that couldn't be right. Moments before their parents had arrived, Amber said she got disappointing news earlier today. She had anticipated an awkward dinner conversation. She *knew* about this.

Amber hadn't guessed that Nick was about to be family, but the thought that she knew and he didn't made him feel even more like a chump. This news was unexpected and disappointing to him too. And the dinner was *more* than uncomfortable.

Nick wondered if Amber was handling this okay. She couldn't meet his eyes. Through most of dinner, she'd kept her arms wrapped around herself and her gaze on her plate. He wished that he could take her hand or put his arm around her or even whisk her out of the restaurant. But he couldn't do any of that, not in light of the big announcement.

"We know it probably seems sudden, but we'd like to get married soon," his mother was saying. "Before all the holidays."

"Thanksgiving is seven weeks away," Amber said softly.

Nick's mom shrugged and gave Tom a goofy, in-love look that belonged on a teenager or something. "So, I guess in the next six weeks, then. I'm sure we can pull it off."

Six weeks?!? His father hadn't been dead a year. Nick's jaw tensed and he could hear the sound of his teeth grinding. At least that would still give him time to talk his mom out of it. Later, in private. If he needed to, maybe it was time to finally tell her what he should have told her years ago.

"Amber?" his mother said.

Nick's gaze snapped up, but his mother wasn't looking at him. She was looking at Amber, who finally looked up. Nick wasn't sure Amber had looked at his mom since the awkward moment they'd made introductions.

"Yes?"

Amber's voice had changed so much in the past hour, losing its color and brightness. Nick hated seeing her stripped of the joy that had drawn him to her in the first place. He noticed her the moment he walked into the restaurant and walked straight to her. He couldn't help himself. And she was only more attractive to him the more he sat with her. She was adorable and too honest and funny and completely beautiful in that unassuming way that made him stare even harder.

Until he found out that she was going to be his stepsister. What was he supposed to do with his feelings toward her now?

Nick's mother smiled at Amber. "We were hoping you could plan the wedding."

Oh, heck no. Nick's protectiveness surged. They weren't going to force wedding planning on Amber. Couldn't they see how upset she was?

Nick's brows furrowed, and the hopeless look in Amber's eyes made his fists clench. He really needed to breathe and focus. His anger had always been an issue, but Nick made real strides in the past year with managing it. The last thing he wanted was to lose his cool now and make a scene.

Lord, let me be quick to listen, slow to speak, and even slower to become angry. Nick silently repeated that verse, which had become something of a mantra in the past year. It took the edge off, but dealing with the full brunt of his emotions would take some time, and maybe a hard run or workout.

Amber twisted her napkin in her hands and glanced between her father and Nick's mom. "I, um …"

Her father reached out and squeezed her shoulder. "We'd pay you of course, sweetheart."

Amber gave a small smile but stiffened at the touch. Nick wanted to rip Amber away from her father and literally carry her out of the restaurant. He could almost imagine their parents' faces if he did. Instead, he found himself rooted to his seat, watching this horror show play out.

"Nick will help," his mom said, reaching over to pat his hand.

"I'll WHAT?"

His voice was almost a roar. All the silent prayers in the world wouldn't remove his anger right now. People at neighboring tables glanced over.

His mom shook her head at him, pursing her lips, then looked back at Amber, who seemed to be sliding down in her chair. In a moment, she'd be under the table. If things weren't already ruined because of their parents, this was about the time that Amber would realize he's the last guy she would want to date.

"It would be a good way for you to get to know Sandover," his mom said. "And make friends."

"Am I five, needing a babysitter? Someone to help me make friends on the playground?"

Amber's cheeks flushed. She was chewing her lip, looking down. Nick hated himself more than a little in this moment. His mom glared daggers, but it was Amber's father who spoke up, his tone harsh.

"Son, I know we've just met. This all may be a surprise to you. But that's no way to speak to your mother."

Was he serious right now? This balding, nerdy-looking man in a shirt with a ketchup stain on his collar wanted to tell Nick how to speak to his own mother?

He scoffed. But Amber spoke before Nick could say a word.

"*Dad.*" She shook her head.

"It's fine. I don't need you defending me."

Before the words were out of his mouth, Nick felt horrible, even worse than he had a moment ago. He was a few levels below scum of the earth. Shame paired terribly with spaghetti.

"Excuse me," Amber said, practically jumping from her seat. Her cloth napkin landed in the center of her almost untouched plate.

Amber's father glared at him. Nick's mom looked both disappointed and furious. Before either of them could say anything, Nick was on his feet.

"I'll take care of it," he muttered, cracking his neck as he walked.

Nick found the door leading to the bathrooms right next

to the bar. He had just stepped into the small hallway when Amber burst out of the men's room, flattening Nick into the wall.

"Oh! I'm sorry!"

Her hands clutched at Nick's shoulders and his hands found her waist naturally, like they'd done it dozens of times, not just the once.

And for exactly six seconds, Nick forgot everything except the feel of Amber in his arms again. His eyes dropped to her lips, which he could still almost taste.

Step. Sister.

Doing his best to keep his temper caged, Nick gently but firmly scooted Amber out of his arms. She dropped her hands, wringing them together. Her cheeks were the red of strawberries, and as she dipped her head, that gorgeous blonde hair hid her face. This was torture.

He cleared his throat, wishing it would also clear his head. "Were you in the men's room?"

"Wrong door. Sorry."

Nick shook his head. "It happens." Not that it had ever happened to him. But he would say just about anything to make her feel better. Especially when he had been part of the cause.

You did that, an accusing voice reminded him. *You were ruthless at the table, snapping at her when none of this is her fault.*

"Sorry," she said again, then shook her head, looking up to meet his gaze straight on. "Gah. It seems like that's all I can say. And I'm not the one who chose this terrible way of making a life-altering announcement. Did that really just happen in there? They're getting *married*?!"

Nick leaned on the wall. "Right? I mean, what were they thinking?"

Amber gave a humorless laugh. "No clue. None."

"You didn't know? At the bar, you said you got news today, and that you weren't excited about the awkward dinner."

Her eyes went wide, understanding and then a sort of pleading look.

"Oh! No, I didn't mean this! It was—" Amber coughed, like she choked on whatever she'd been about to say. "It wasn't *this*. I had no idea he was even dating anyone, much less getting married."

"Oh."

Idiot. I'm an idiot and a first-class jerk. Nick shoved his hands in his pockets. "I owe you an apology. Several, in fact."

Amber laughed, this time a real one. The sound hit him right behind the ribs, especially when he saw the dimples appear in her cheeks. Nick wanted to do whatever he could for however long, if it would mean making those dimples appear.

"None necessary," Amber said, still grinning. "I think tonight, you and I get a pass. On *everything*."

At that moment, the men's room door opened again. A man emerged, hands still working on his zipper, and leered at Amber. Her smile disappeared.

"Like I said in there, the invitation's open, sweetheart."

As his fist flew into the man's jaw, Nick hoped Amber was right about getting a pass on things. Especially about the words that left his mouth next, which he immediately wanted to forget.

"That's my sister!"

CHAPTER FOUR

I f Amber had any question as to how Nick viewed her after the bar and dinner fiasco, he answered clearly in that hallway. First, he felt protective, as evidenced by that impressive punch. Second, worse, and most importantly, he saw her as a … sister.

Of all the friend zones to be placed in, this was the friend zone in the outer realm of possibility. That amazing kiss would be forever etched in her memory. *But it's for the best,* she tried to tell herself. *I'm starting cancer treatments in a few days. It's not exactly the best time for romance.*

"It can't have been that bad," Ripley said, not for the first time. They were eating sushi in Amber's car, tucked away where their nosy office mates wouldn't have to hear about Amber's utter humiliation.

"It was worse than bad," Amber insisted, pointing a chopstick at Ripley. "Nick almost got arrested for assault. My dad tried to take his new stepfatherly duties to the nth degree by yelling at him, and then the two of *them* almost got into it. But then, you already know that."

Ripley scrunched her nose. "Sorry. The downside to being engaged to a cop. I know everything."

"The upside being the fact that Cash is also really sweet. Underneath that grumpy exterior."

"Let's not forget *hot* exterior," Ripley said, pointing a chopstick.

"Yes," Amber said, rolling her eyes, "your fiancé is attractive. Objectively speaking."

"And how hot, objectively speaking, is your new stepbrother?"

"Almost stepbrother. And it doesn't matter, because I haven't told you the worst part," Amber said. "He called me his sister. Not stepsister, but *sister*."

"How exactly did that come up?"

"When he was punching the bathroom-jerk in the face."

"Ah." Ripley tapped her chopsticks against her lips. "I mean, the sister thing is not great. But punching someone for you—that's pretty chivalrous, considering the guy deserved it."

Amber sighed in resignation. "He's really nice too." Then, she remembered his petulant behavior during dinner. "Mostly." He got a pass for that though, considering the circumstances.

Nick was the whole package—the kind of guy who made her heart stutter, made conversation feel effortless, and kissed like nobody's business. All wrapped up in the package of her future stepsibling. Totally unfair.

"I'm sorry about the wedding," Ripley said.

"You and me both."

"What did you say to your dad?" Ripley asked quietly.

"Nothing." Amber had a lot of things she wanted to say but kept quiet. For now. "We're having breakfast tomorrow. I agreed over text but haven't spoken to him since last night. Things ended abruptly."

Which Amber hadn't minded in the least. She barely made it to her car before she burst into tears and had spent the rest of last night crying into a carton of her emergency grief gelato. She typically kept at least one carton in the freezer for moments when the grief hit her hard. A tiny, cold and creamy pick-me-up. Last night, it hadn't worked.

"Can we circle back to the fact that you kissed him? I mean, that's so not like you."

No, it wasn't. But with everything else, Amber wasn't about to launch into her *other* big news. For today, this nightmare is enough.

"I'm blaming the wine. I was just in a mood. And Nick is … sweet and fun. We had a good conversation."

"And then you just asked him to plant one on you?" Ripley arched a brow, but Amber only shrugged. "It's got to be more than that."

It was. There was the diagnosis, poised behind Amber's lips like a curse she was afraid to speak. And seeing Emily and Jimmy. Ripley would at least understand *that*.

But those things weren't really her reasoning. It was simply Nick. Something drew Amber to him even from the first moment he brushed by her at the bar, making her drop the wineglass.

Like fated mates, she thought suddenly, remembering a fantasy book she'd read about wolf shifters. Then, she snorted. Because the idea was as dumb as the book had been. Fated mates, instalove—those were the things of stories. *Remember? No instalove*, she told herself.

"Jimmy and Emily were there," Amber said.

"Oh. Now *that* reasoning I get. But aren't you over him?"

"Of course!" Amber thought of how it felt to see Jimmy

and Emily last night. She hadn't felt jealousy, but more envy at what they had. And that stupid, awkward cloud that never quite got resolved. "It's just so weird with them, you know? We never talked about it, and Emily looks at me like at any moment I'm going to try and rip Jimmy away from her."

"Can't we just, like, have a truce and talk it out? I hate that you can't hang out with all of us. Emily's really—well, *nice* isn't the word I'd use. I like her, but she's different. You'd like her if you gave her a chance."

"I'm not going to be the seventh wheel in your perfect little couples' group," Amber said. "Especially when I make them both uncomfortable. Anyway."

Ripley sighed. "I know all of this stinks, but selfishly, I can't wait to meet Nick."

Amber groaned, and her gaze caught on a truck slowing in front of their office, then parking right out front. She dropped her chopsticks and started getting out of the car.

"Looks like you get your wish," she muttered, before shouting, "Nick!"

Amber pinwheeled her arms, desperate to get his attention before he walked into the office and became fodder for gossip. That would happen soon enough, when she spoke to Deondra about being asked to plan her father's wedding.

Nick turned, and was somehow more handsome in the midday sun. Amber's breath caught in her throat and she clung to the car door. Her chest physically ached as she watched him walk toward her, a tentative smile on his face and the sun glinting off his golden brown hair.

Why?

Why did he have to be so handsome? Why were their parents bent on some quick engagement?

A deeper, quieter voice that she pointedly ignored added,

And why did I meet someone like him right when I found out I have cancer?

The only upside to all this drama was that she had been able to shove the reality of her diagnosis to the back of her mind. She hadn't told her father yet either. One more fun topic for their breakfast tomorrow. Until she told her dad, maybe this quiet secret could be hers alone. Not real until it had to be.

Ripley gave a low whistle from inside the car. "Wow. Okay, I can see a little more now why you decided to kiss him. Can you just consider it a technicality that he's going to be your stepbrother? Really, who cares? We're all adults here …"

"Shush!" Amber hissed, as Nick reached the car.

"What are you doing out here?" Nick asked, glancing through the windshield and giving Ripley a friendly smile.

"Lunch break. Hop in the back. I'll move my seat up since you're so tall. I've got short legs."

Of course, then Nick looked down at her legs, bare beneath her favorite flowy knee-length dress. Her legs weren't her best feature, but they were still tan from summer and rides along the beach road whenever she got the chance. She hated running with a passion, but she could bike all day long.

Nick tore his eyes away, shuffling his feet, and Amber ducked inside the car. She yanked the lever under the seat, sliding herself forward as far as she could go. Ripley stared with wide eyes.

"Not a word," Amber growled as the back door opened.

Nick folded himself in the back seat and Ripley turned to him with a bright smile. When she held out her hand, he shook it, but Amber couldn't see his face since he sat directly behind her.

"I'm Ripley. I think you met my boyfriend, Cash, last night at the restaurant."

"Cash? Hmm ..."

Ripley laughed awkwardly. "Oh, um, the cop. Police officer. He prefers that I call him an officer."

"Oh, right." Nick chuckled. "I guess we didn't quite exchange names."

It was killing Amber that she couldn't see Nick's face. She swiveled in her seat and disengaged the head rest. It slid out, and she tossed it onto the back next to Nick, who stared at it, then looked at her with amusement in his eyes.

"You just pulled off the headrest," he said.

Amber shrugged. "They come off. And go right back in. You just push the little button. It's a thing."

Ripley's shoulders shook with silent laughter. Amber wanted to smack her, but she couldn't without drawing attention. And she already had enough of that with Nick staring.

Heat climbed her spine at the intensity of his gaze. It was hard not to look at him and remember that kiss. She suspected that years from now, she would still be thinking about it. Any future guy was going to have a lot to live up to in that department. Which was ridiculous considering how quick and how chaste it was.

And what would a passionate kiss with him be like? It would probably be the kind of kiss that women talked about —toe curling and knee wobbling. Amber realized she was staring at Nick's mouth and turned away, only to find Ripley smirking at her.

Nick stared between them, and Amber hoped he couldn't guess the reason for the blush in her cheeks.

"Is Sandover the kind of place where everybody's in

everybody's business?" Nick asked. "And people eat sushi in parking lots?"

"Pretty much," Amber said, thankful for the question. Anything to get her mind off kissing the man currently taking up space in her back seat.

Ripley nodded. "Kind of the opposite of Vegas. What gets mentioned on the police scanner, doesn't just *stay* on the police scanner."

"Right." Nick ran a hand through his hair, leaving it tousled.

Amber tore her gaze away, shoving down the desire to fix the wayward strands. "But we're the only ones I know who eat sushi in a parking lot. That I know of, anyway. Do you like sushi?"

Amber held out her container, offering it to Nick. She really didn't want to share. Like always, she had saved the best for last. Philly rolls with avocado, salmon, and cream cheese. She could be a little territorial when it came to food she liked. Ripley knew this, and Amber could see her grinning still.

"I do. Maybe just one," Nick said, reaching for a roll and popping it in his mouth.

Amber tried not to stare and failed as he chewed, that hard jaw flexing as his lips moved. She had already spent way too much of the last eighteen hours thinking about his mouth. Especially in the last five minutes.

"Thanks. Not bad," Nick said. "I haven't had a chance to check out the local restaurants yet. Other than the one."

His eyes met Amber's for a moment, and she couldn't tell what he was thinking about the dinner from the night before. Was it regret? Anger? Something else? Maybe, like her, he was still processing it all.

Amber hadn't gotten a chance yet to talk to her father. Or,

more accurately, she had been avoiding his calls. Not the most mature response, but she needed time to let the reality of everything settle. She usually held fast to the "don't let the sun go down on your anger" verse in Ephesians, but this felt different. Maybe Nick was struggling through the same thing with his mom.

"Don't order the sushi from Moe's," Ripley said, waving her chopsticks and breaking up the tension. "Or anything else. That place is food poisoning central."

"Sushi from a place called Moe's?" Nick laughed. "The name seems like warning enough."

Amber nodded. "It's the first indication there's a problem. The second is that they serve sushi, Mexican, and pizza."

"That's a terrible combination," Nick said.

"I don't know how it's still in business," Amber said. She held out her Dr. Pepper to Nick. "Thirsty?"

He raised an eyebrow. Amber raised one right back. *Your mouth and mine got a lot closer than this last night, buddy.* As though he could sense her thoughts, Nick reached for the bottle and then took several long swallows without breaking eye contact.

His icy blue eyes pinned her in place, conveying … something a lot like a challenge of some kind. Definitely nothing *brotherly*. The car suddenly seemed to ratchet up a few degrees. Maybe a few dozen.

Amber tore her eyes away from Nick. She and Ripley rolled down their windows at the same time, letting a bit of ocean breeze in. Amber took a deep breath.

I guess I'm not imagining this tension between us. Okay, then.

The realization made her heart quicken. At least until she reminded herself that Nick was off-limits. He leaned forward, his face way too close to Amber's, and placed the soda in the cup holder.

Ripley waved a hand over her cheeks. "That's hot. The wasabi, I mean."

Amber shot her a look, and Ripley only shrugged.

Nick cleared his throat. "So, when you're not eating sushi in the parking lot, you work there?"

Amber nodded. "Sandover Events. Weddings, parties, charity events. But mostly weddings."

"Ah. Now my mom's request makes more sense," he said with a grimace. "Still, I'm sorry she asked that of you."

Amber swallowed, looking down at her lap. "Thanks. But it's not your fault. You don't need to be sorry."

Ripley suddenly started gathering her things. "I'm headed back in so y'all can talk. Or whatever. Nice to meet you, Nick! Hope to see you around. And not in the back of Cash's squad car. That was a joke."

She grinned before marching across the parking lot, her neat blonde ponytail whipping in the breeze. There were a few beats of silence. And then, in a fluid motion that shocked Amber, Nick climbed into the front seat.

He was graceful, but so tall that his shoulders and hips whooshed right by Amber. She inhaled that spicy leather scent again, wishing she could bottle it up. Or maybe ask to borrow Nick's shirt and wrap her pillow in it.

As soon as he was settled, he pulled the lever and moved the seat back as far as it would go. "You said it. I'm tall." He grinned.

"Are you also some kind of gymnast? That was a smooth move."

"Just used to climbing in and out of the back seat."

Amber's eyes went wide. There was only one reason that immediately came to mind for a guy to be used to climbing in and out of the back seats of cars.

Nick's brows furrowed, then shot up as he seemed to

realize what he'd said. "No! Not because of any, um, whatever you're thinking. I have brothers. Lots of them. Riding shotgun was the highest honor. We'd fight over it, and if someone got out, you had to be the first up there."

Amber laughed. "That makes me feel better. Not that it's any of my business about you and back seats. I mean … wow. Let's strike all this from the conversation, please."

Nick laughed. Amber shook her head, then went to lean back. Only, she had forgotten the headrest was gone and her head started to drop. And then, Nick's hand was there. He cupped the back of her head, fingers briefly stroking her hair, before Amber pulled away.

She could not handle that kind of touch from him right now. Even if he was saving her from mini-whiplash.

"Thanks."

Nick reached into the back for the headrest. He set it back into place, fiddling with the button to secure it again. Amber tried not to visibly sniff him as his hands worked beside her head. He just smelled so dang *good*.

"There's a reason you don't take the headrest out," Nick scolded teasingly, his fingers lightly grazing her cheek as he pulled his hand away.

The touch, just like his hand on the back of her head, stirred something to life in her that had no business waking up. Especially when it had probably been an accident.

It *had* been an accident, right? Or was that a slight ruddiness to his cheeks that hadn't been there before?

Amber turned back to her sushi, untouched in her lap. She had lost her chopsticks somewhere in the car, but she plucked one of the rolls between two fingers. Not the most sophisticated way to eat, but Amber read an article saying this was how sushi was eaten in Japan. Some people liked reading celebrity gossip online; Amber enjoyed collecting random trivia.

"You're welcome to have more," Amber said, holding out the tray.

"Thank you."

For the next few minutes, they finished her last rolls together in a companionable silence. Licking soy sauce off her finger, Amber set the tray on the dashboard and angled her body toward Nick. He did the same, both of them leaning against their respective doors. The ocean air blew softly, carrying his scent toward Amber.

"So," Nick said.

"So?"

"I said it already, but I'm sorry my mom put you in that position. Asking you to plan their wedding."

Amber shot him a look. "Don't think I've forgotten that she roped you into it too."

"Why do you think I'm here?" he asked.

"Oh. Right." Amber hadn't given it much thought. She had been excited to see him, and thought maybe some part of him was excited to see her too.

"It's so weird, right? The whole thing." Nick ran a hand over his cheek, and Amber could hear the rasp of the light golden stubble. The sound made her shiver.

"It is."

It was more than weird. The idea of her father moving on so quickly crushed Amber. She could not fathom how he could have loved her mom and yet marry another woman so soon. She wanted to hate Nick's mom because it was easier than focusing her hurt and anger on her dad. But it wasn't Linda's fault. She hadn't lost her husband a few months before. At least, not that Amber knew.

She felt simply sick thinking about her dad. It felt like the deepest kind of betrayal. They had been walking through their grief together and then he just met someone and, like *that*, wanted to replace her mom? Amber almost had whiplash at the idea. And it would have killed her mother, she felt sure of it.

"I'm sorry," Nick said, brushing his fingers over her arm.

Amber jumped at the touch, and Nick dropped his hand. "You've said that already, and you don't need to apologize for your mom. You and I can't control what our parents do. Even if we'd like to," she muttered.

Nick waved a hand. "I owe you an apology for more than that. For a lot of things I did and said last night."

If he said he was sorry about the kiss, Amber might punch him. She leveled her gaze at him. "I don't think you need to apologize for anything else either. I'm not sorry about any of it." She flinched, realizing that wasn't quite true. "Well. Other than you calling me your *sister*."

Nick grimaced and covered his mouth with his hand. Amber tried not to stare at his fingers, the ones she had studied last night in the bar and felt on her waist while he kissed her.

"I *am* sorry about that. I don't know where that came from. I was trying to remind myself that you are ... off-limits."

Off-limits. Amber knew in her head that was the case. She'd been telling herself the same thing since last night, hating the reminder. But hearing him say it, making it more official ... she hated that even more.

"Can we forget the awkward family terms and consider each other as ... friends?" Amber asked, hoping that her face didn't give away her disappointment at the term.

Nick studied her for a long moment, his eyes bouncing

over her face, from her jaw to her lips and nose, back up to her eyes.

"No matter what I said last night, I don't think of you as my sister. Or future stepsister." Nick paused, his mouth tightening. "I guess, if that's what you want, friends will have to be enough."

Maybe she was imagining it, but Amber could have sworn she heard an unspoken *for now*. And there was still something more in his blue eyes, a spark of attraction or hint of promise. Is that what she wanted? No! Definitely no.

But given the situation they were in, it *had* to be no. Didn't it?

She forced herself to swallow. "I guess so. Friends and co-wedding planners?" She wrinkled her nose. "You really don't have to help. I can tell your mom—"

"I want to." Nick blinked, almost looking surprised that he'd said the words, or for how quickly they'd come out of his mouth. "Let me qualify that—I don't want to help plan a wedding. But we're in this together. I'm not letting you have to do this on your own."

"But it's my *job*."

"Don't care. You can't stop me. Although ... I did have one idea I wanted to run by you."

Amber tried to hold back a smile. Nick wanted to help her. She wouldn't have to do this awful, awkward thing on her own. They were in it together. The thought warmed her. And the cherry on top? It meant more time with him.

"I'm all ears."

He cleared his throat. "What are the chances we could reverse Parent Trap them?"

Amber barked out a laugh, covering her mouth. Nick's eyes danced.

"Reverse Parent Trap?" she asked.

Nick shifted in the seat, leaning closer as he turned toward her. "You know, try to break them up rather than bringing them together."

"I knew what you meant. I just—are you serious?"

Nick groaned and closed his eyes for a moment. "I guess not. Unless you think that would work?"

"I wish. No offense to your mom. She seems nice."

Nick smiled. "She's the best. Usually."

"I'm sorry about my dad. I know he wasn't great to you last night. He's not typically so hostile. Normally, he's a good guy. Though he can be overprotective of me. I'm an only child, and after my mom …"

Amber closed her lips, not wanting to think about her mom right now.

"And I'm not normally a man-child who sulks through dinner and throws temper tantrums."

Amber had to smile at that. And she didn't even try to argue the point. Nick had been putting off hostile vibes that were nothing short of scary. If she hadn't met him before, he would have made a terrible first impression. The total opposite of the charming, easygoing guy she'd met—and, let's not forget, *kissed*—at the bar.

"I'm planning to apologize to your dad this week."

Amber bit her lip. "I haven't spoken to him since last night. I've been ignoring his calls. *Now* who's throwing the temper tantrum?"

Nick surprised her by reaching across the car and covering her hand with his. "Hey, this is hard. I've been avoiding my mom too. A little harder since I live with her. They really didn't do a good job handling this."

"No, they didn't."

Nick's face grew more serious, and the light in his eyes dimmed a little. "I'll admit, I had planned to talk Mom out of it last night. But then, I started thinking ... I guess if they're happy?" He sighed.

Amber's dad *had* looked happy last night. At least, until dinner turned into the kind of drama that would have been perfect for reality TV. But how could he move on so quickly? Amber's emotions shifted from anger to betrayal to disbelief with a speed that left her dazed.

Not long after her mom died, Amber's boss, Deondra, had gently warned her that men sometimes remarried quickly after losing a spouse. Amber had been in the throes of grief at the time and dismissed the comment. The idea had been so ridiculous. And now ... here she was, about to help plan his wedding.

"My mom has only been gone three months. I just don't know how—"

Amber's words caught on the knot of emotion forming in her throat. She blinked, looking down where Nick's warm hand covered hers. His touch, which had the ability to make her pulse race, carried the weight of true comfort. She felt like she had known him for years, not less than a day.

"I'm so sorry for your loss." Nick's voice was soft, but it still hit hard. "I didn't realize it was so recent. That's ..."

He trailed off, shaking his head. What was there to say? The situation just plain sucked. All of it.

Tears threatened, stinging the backs of her eyes but not falling. Amber could measure her grief in how quickly the tears came. Even a few weeks ago, she would have been a sobbing mess by now. This was better. So, why did it feel somehow worse?

"Did your parents get divorced? Or ..." She didn't want to finish the question.

Nick shook his head, and her heart sank. "Eleven months and four days."

He knows the number of days. The knowledge of that squeezed her heart. But he had an edge to his voice, almost a bitterness. Was that because his mother had moved on so quickly or was it something else?

"Does it get easier?" she asked, twining her fingers with his. The movement felt natural, and she needed the touch right now. Embarrassing? Yes. But she found that she didn't care. She would take any connection with Nick she could, and not just because of her mood. No, even as she felt guilty for it, Amber relished in Nick's vulnerability and his closeness for totally selfish reasons.

Nick didn't answer immediately, as though weighing the question. "Never easier. Just … more resigned."

"Such a terrible word," Amber said, without thinking.

"Terrible?"

"*Resigned* means to give up. To surrender." Amber licked her lips. "It's acceptance."

"We have to accept it, don't we?" Nick asked, emotion coloring his voice. "They're gone. Acceptance is literally one of the stages of grief."

Amber stared at Nick, finding his eyes dry but his gaze intense. His jaw was tight, and she had been right about the bitterness in his voice, which was mirrored in his expression.

She spoke carefully. "Yes, we must accept it, at least in the sense that it is true. We can't stay in denial. But it doesn't mean we simply roll over and allow grief to alter the course of our lives. We don't lose our way or ourselves in our acceptance. It's not passive—that's why I don't like the word resigned. We must fight. For our lives. For joy."

Amber realized the moment her words dried up that she had said too much. She'd babbled stupidly, going on about things that you didn't say to someone else who had suffered loss. She struggled to believe those words herself.

Grief was personal. It was one's own. You didn't try to tell someone how to walk through it. Or how they should—

"You're right."

Nick's fingers squeezed hers, and his thumb stroked the back of her hand. Amber hazarded a glance at him, unsure what she would see. His eyes burned, twin blue flames that lit a matching fire in her chest.

He opened his mouth, then closed it again, blinking until the fire turned to a slow simmer, then almost nothing at all.

"Well," he said finally, with a small smile, "I guess you and I have a wedding to plan."

CHAPTER FIVE

Despite the polite small talk they had kept up so far, two things hung in the air in the diner between Amber and her father. As she sliced into a stack of pancakes, Amber tried to decide where to start. By telling her father she had cancer? Or that she was devastated by his surprise, quickie marriage?

Then there was the other thing, the one she couldn't tell him—how she had kissed Nick. And would very much like to do it again, even if they had agreed to be just friends, an agreement she already wanted to break.

Eeny, meany, miny, moe...

Amber finished her mouthful, then gripped her fork and knife like they were weapons. "Dad, why didn't you tell me you were dating anyone?"

The words forced her to think about the reality of it again: her father was going to marry someone else. He was *in love* with someone else. Suddenly, the sweet scent of syrup was cloying, and her stomach turned.

How could he?

Her father set down his fork and wiped his mouth before meeting her gaze. The apology was in his eyes before it reached his mouth.

"I didn't plan for this. Linda and I met and then I started having feelings. We went on a few dates, and I told myself I would tell you after every date. I meant to tell you."

"But you didn't." Amber squeezed her eyes shut, not wanting to think about her father dating someone else, kissing someone else.

He sighed. "I know, and I'm so sorry. At first, it was casual, and I thought I would wait until I knew it meant more. Before I knew it, we were suddenly serious. And then I didn't tell you because I felt guilty that I hadn't told you."

"So, you thought you'd get engaged. Better to ask forgiveness than permission?"

"Maybe a little bit. It just never seemed to be the right time, and things happened so quickly ..."

He trailed off and shrugged, like this was something simple he'd forgotten, like to return a phone call or mail a letter. Not an entire relationship he had intentionally not told her about.

Amber held back an eye roll, but barely. She couldn't remember being this angry with her father since she was a teenager. In the months since her mother's death, they had grown closer than ever before. At least, she thought they had. Meanwhile, he had been dating Linda behind her back. Amber had even considered breaking her lease and moving home with him. If she had, he wouldn't have been able to keep it a secret.

"How long?" she asked.

His mouth opened and closed for a moment. "Two months."

For a moment, Amber felt like her heart stopped beating

in her chest. Her father started dating Linda only a month after his wife died. Four weeks. Some part of Amber knew that this didn't negate the love her father had for her mom, but then again, how could you really love someone and move on so quickly?

"If I could have planned this out, if I could have met Linda later on, I would have. It happened when it happened."

"You could still wait. Give things more time." *Give* me *more time.*

"If there's one thing I'm more and more aware of at my age, it's how little time we may have."

Amber suddenly wished for Nick. To have him beside her, his warm and comforting presence. She wanted to call him the moment she left the diner and tell him everything—only Nick would understand how hard this was. They could commiserate together about how selfish their parents were being.

"I don't regret this, though I'll admit Linda and I made a mistake in how we told you." His expression darkened. "Not that it excuses how her son behaved."

Amber scoffed. "All things considered, I think Nick and I were both pretty tame. Honestly, you were terrible to him. If anything, you owe him an apology."

Her dad looked like he was about to argue.

Amber held up a hand to stop him. "Don't say another word about him. Nick is my *friend.*"

"I don't think that's a very good idea."

Amber arched an eyebrow. "Really? You want to talk to *me* right now about good ideas? You're the one who decided to make us *family* without even telling us. But I can't be friends with the son of your fiancée?" Amber refused to say stepbrother. She crossed her arms over her chest.

Maybe I could tell Dad that Nick's a great kisser. I'd love to see the look on his face.

The waitress suddenly appeared at their table. "More coffee?"

"Just the check," Amber said. "We're done here."

"You've hardly touched your food," her father said.

"Forgive me if this conversation has killed my appetite." Amber's voice rose as she continued. She wished she could quiet her raging emotions, but it was like all the things from the past few days came flooding out.

"All you had to do was give me some warning. That you might consider getting remarried someday. That you were thinking about dating. That you were dating. That you'd thought this out enough to buy Linda a ring and propose."

"And how would you have reacted?"

Amber threw her hands up in the air. "Probably like I'm reacting now! But I would have had some time to get used to this idea. Right after this breakfast, I'm meeting Linda to plan your *wedding*. Do you know how this makes me feel?"

Her father spoke quietly, but that didn't keep his next words from crashing over Amber like a rogue wave, taking her under. "I should have told you. But I don't need your permission or approval. That's not something I owe you."

Wow. Amber's heart felt like it was breaking. A new crack, right beside the one that formed when her mom died.

Amber was on her feet in seconds, tossing a bill from her purse on the table as she turned away. Her father followed her, grabbing her wrist. She refused to face him.

"Honey, wait."

Amber bristled at his touch and the term of endearment. "Why? Do I *owe it to you* to listen?"

She threw back an echo of his words to him, not even caring how many of the other patrons were watching or listening to their argument. She couldn't see them anyway through the blur of her tears. All she could think about was her mother. There wasn't a day that went by that Amber didn't ache from missing her, that she wasn't aware of the hollow, carved-out space in her life that her mom used to fill.

And her dad was marrying another woman. Tears spilled down her cheeks.

"Amber. I'm sorry. You're right, and I'm sorry. I didn't mean to be so harsh. I just … Let's talk through this. *Please*. I can't lose you too."

The crack in his voice melted away most of her anger, even as a deep sadness swept through her. No sooner had she turned than her father pulled her into a hug.

He was so familiar and soft, his Old Spice aftershave tickling her nose and surfacing so many memories of his hugs.

"I'm sorry, Amber. I kept putting off telling you and it got bigger and bigger and then it was even harder. I don't want to disappoint you."

His voice broke, and for a moment, there was only the shuddering of his uneven breaths. Amber tried to hold back a sob, aware suddenly that they were in a crowded diner, where music played and people laughed and bacon sizzled on the stainless steel cooktop a few feet away.

He didn't want to disappoint her, but he did.

"Linda is so good for me. She isn't—she couldn't ever replace—" He sighed, his voice and breath steadier now. "She's completely different. And she understands what I'm going through. I don't feel so alone."

"You have me," Amber said, knowing even as she said it that there wasn't a comparison. Her dad didn't just need her. He needed something more, and Linda gave him that.

Suddenly, his words rushed into her like a roaring wind in her ears, *I can't lose you too.*

Now, when she had raked him over the coals for keeping secrets, now is the time she needed to tell him about the cancer.

I have cancer, she thought, trying to force her mouth to say the words. It would be easier now, as he held her, when she didn't have to see his face.

I have to tell you something, she thought, testing out the phrase. *I got some news from my doctor.*

Of all the pamphlets he had given her, Dr. Espana hadn't provided literature on how to announce you had cancer to your father, who had just lost his wife.

I can't lose you too.

Some part of her knew what his reaction would be. He would drop everything in his life to help her and support her. He'd insist on going with her to treatments and talking to Dr. Espana. He would make her move home.

He might even break off the engagement with Linda. And as much as Amber didn't want him getting remarried, she didn't want to be the cause of the breakup. If her dad really was finding comfort and life again, as much as it killed her, she wanted him to have it.

There was no way she could tell him. Not now. Not yet. *After all my protests, I'm doing the same thing to him that he did to me with Linda. He'll just have to forgive me later.*

And I'll have to go through this alone. The thought made her shake. When she really let herself think about the cancer and the treatment she was about to start, she was terrified. No matter what Dr. Espana said about survival rates.

As her father finally released her from the hug and stepped back, one of her mother's favorite verses rose up from her memory: *When you pass through the water, I will be with you.*

In her consultation with Linda so far, Amber had been totally professional. *I'm a compartmentalizing champ*, Amber thought, pen poised above the page. Then again, she also felt like she was dying inside.

Which, technically I am.

Internally she groaned. It was too soon for cancer jokes. But maybe because of the emotional upheaval during breakfast with her father, she'd run out of feelings and was just ... numb.

"I really love flowers," Linda said. "So I want special attention paid to the floral arrangements. I was thinking about peonies and hydrangeas."

Both of which are expensive and out of season, Amber thought, even as she chided herself for it. *Don't get nosy. Don't worry about where the money is coming from, whether she or your dad are paying for this small but extravagant wedding. She's just a client. Just. A. Client.*

Amber dutifully took down notes. Later, she would compile everything in a document, but she liked to make the original notes by hand. It kept them clearer in her mind. She had read a few articles about how the brain stored information written by hand more than what was typed.

Maybe in this particular case, that isn't such a good thing. I'd prefer to forget all of it.

"I'm picturing big centerpieces on all the tables, bouquets with sprigs of lavender, set in crystal. Flowers and silk on the end of each pew at the church. And, of course, a few large arrangements up front."

Amber's hand was starting to cramp. "And as for colors—you mentioned using lavender. Are you thinking purples?"

"Purple and mint," Linda said. She pulled her tablet from

her purse. "Maybe this would be easier if I just showed you my Pinterest board."

And ... here we go. If Amber had a nickel for every consult that included those words. Pinterest was helpful for getting a visual idea of what clients wanted, but it usually gave them highly unrealistic expectations. Or, they would decide on something, then see a new idea on Pinterest and want to change the whole color scheme of the wedding.

"Of course."

Amber set down her pen as Linda came around the conference table, taking the seat next to Amber. The strong floral scent of Linda's perfume rose around them as she began to talk through the various images and ideas she had saved.

It's totally the opposite of my mom's perfume.

The thought made Amber's stomach tighten. She found herself only half listening, studying Linda instead. The other night at dinner, she had been too shocked to pay much attention to her father's new fiancée. Now, up close, she could do so more easily.

Her hair was a light blonde mixed with gray, where Amber's mom had kept hers honeyed up by regular salon appointments. Linda was softer and rounder. She had a brightness to her, a warmth that Nick also shared. If not for the circumstances, Amber probably would have enjoyed working with Linda.

The woman positively lit up as she continued to scroll through photos of flowers, table arrangement, dresses, and cakes. Which would have been endearing (again, if she weren't marrying Amber's dad) but was also ... surprising.

Amber didn't have a lot of older clients, but the ones she did work with never had this level of excitement. This was more on par with a young twentysomething woman still starry-eyed and in love for the first time.

She's in love with my dad. The thought still made her stomach tilt. Almost impossible to believe, even though she had seen them together. The dinner went downhill so fast that neither her father nor Linda had seemed particularly enthralled with each other.

Was there some reason Linda was so excited about this and was planning with all the enthusiasm of a twentysomething first bride? Maybe she didn't have the money or means to have her dream wedding when she was younger.

Amber doubted any of her excitement had to do with her father. Most men cared very little about these kinds of details, and Amber's father absolutely did not. Even so, none of the plans Linda made seemed to have anything to do with Amber's dad. Nor did Linda mention him often.

Maybe it's because she doesn't want to upset me? Or ... is it because she's more interested in the wedding itself than the man she's marrying?

The second question made her uncomfortable. According to her father, they had been dating for two months. Two months, from meeting to engagement, another six weeks until the wedding. It was shotgun-wedding fast, though that clearly wasn't the situation.

Which begged the question: how fast could you fall in love?

Though she wasn't in love with Nick by any means, the question made Amber think of him. Because even after being around him twice, she had big feelings. Way too big, all things considered. Maybe losing someone made you more emotionally vulnerable? That must be it. Her father sure moved on quickly. Maybe the same held true for children who had lost a parent. Amber made a mental note to search for articles on love after loss later.

"And are these the kinds of dress styles you're looking for?" Amber forced herself to focus and pointed at one of the collections of images Linda had created.

"I'm not sure what I want yet," Linda said, for the first time looking a little subdued. "Is it poor taste for someone my age or situation to wear white?"

Amber smiled, hoping it looked more natural than it felt. "No. I love a bride in white. It's classic. How many brides-maids are you planning to have?"

Linda set down the iPad. "Do you think I really need them? What's the custom for situations like ours?"

You mean, situations like where neither of you waited until your spouse had been gone a year before you started planning to marry another person?

Amber really needed to get rid of that snarky voice in her head. It definitely wasn't helping. She sent up a silent prayer: *Lord, give me sweetness that I don't feel or have. And pronto, if you please.*

"What would *you* prefer?" Amber asked. "Maybe you should think about the ceremony overall, then decide if you want to have bridesmaids and groomsmen or not."

"I'd like a simple ceremony. Beautiful and elegant, but simple."

Amber nodded, jotting a note down: *Second marriage, barely mourned loved ones, BUT beautiful and elegant. Yeah, right.* She really might need to double or triple up on her prayers. Clearly, one wasn't enough.

"My sister is coming to town for a bit. Maybe I'll ask what she thinks."

"Sounds good," Amber said.

"Would you want to come with us?" Linda asked.

"Hm?" Amber closed her notebook, more than ready to move on to her next appointment, set down her pen. "Come with you where?"

"To look at wedding dresses."

Amber's mouth felt dry and hot. She took a sip of the bottled water Ripley had given her, along with a pitying glance, at the start of the consultation.

"You want me to help choose your dress?"

While some brides like to look for a dress with only family, it wasn't unusual for Amber to be asked to come dress shopping. Of course, none of them had been marrying Amber's father.

Linda touched Amber's hand. Her skin was cool and dry, and Amber tried not to flinch away.

"I don't have any daughters," Linda said. "And, because my sons refuse to settle down, not even any daughters-in-law. My sister would love to meet you, and we both thought it would be good to bring you along."

The moment stretched out, with Amber trying and failing to come up with some kind of excuse. Saying yes felt like the worst kind of betrayal to her mother. But could she really say no?

"Why don't you text me when and where to meet you," Amber said, finally able to make her mouth form coherent syllables.

I'm sorry, Mom.

Linda beamed. "Wonderful. I really look forward to having you as part of my family."

She knew Linda meant well, but the way she worded it rankled. Like Amber would just be absorbed into their family. Also, did she mean *my family* as in, the new family Linda was creating with Amber's dad? That definitely didn't work for Amber.

"Are you dating anyone right now? You could always try on dresses of your own."

Linda smiled, as though this was some kind of brilliant idea, and not just one in a long string of hurtful things people could say to someone single. Also, Amber immediately thought of Nick and felt like she was lying when she said no.

"No need for me to try on dresses. This is all about you," she managed to say, trying to channel all the professionalism she could muster. Instead, she felt like a dog, baring its teeth.

"Oh, before I go, your father and I talked. I shouldn't have tried to push Nick into helping you. We've decided it's best not to push him into it."

They decided? Amber's blood pressure was reaching dangerously high levels. Her father and Linda didn't get to decide *anything* else for her. And why didn't Amber get that same option?

Disappointment followed closely on anger's heels. Amber had really looked forward to seeing more of Nick and not having to deal with this on her own. But of course, he probably would take the first chance to get out of this task if he could. Amber knew she would, and it was literally her job.

Maybe it was time for a new job. Or a new island to call home.

CHAPTER SIX

Though the fire station here was a lot smaller than Nick's old one, the view more than made up for it. "Wow," Nick breathed, setting his hands on the low wall at the edge of the roof. Just across the road, the waves tossed themselves against the beach as gulls circled.

He turned around, glimpsing the calmer waters separating Sandover from the mainland. The sound—Amber had called it the *sound,* not a bay or harbor as Nick would have done. He smiled at the memory of her calling him an Off Islander.

"I know, right?" Jimmy, who had been giving Nick the tour, grinned at him. "I never get used to it."

Nick shook his head, trying to remember what they'd been talking about. Had they been talking?

"What?"

"The view." Jimmy tipped his head toward the beach. "The sand and the waves and just … all of it." He leaned on the wall, eyes fixed on the beach, the perfect picture of a surfer with this tousled blond hair and sun-kissed skin.

"Oh, right. Yeah, it's pretty amazing. You didn't grow up here either?" Nick asked.

"I'm a full Off Islander. Have you heard that expression yet?"

"Yep."

Jimmy stretched his arms wide. "This island is both welcoming and insular. It's become home to me, but that doesn't make me an On Islander."

Nick raised his brows. "Seems like out of anyone, firefighters would be an integral part of things. Enough to fully embrace them."

Jimmy laughed, tossing his head back. "You'd think. I'm welcomed enough, but my title won't ever change. Trust me, you'll be welcome too. It's a good place."

Nodding, Nick glanced out over the beach again. Being here did give him a strange sense of homecoming, of rightness. As though Sandover was where he should have been all along.

It was the same with Amber, Nick realized. He had known her a matter of days, but it felt like longer. And the feelings he had ran deeper. Not just physical attraction, despite the kiss in the bar, and definitely not friendship, as he'd tried to tell her the day before in her car.

Being around her felt like being on this island. A deep sense of belonging. Of *home*.

He knew, logically speaking, that it was ridiculous. But his logic didn't change the depth of his feelings for Amber, which ran far deeper than his connection to any other woman. The thought scared him a little bit. But not because it felt wrong; only because of the ridiculous situation they found themselves in.

Jimmy clapped a hand over Nick's shoulder. "So, ready to get tossed into the fire?"

Groaning, Nick stretched. "Drills?"

"Yep. Beau knows you're fine. We've all seen your file. But he likes to see every guy here pull his weight. Literally. It won't be fun."

"Depends how you define fun," Nick said, grinning. He could use a little physical exertion to wear the edges off his anger. Running on the beach the past few days had been good, but he still felt on edge.

Jimmy's eyes gleamed. "How about a little friendly competition?"

"You're on."

"Loser buys beer next time we go out," Jimmy said, walking backward toward the door leading to the stairwell.

Nick loved the easy way Jimmy just included him, assuming they would spend time together outside of work. The other guys he'd met downstairs had been the same way, only furthering this feeling of belonging.

"Tomorrow night, Beau and I are off. We're going to a cookout at a friend's house on the beach. You in?"

"Wouldn't miss it," Nick said. He paused, then added, "Can I bring a friend?"

Jimmy lifted a brow, smirking. "Already met someone? You move fast."

Not usually, Nick thought. *Just with Amber.*

"It's complicated. Very complicated."

"Invite away," Jimmy said. "And later, you'll have to explain. We can all share our complicated stories and see who wins the prize. You might be surprised."

So might you, Nick thought.

———

It's reckoning time, Nick thought as he walked inside at dinner-time. Out loud, he said, "Hey, Mom."

"Hello." She smiled, though her tone was cool.

Despite the fact that he was living in one of the guest bedrooms, he hadn't seen or spoken to his mother since leaving the restaurant two nights ago. She had left enough coffee for him each morning before she left for work, though she had made pumpkin spice. As far as Nick was concerned, pumpkin spice anything had its own special circle in Dante's Inferno. Which his mother definitely knew.

He leaned against the kitchen island, watching her put together a salad. His mom had been making hot meals for Nick most nights. Not that he had asked for them—he had actually protested, as much as he loved her cooking. Last night when he got home late after driving around and exploring the island, she had been in bed. Whatever she'd made, there were no leftovers.

Tonight, salad. Not just salad, he realized as she opened a container. A leafy salad topped with tuna salad. *Gross.* The smell alone made him want to leave the kitchen. Canned tuna was basically cat food, unfit for human consumption. Another fact Nick's mom knew.

Yep. It was definitely intentional.

"How's it going?" he asked, raising a brow.

She set down the knife she was using to chop tomatoes and gave Nick her full attention, raising an eyebrow right back. "Have you been avoiding me?"

It would be an easy white lie, but Nick had grown to hate even innocent lies. "Maybe. Have you been making pumpkin spice coffee because I hate it?"

She bit her lip, holding back a smile. But only for a moment. Then she gave a small laugh. "Maybe."

"And the tuna salad?"

"I happen to like tuna salad." When Nick continued staring without speaking, she threw her hands up in the air. "Fine! Yes. I'm making tuna because you hate it."

"Now that we've got that straight, should we clear the air?"

"Let me start," she said, her expression softening. "I owe you an apology. Tom and I made a miscalculation in how we handled our announcement."

Nick chewed the inside of his cheek to keep from commenting on her wording. Miscalculation? He had a few stronger words for it.

She continued, "I'm so sorry we didn't tell you ahead of time, and that we told you and Amber together. I know how you feel about people hiding things, about lies."

Nick tensed. *Because of Kim.* But also—and his mother didn't know this—because of his father.

"I kept meaning to tell you, and then I thought I'd wait to tell you in person about Tom." Her eyes lit up when she said his name. "When Tom proposed … I was shocked. I hadn't realized he was thinking about moving so quickly, but I'm so excited! I couldn't say no. I hope that you can be happy for us."

"You deserve happiness," Nick said quietly. "And a man who really loves you."

He hoped Tom was that man for his mother. Their first impression hadn't gone over well, but under the circumstances, what could he expect? His father definitely hadn't deserved her.

"Will you forgive me?" his mom asked, her eyes looking watery.

"Of course." The words were easy, though forgiveness wasn't always. That was one thing he wished he had inherited from her. Forgiveness seemed elusive, always just out of his grasp.

He weighed his next words carefully. "I do wish you had let me know you were even dating someone. The surprise wouldn't have been so … shocking."

"You're right. We were just … caught up. It was selfish. But after losing your father, it felt so good to have a piece of happiness. Things moved faster than I thought."

Yes, they sure did. If his mother had been worth a lot of money, Nick might even wonder if there were other reasons for the timeline. But his parents had invested most of what they had into this beach cottage. Even now, his mom kept the books working for a local decorator.

"And I'm sorry for my behavior at dinner. I acted like a child. Will you forgive me?"

Her lips twitched. "For which part? The attitude or the fistfight?"

Nick chuckled. "I'm not all that sorry about punching that guy."

"Nick!"

"Punching someone isn't usually the way I would handle things, but he had it coming."

"What did he do?" she asked. "I never got the full story. Not that I'll approve. You've made such big strides with your anger."

Nick ran a hand over his jaw. His mother was right. Not that he had ever been out of control. The man was the first person he had ever punched that wasn't one of his older brothers, and they all had it coming. With so many boys in the family, you had to be scrappy as the youngest.

Even though he didn't like the loss of control, what he said was true—he didn't feel sorry in the slightest. Even now, he was furious thinking about the man's lewd looks and what he'd said to Amber.

Nick literally felt like his body temperature climbed a few degrees just thinking about that idiot. "He said something inappropriate to Amber."

Her eyes widened. "Well, then I'm not sorry either. Though I'd prefer not to bail you out because of assault charges."

"I think we can both agree on that."

"That's very sweet that you protected Amber. I hope the two of you can get along."

Oh, we more *than get along.* Nick had to bite back the words. No, he didn't like hiding things or keeping secrets. But there was no way he was going to confess that he kissed Amber the other night.

"Speaking of which, I'd like for you to apologize to Tom," his mom said.

"I already planned on it." Though Nick was looking forward to it as much as he would a visit to the dentist's office. Tom already seemed to despise him.

"Good. Also, Tom talked to me, and I should never have tried to force you to help Amber plan the wedding. You're free from that commitment."

Nick didn't *want* to be free. He liked the easy excuse wedding planning gave him to hang out with Amber. Not that he cared a lick about the wedding or wedding planning in general.

"What if I want to help?"

She blinked at him. "Do you?"

"I—yes. I want to be involved."

Involved with the wedding *planner* that is. Even if it was a flimsy excuse for spending time with Amber, Nick would take it.

"That means so much to me. If you weren't so sweaty, I'd give you a hug."

Nick held out his arms as though to hug her, and she squealed and ran around the other side of the island.

"Don't you dare!"

Chuckling, he held up his hands. "Fine. No hugging until I've showered."

"And maybe while you're showering, I'll make you something for dinner that doesn't involve tuna."

"Mom. You don't have to. I'm totally capable of fixing my own dinner. I've been doing it for years."

She moved close enough to pat his cheek. "Don't take away my joy in serving you while I can."

"Hopefully, I'll find a place soon," Nick said. He'd asked around the station, hoping someone would need a roommate. No such luck.

"No rush. You know I don't mind having you here. As long as you need. Oh! Your aunt Jill is coming this weekend. Maybe for a little longer."

He groaned. "Jilly? Here?"

Nick and his mom's much younger sister had more of a sibling relationship than a typical aunt-nephew one. She was about halfway between his mother's age and Nick's age. Both of them liked poking the bear and took equal turns being the bear and the poker.

As Nick went to shower, his phone buzzed with a text from Jimmy, giving him the address for the cookout. Nick had almost forgotten. He let the water warm up while he tried to compose a brilliant text to Amber.

Giving up, he finally went with basic rather than brilliant.

Nick: I got invited to a beach cookout tomorrow night. Want to join me?

Amber responded almost immediately, and Nick grinned as he read her message.

Amber: Scared of the On Islanders?
Amber: You need backup? Or a wingwoman?

He frowned at the second text and paused, wondering what to say as steam billowed into the room. Did Amber want to see him date someone else? Or did she maybe think he *wanted* to date someone else?

Nick: I definitely don't need a wingwoman. Or a wingman.
Nick: I'm not looking to meet anyone new.
Amber: Got it.

And this is why Nick hated text messages—it was so hard to read tone and any underlying meanings. He ran a hand through his hair. Amber's reply felt short and snippy. He had been trying to hint that he had already met someone—*Amber* —whom he wanted to date. That probably didn't come through at all.

He was totally overthinking this. Meanwhile, the hot water was probably running out.

Nick debated texting back that he already felt spoken for, but didn't know how far he should push things. Especially when he'd been dumb enough the day before to agree to *friendship*. He did want to be Amber's friend, but he also wanted *more*. Much more.

And he'd come by her work not to plan the wedding, like he'd told her, but to apologize for the sister comment. There was a whole joke he'd planned out about it, one that segued into asking her on a date for the second time, which somehow made him more nervous than the first. She had already said yes once, but that was before their parents dropped a bomb on their lives. Ultimately, he chickened out.

He hadn't given up on his plans to ask her out though. He wanted them both to forget what they would soon officially be to each other because of their parents' marriage, to push past the friendship he'd agreed to.

This felt like a delicate balancing act on a razor-thin wire. Hopefully, with some kind of metaphorical safety net below, because Nick felt sure he would need one.

Amber: Want to meet there or want to pick me up?
Nick: Definitely pick you up. Send me your address.

She did, and he plugged it into his phone, which was starting to fog up. He wiped the screen with his palm before entering another message.

Nick: It's a date.

No way to misunderstand that, right? Maybe not as up front as telling her he wanted it to be a date. But still. He said the word date, right there in the text. *It's a date.*

Amber: Ha ha

Or … maybe it didn't come across how he meant it. Nick groaned and turned his phone off, dropping it on the counter before he stepped into the shower, which had now turned cold.

CHAPTER SEVEN

It's a date.

Nick's words, his rash, stupidly texted words echoed in his mind that next day, like a drumbeat in his mind. They still echoed as he climbed the stairs to Amber's apartment, wiping his damp palms on his shorts. Amber thought he was joking. Now, he felt unnerved and unsure how to act, how to behave.

He should have just been clear and honest, telling Amber he really *did* want to date her. Wasn't honesty the thing he prized above everything else?

I don't want to just be friends, he should have said.

Why did the right words always come to Nick far too late? Tonight. He could talk to her tonight about moving out of the friend zone. Taking things slow, but taking them somewhere. He knew he wasn't imagining the chemistry that crackled between them. It was heat and energy and something soul-deep.

It scared him, if he was being honest.

Take it slow, he told himself. *If you're scaring yourself, you'll definitely scare her. Friends first, like she asked. For now.*

He knocked twice on the door, and it flew open almost immediately as though she had been waiting behind the door. Amber flashed him a brilliant smile, her dimples flashing. Nick barely restrained himself from wrapping his arms around her.

"Hey!" she said.

"Hey yourself." She looked beautiful, but he couldn't unstick his tongue from the roof of his mouth to say so. He stepped back so she could lock the door, putting his hands in his pockets to resist the urge to put an arm around her shoulders or take her hand.

"How are you?" he asked as they started down the stairs.

"Fine. You?"

"I talked to my mom," he said. "I feel better about that."

"Good! I had breakfast with my dad." She sighed. "I wish I felt better."

"Not a great conversation?" He glanced at her sideways as they reached his truck.

Amber shook her head. "Just … awkward. Hard."

He opened the door for her, making sure her legs were tucked inside before closing her in. Rounding the front of his truck, he watched her buckling, her blonde hair sweeping over her cheeks. Glancing up, she caught him watching and gave him a tentative smile.

Look away. Look down. Look anywhere but at her face.

Nick smiled back instead.

The conversation dried up between them, and it was only when Nick had pulled out onto the main road that he broke the silence.

"How are you?" he asked, only then remembering that

he'd already asked when she opened her apartment door. *Smooth*, Nick.

Amber giggled. "Still fine. Anything changed in the last few minutes for you?" she teased.

"Tons," he deadpanned.

Amber shifted her body so she faced him. "Do tell! I'd love to hear what's new in the last five minutes."

It was hard to concentrate on driving with her watching him. Thankfully, Nick had already driven by the address Jimmy had sent him, so he wouldn't have to rely on GPS. He wanted to learn his way around Sandover, and the best way to do so wasn't using an app. They were only a few minutes away from the massive beach home, which was a newer construction made to look like the smaller, weathered beach cottages that looked like they had always existed here.

Nick glanced over at Amber. The only thing that had changed in the last few minutes was the speed of his pulse and the nervous excitement in his belly. He couldn't exactly admit that. Instead, he changed the subject to one that killed the vibe completely.

"Mom really enjoyed meeting with you about the wedding."

Amber groaned, then seemed to catch herself. "Sorry."

Nick chuckled. "So, it's *not* going well?"

"It's … fine." Amber thought for a moment, and Nick could see her running her hands over the truck's interior, like she was trying to memorize the contours of the dashboard and the center console.

"I like your mom. It wouldn't be weird except …"

"That she's marrying your dad."

"Yep."

She sighed, and once again, silence filled the car. It wasn't uncomfortable, but their weird reality seemed to hang between them. Rather, it felt like the pulling back of a wave, as though they both were holding things close, trying to keep the natural momentum of the waves from slapping against the shore.

"Let's make a deal," Nick said after a moment, and the tension between them immediately dissipated.

Even from his peripheral vision, he could see Amber's smile.

"Ooh. I love that game. What kind of deal?"

Nick laughed. "This one may be less fun. Here's my proposal. Let's keep being honest with each other, but we should avoid bad-mouthing the other person's parent. Not that you were," he added quickly.

"No, I get it. That makes sense. I wouldn't want to cause more conflict. That could get ugly." Amber paused. "Can we complain about our *own* parent? Like the fact that my dad is making me nuts and I think he was a jerk? I told him to apologize to you."

Chuckling, Nick said, "Only if I can tell you how fast I need to move out of the house with my mom."

Amber held out her hand, and Nick lifted his from the steering wheel, trying to keep his eyes and focus on the road. It was hard with her smile and her melted-chocolate eyes glittering at him.

"Deal," Amber said, as a riot of sparks exploded underneath his skin at her touch.

Nick pulled away quickly, so distracted that he almost missed the driveway. Braking hard, he managed to recover and pull in behind a Jeep.

"Nick?"

"Sorry. I almost missed the turn."

Nick realized she wasn't even looking at him, maybe not even thinking about him jamming his foot on the brake. All amusement had washed from her face as she stared up at the big house on stilts in front of them.

"What's wrong?"

"W-where did you say you worked?" Her voice shook.

Nick frowned. "I'm a firefighter. I got a job at the station here."

Amber's eyes fluttered closed, and for a moment, her lips moved, almost like she was saying a silent prayer. Maybe she was. Nick hadn't been to church in a while, since before Kim, so if praying silently in front of other people was a new thing, he didn't know about it. Somehow, he had the feeling it was just Amber.

"Is that … okay?"

Usually women loved firefighters, or at least, the idea and the appearance. Maybe Amber was the one woman in the world who didn't like men in uniform?

She opened her eyes, still staring at the house. "It's just—"

Before she could answer, Jimmy jogged under the house from the beach, smiling and waving, heading toward Nick's truck.

When his gaze moved to Amber, the smile dropped. He stopped running, putting his hands in his pockets and waiting for them by the stairs leading up to the house. Something uncomfortable twisted in his gut.

Nick held up a finger, indicating they'd be there in a minute. Jimmy nodded and turned away, walking back toward the beach.

"You dated Jimmy."

Why did that thought bother him so much?

Amber picked at the hem of her shirt. "Briefly. Barely."

Wow. This island really is small, Nick thought. *Or I'm just totally a magnet for weird coincidences.* He wanted to ask more, to know more, to know everything, even as he wanted to pretend like it didn't exist. He turned to Amber, whose face had lost the happy glow from a few minutes before.

"If you want, we can go. Or I can take you home. Totally up to you."

"I should have thought about it. I think if I'd known where you worked, I would have realized. This island is so small. Everyone knows everyone, or if they don't, they'll meet them tomorrow," Amber babbled, then seemed to realize she was doing so and clamped her mouth shut.

"Say the word," Nick said. "We'll go."

Amber looked up, meeting his eyes with a smile that had dimmed from its earlier brilliance.

"No. I'll stay."

"Do I need to punch Jimmy? I mean, I know we have to work together, but still." The thought of Jimmy hurting Amber was even worse than the idea of him dating her.

Amber laughed, and it eased the hot anger building in his throat.

"No more punching people for me! No, it wasn't like that. We were casually dating and then Emily came to Sandover. I guess they'd known each other for years. Anyway. I'm over it, and it's not still painful or anything. Unless painfully awkward counts. Getting over the weirdness is long overdue. Unless … this makes it awkward for you?"

Nick shook his head, opening the door. "No way. But any time you need to get out of here, just say so. I'll do the same. We can have a code word."

"Chinchilla," Amber said.

"Chinchilla?"

"You know, adorable, fluffy, gray."

"They're rodents," Nick said. "Like rats."

Amber gasped. "No! Don't tell me you just compared my favorite animal to the ones that started the bubonic plague!"

"Fleas started the bubonic plague, if you want to get technical. And how are we going to work *chinchilla* into normal conversation?"

"I guess we'll have to have a good time, so we don't need to use it," Amber said, laughing as she got out of the truck.

I already am, Nick thought.

He already felt like he'd known Amber for weeks or months, not days. Maybe part of it was that she was so easy to read, even when she was trying to hide her feelings.

Like the way she made an effort to keep her shoulders and chin up as they made their way toward the beach.

"Can I carry something?" Amber asked as they emerged from under the house.

Nick had a grocery bag in each hand, one with beer and the other with some chips and dips he'd picked up at the grocery store. "I got it."

Amber touched his arm, and the feeling of her fingers brushing his biceps pulled him to a stop just as the ocean came into view beyond the dunes. She looked up at him, her eyes trying to look steady, even as he could read the nervousness.

"It would give me something to do with my hands," she said.

"Say no more."

Nick handed her the bag of chips, and she rewarded him with a wide smile. As they continued on and a small group came into view on the beach in front of the house, Amber took a deep breath. Nick could feel her tensing up, and without letting himself question it, he threw his free arm around her shoulders.

She immediately relaxed into him with a sigh, leaning into him.

"Thanks," she said. "Sorry to be so lame."

"You're anything but lame. I've got you."

Amber smiled up at him again, and it was one of those moments he just wanted to remember forever—the way the sun glinted on her hair, the brown in her eyes turning to warm caramel, the slightly crooked smile and full pink lips. And those dimples! Her cheeks were flushed, as though his words had been the best kind of compliment.

"Nick!" a voice boomed. Beau jogged over.

He could have been Jimmy's older brother, blond and broad and friendly. Nick noticed Jimmy watching from a nearby chair with a tall blonde in his lap. Amber clearly noticed too, though she pretended not to.

Nick tightened his arm around her, squeezing her shoulder. He liked the feel of her, small and trusting, tucked against him. He liked feeling needed. Though he hoped whatever awkwardness there was between her and Jimmy would dissipate.

Beau patted Nick's shoulder. "Good to see you, man! Amber, hey! It's been a while. Glad you're here."

His smile was wide and so genuine that it was hard not to smile back. He was like a big, happy golden retriever.

"Hi, Beau," Amber said softly.

A dark-haired girl appeared next to Beau and his arm curled almost automatically around her. His smile widened before he kissed her on the cheek.

"This is my wife, Mercer." He looked so proud when he said the word wife, and Nick felt an unfamiliar jolt of envy. "Mercer, you may know Amber already, and this is our new recruit, Nick."

Mercer's smile was shy, and she gave a small wave. "Hi.

Good to meet you, Nick. Welcome to Sandover. Amber, we haven't formally met, I don't think. Which is a shame. Nice to officially meet you."

"Thanks," Amber said. "I'm a big fan of your singing." She turned to Nick. "Mercer sings at church and also performs locally."

"And Off Island too," Beau said, beaming down at Mercer, who was squirming a little, even as she smiled. "She's had a few gigs in Raleigh and has one in Asheville at the end of the month."

"That's great!" Amber said. "We'll have to come see you sing soon."

As the two women started talking about dates and times for Mercer's performances, Nick realized what she'd said. *We'll have to come. We.* He found himself grinning.

"Yes. We will."

CHAPTER EIGHT

Amber was shocked to find how easily she slid right back into the small group of friends she had once been a part of. It felt almost as though she'd never left. Other than Jimmy and Emily, who gave her a wide berth. But Jackson and Jenna, who lived in the big house, were more than welcoming. Amber volunteered in the church nursery, and their five-month-old daughter, Patty, loved her. The feeling was mutual.

You weren't supposed to pick favorites in the nursery, but Amber ignored that advice. "Do you mind if I hold her?" Amber asked, as soon as Jenna brought Patty down from her late afternoon nap.

"Mind? No way!" Jenna handed over the baby, who was already reaching for Amber.

She shifted so Patty was propped on her hip, gurgling happily and waving her chubby fists.

"Thank you," Jenna said, stretching. "I swear, you wouldn't know it from looking at me, but carrying around a baby all day is making me discover muscles I didn't know I had."

Holding Patty wasn't uncomfortable, but Amber could see how the weight would wear on her day in and day out. Especially with the way Patty constantly moved, waving her arms or wiggling against Amber.

"I can see that."

"I'm going to grab food while I've got two hands to eat it. Even if I have to pry a half-raw burger off the grill, it's worth it." Jenna wandered off toward the table with snacks and fixings next to the grill.

Amber caught Nick grinning at her from where he spoke to Beau a few feet away. Amber smiled back, picking up one of Patty's wrists and waving her tiny hand at Nick. When he gave an exaggerated wave back, Patty squealed and thrashed in Amber's arms.

Her heart echoed the movement. *Nick likes kids.* The thought made her almost giddy. She was just in the process of mentally censuring herself for caring about that too soon, when she realized another reason she shouldn't care.

Nick likes kids. I can't have kids.

Amber almost gasped when that voice in her head, which sounded like Dr. Espana, reminded her of a truth she had successfully ignored for a few hours in a row. *I won't be able to give him kids.*

Not that we're even dating. Talk about jumping a lot of steps ahead.

Still, the pain was acute. Amber turned away from Nick, walking Patty toward the ocean and effectively hiding her tears. Amber had kept herself from thinking about the diagnosis. Her father's announcement, awful as it was, made for a great distraction. So did Nick.

The unfairness of it all hit her again, and she remembered

thinking in Dr. Espana's office that she still wasn't angry with God. How about *now*?

Amber kicked her shoes off and walked Patty closer to the shore. Her feet sank in the wet, heavy sand as cold water washed over her toes. Despite the stinging reminder of what she was going to lose, Amber's heart lifted as she watched Patty wave her chubby arms, gurgling at the waves and the gulls circling overhead.

There was adoption. Fostering. This didn't mean Amber couldn't have kids. Just that she wouldn't carry them in her own body.

"Those are seagulls," Amber told Patty, pointing. "Whatever you do, don't feed them, okay?"

"Who have you got here?" Nick was suddenly beside her.

Amber swiped a hand across her face before turning to face him. "Nick, this is Patty. Patty, meet Nick."

Patty held her arms out, squirming and reaching for him. Nick looked surprised but pleased. "May I?"

"Sure," she said, her voice a little wobbly as she handed Patty over. The baby immediately looked up and grabbed Nick's chin in a chubby fist, then squealed, waving at the birds again. Nick held her easily, as though he did it all the time.

Amber sucked in a breath. The sight of Nick holding Patty with such ease both made her heart soar and then plummet. She wanted the picture right there, Nick and a baby, and she realized with an unnerving clarity that she didn't just want a man and a baby. A very real part of her wanted Nick and *their* baby.

It made no sense. Amber shouldn't feel this depth of emotion for Nick. Less than a week. That's how long she had known him. Maybe it was some kind of hormone thing? Her cancer? Maybe kissing him at an emotionally vulnerable time confused her heart?

That must be it.

A breeze blew Nick's hair across his forehead, and Amber curled her hands into fists. Patty managed to grab a handful and give it a good yank. Nick only laughed, using his free hand to pry her fingers loose, and bouncing her until she giggled, flailing her arms and squealing.

His eyes met Amber's, and longing passed between them, deep and rich and warm. Far too intimate. Amber turned away.

I can never give him that.

Amber could make peace with losing the ability to have kids. But most guys would want a chance to have sons and daughters with their own DNA. Wouldn't they? She felt suddenly like she was a used car in a lot for sale, and her condition made her unattractive even for a test drive.

Amber stared out over the ocean. A pelican dove down to the surface of the water and came up empty. It took to the sky again, circling and circling over the water.

Amber tried to will all the thoughts of cancer and having babies and dating Nick from her mind.

"So, does this little one belong to Jackson?" Nick asked. "And this is his house?"

"Right on both counts. Jackson and Jenna live here. Pretty amazing, right?"

"It's some place."

"Jackson owns half the island. If he's not a billionaire, he's close."

Nick glanced back toward the house. "Seriously? I mean, the house is big, but not *Lifestyles of the Rich and Famous*. He's so young."

"His dad started buying properties and developing before

the island exploded. They also owned a grocery store that just went out of business this year. The island practically had a funeral for it. Anyway, Jackson could probably help you find a place if you're looking," Amber said. "I mean, unless you want to live with your mom."

Nick shook his head almost violently. "Um, no. I want to be out as soon as possible."

Someone whistled from behind them and shouted, "Burgers are done!"

As they walked back toward the house, Patty continued squealing and burbling happily. Nick talked right back to her. If he wasn't around kids often, he was totally a natural. Whatever pull Amber felt toward Nick before only intensified.

Just before they reached the group, Nick nudged her lightly. "Hey, are you doing okay?"

Amber nodded. "Sure."

"No need to call out our password? What was it again? Plague-carrying rodents?" He flashed her a grin.

Amber laughed. "Don't you dare call them that. And no, no need for the password."

Not yet, anyway. But as they reached the group, Amber couldn't help but notice the awkward tension still between her and Emily. The night was still young.

———

An hour later, Amber helped Jenna carry Patty up to the house to eat. She had started fussing mildly, nuzzling into Amber's shoulder with an open mouth and a surprising ferocity.

"You're not going to find anything there," she had said,

signaling Jenna, who had laughed seeing Patty gumming Amber.

"Thanks for the reprieve," Jenna said as they began the three-flight climb to the main living area, which was apparently on the very top level.

"I didn't mind in the least. Call me anytime for babysitting. I mean it."

"Seriously? Because I will take you up on that."

"Please do. I'll make sure you have my number."

Jenna smiled through a yawn. "I won't forget."

They reached the top floor with a living area open to the kitchen. Amber was practically panting when she handed Patty over to Jenna, who wasn't even winded.

"You get used to it," Jenna said with a smile. "Or there's an elevator, but getting stuck once was enough for me."

Amber shuddered. "Stairs it is. Could I use your bathroom?"

"Of course." Jenna pointed out where the bathroom was, then disappeared into the master bedroom next to the kitchen with Patty, who was starting to squawk in earnest.

When Amber finished up, the bedroom door was still shut, and she stood looking around the room for a moment, taking it in. The house was gorgeous—new and modern, yet with the look of the older Sandover homes. The front of the house facing the beach was all glass, and Amber stepped out through the sliding glass doors.

She breathed in deeply, leaning on the rail. In front of her, the sky was the deep blue-black of a velvet dress, but if she turned her head, she could see the strains of pink and gold that bled into a beautiful sunset off behind her on the sound side of the island.

Amber located Nick down below. He was in the middle of a heated two-on-two volleyball game. He and Jimmy were taking on Beau and Jackson. All four were ridiculously athletic, even Jackson, who was ten or more years older. Shirtless, their muscles flexed and bunched, visible even from here. *Probably visible from space*, Amber thought, staring as Nick leaped for a ball.

Amber sighed, leaning on the railing, imagining the reel of her life spinning forward. She could see this being her life in ten years, twenty. Not watching from the balcony of a multimillion-dollar home, but the idea of friends and family on the beach.

Will I get ten or twenty years? Will I get a family?

Will I get Nick?

It wasn't cold, but Amber wrapped her arms around herself before stepping back through the balcony door.

As she stepped inside, a voice startled her. "You can still see the sunset from up here."

Amber glanced up a small set of steps she hadn't even noticed earlier. A small room perched almost on top of the house, like a little crow's nest enclosed with windows on all sides. And reclining on a love seat was Emily.

Amber swallowed, hesitating where she stood.

"Join me for a minute?" It was more of a command than a question.

Here we go, Amber thought, as she began to climb the small set of stairs.

It wasn't that she didn't *like* Emily, and as she'd told Nick, Amber and Jimmy hadn't been serious. Still, she'd been incredibly hurt and humiliated when Emily showed up out of nowhere on Sandover. Amber remembered introducing herself to Emily as Jimmy's girlfriend, having no idea who Emily was.

Now, Amber could see that she'd gotten ahead of herself. Jimmy had never even kissed her. It shouldn't have hurt as much as it did. But that's the thing: feelings didn't have to play by logic's rules.

Amber sank down into a chair beside the love seat where Emily was sprawled with her long legs tucked up on the cushions. Emily was right, the view up here was amazing. The sky looked like a beautiful bruise, pinks and purples fading into deep blue. Only a faint gold lined the horizon over the sound and the distant mainland.

"I wanted to say I'm sorry," Emily said.

Amber blinked. "What?"

Sighing heavily, Emily crossed her legs and leaned forward with her elbows on her knees. "I know that I totally made things awkward for, like, a year. More than a year. I didn't mean to. I'm not, like, good at girl stuff. Or ... talking."

Amber couldn't help it. She laughed. "Girl stuff?"

"You know," Emily said, waving a hand in the air. "Feelings. Heart-to-hearts. It's never been my strong suit. I should have cleared the air a long time ago, but didn't know how or what to say. This is me making up for lost time."

She paused and cleared her throat, while Amber simply stared. This was ... wholly unexpected.

"I didn't mean to steal Jimmy from you. I'm sorry how everything happened."

Amber blew out a breath and sagged back against the cushion. "I don't think he was ever mine to steal."

"Yeah, but you guys were dating when I came. I thought mean things about you even if I didn't say them. I was horribly jealous."

"Of *me*?"

Emily's head jerked back slightly in surprise. "Are you kidding? You're adorable, you live here, and you were dating him."

"Oh."

"At the time, I'd been trying to tell myself for two years that I wasn't in love with him. That I hadn't made the biggest mistake of my life rejecting him. I didn't come here for him, at least not consciously." She shrugged, then grinned. "I'm not sorry Jimmy and I got together, just about how it happened. I didn't want you to be hurt. I just wanted Jimmy."

"You seem just fine at talking about your feelings," Amber said drily.

"Yeah, right," Emily said. "I'm too blunt, too honest. I don't know how to sugarcoat things. The point is: I'm sorry I hurt you. I'm sorry I've been weird or awkward. Sometimes that's just me when I don't know how to be."

The small room fell into darkness as the light finally faded completely. Only a light from downstairs in the kitchen illuminated the space. Emily's face was still beautiful in shadow, like some centuries-old sculpture.

"I forgive you," Amber said. She hadn't even been mad, truth be told. But things had been awkward, incredibly so. If Emily could be honest, Amber could too. "I was never mad. Just hurt. And I … lost more than Jimmy. I lost my friendships."

Emily's lips parted like she was going to speak. Then she twisted her lips, like she was wrestling with her words.

"You can have them back. I'm done being awkward and weird. I actually like you." Emily sounded surprised when she said this. "I think we could be friends. I mean, as long as you know that I'm not good at being all … feeling-y."

Amber burst out laughing. It took a moment to stop, and she saw Emily grinning at her, looking pleased. "Feeling-y?"

"You know. Touchy-feely. Woo woo. Hugging. Flowers

and butterflies and rainbows. I'm bad at that. I don't know how to braid hair or do manicures—what?"

Amber was laughing even harder, clutching her stomach as it started to cramp. She didn't know what it was about Emily's words, which weren't all that funny. "I'm sorry! It's just—I don't know." She wiped a few tears that had escaped, running down her cheeks. "This whole conversation was just the last thing I ever expected. You're different from what I thought."

Emily tilted her head. "What did you think?"

"I didn't know much about you." And then things she had known, she didn't like. "I just knew that you and Jimmy seem happy together."

"Boo! Where'd your honesty go. That's way too nice. I'm sure you had some mean thoughts in there too. Girls usually do when it comes to me. Woe is me, right?" Emily rolled her eyes. "The poor, pretty model can't make friends. But you *have* to be friends with me. I just figured it was time to end the bizarre awkwardness."

Amber giggled. "I'm sure I contributed a lot to the awkwardness. I didn't want you to think I was still after Jimmy or not over him or mad. I just wasn't sure how to *be*."

Emily grinned. "So, basically, to sum up, we could have ended the long-term awkwardness last year with a short-term awkward conversation. Great."

"Pretty much."

"Now that we've established that, we could get on with being friends. Or—being more normal. You don't have to be my friend."

It was the second time Emily had said that, and though Amber couldn't imagine this brash, honest, beautiful woman being insecure, she could read the signs.

"I'd like that, actually."

Amber wasn't just saying that to be polite. Emily was nothing like she had previously thought, and without feeling like the whole Jimmy thing hung between them, she could really see being friends.

"Good. Now that we've got that settled, I think there was talk of s'mores on the beach."

There were s'mores, though by the time Emily and Amber got down to the beach, most of them had been eaten. The folding table on the beach was littered with trash from chocolate bars and empty marshmallow bags. The sweet smell hung in the air.

"Don't worry," Jimmy said, holding out a plate for Emily, "I saved you some. Blackened to a crisp, just the way you like them."

As Amber watched, Emily put a hand on Jimmy's face and gave him a quick kiss. "Just like my heart," she said, taking the plate.

Amber's stomach shifted. It had nothing to do with jealousy or weirdness, and everything to do with the fact that she wanted that. Not with Jimmy. She hadn't kept feelings—beyond hurt—for a long time. She wanted her own Jimmy. The kind of guy who would save s'mores for her. Honestly, it was a small thing that she wanted, but the yearning for it felt huge. She wanted someone who would *consider* her.

"Hey! I thought you left me." Nick stood beside her, smiling.

"No way. Just got caught up in a conversation."

"Good or bad?" His gaze flicked to Emily, who was licking marshmallow off her fingers.

Amber smiled up at him. "Very good. I'll fill you in on the way home."

"Good. Here." He shoved a plate toward her. "I didn't know how you liked them, so I made you one set extra black and crispy and disgusting and one golden brown, cooked to perfection as they ought to be."

"Blasphemy!" Emily said. "You've got it all wrong. Black is best."

Nick blinked in surprise at the interruption, then found his smile again as he turned to Amber. "What's the verdict?"

Amber stared at the plate. Nick had even managed to cover it with foil, keeping the s'mores warm. Her throat felt thick and her eyes pricked with tears. How embarrassing! Getting worked up over something so small as a plate of s'mores.

But it wasn't small. It was exactly what she'd been thinking moments ago watching Jimmy and Emily. Amber wanted a guy who would be thinking of her, considering her. And here was Nick, a knight in shining armor handing her a plate of s'mores. He wasn't just any guy, but the guy that every part of her seemed to want, despite the reality of their parents. Despite her cancer diagnosis and its impact on her fertility, which she needed to tell him about.

"Golden brown perfection."

She managed to blink back the tears and smile brightly as she took the plate. Emily groaned, and Jimmy laughed. Nick shoved his hands in his pockets and dragged a toe through the sand, watching as Amber took a bite of the blackened one first.

"You save the best for last, huh?" Nick asked.

Amber licked the chocolate from her fingers. "Always."

CHAPTER NINE

Amber had come to this bridal boutique with dozens of brides, but it took a lot of mental prep before she could force herself to even get out of the car. After ten minutes of breathing exercises, silent prayers, and two Gwen Stefani songs, she walked through the front door feeling like she could make it through dress shopping with her father's fiancée.

It wasn't just the fact that Linda was in a relationship with Amber's father, shopping for a dress to be his new wife. That would have been bad enough on its own. But especially after the cookout last night, her feelings for Nick just kept expanding. Amber felt like his mom and aunt were going to see evidence of it all over her face.

Evie, one of the women who worked at the boutique, greeted Amber inside the door. She bounced on her toes, and her blonde curls bounced with her. Evie was one of those effervescent women, always bubbly, always in motion.

"Hey, Amber."

"Hi, Evie. I'm meeting Linda for her nine o'clock appointment?"

"They're already here in salon one. You can go on back. And let me know if you need anything. Extra strong mimosa, maybe?" Evie gave her a quick smile, her eyes pitying.

Word traveled fast. Amber had hoped maybe Evie wouldn't know Linda was anything other than a normal client. Then again, this was Sandover. Gossip traveled faster than a brush fire.

"Do you have vodka?" Amber deadpanned.

Evie laughed. "No, but I could get some."

"I'm kidding. I'll be fine." *Probably. Maybe.* "Actually, a mimosa would be great."

"Oh, and your dress for Ripley's wedding is ready to try on," Evie said. "I'll bring it back in a few minutes. With a glass."

"Sounds perfect."

Ripley and Cash had gotten engaged earlier in the year and had planned for a wedding just after Christmas, since that's when they had fallen in love the year before. Amber was going to be the maid of honor, with Emily and Mercer being the other two bridesmaids. So far, Amber had managed to avoid Emily. She had known it would be inevitable with bridal showers and a bachelorette party she still needed to plan. After clearing the air at the cookout, Amber could now look forward to it all instead of dreading it—the way she was dreading this next hour or two.

Taking a breath, Amber walked down the hall toward the spacious private dressing area, feeling like she was walking toward her doom. Okay, maybe that was a little dramatic. Then again, all things considered, her life *was* dramatic right now.

Amber had promised herself a treat once she got through

this. A bribe in the form of a pint of her favorite gelato from the grocery store, and at least three episodes of *The Vampire Diaries*, one of her favorite guilty pleasures.

This is nothing, she told herself. Nothing a little Klaus can't fix. The bad boy vampire from the show wasn't the kind of guy she'd ever want to date in real life. But that's why he was a TV boyfriend. Amber could appreciate a hot, centuries-old bloodsucker with a delicious accent and a penchant for the finer things in life. He was an escape, and if anyone deserved an escape right now, it was Amber.

Here we go, she thought, stepping into the dressing area. But all the breathing exercises and prayers and Gwen Stefani songs couldn't have prepared her for the sight of Linda, standing in front of a full-length mirror in a wedding dress. Her heart felt like it had been slammed in a car door.

Linda caught sight of Amber in the mirror and spun, the dress lifting a little as she did so, reminding Amber of a little girl playing dress-up. "Amber! You came!"

"I'm here! Sorry I'm a little late."

A gorgeous woman with sleek blue-black hair, what looked to be a designer dress, and a champagne flute in her hand crossed the room with a confident stride. This was Linda's sister? The two women looked like flip sides of a different coin. No, not even like the same currency.

"I'm Jill. Does that make me a step-aunt?"

Amber shook Jill's hand, forcing a smile. "I ... guess so? I'm not sure about how all that works."

"You should know!" Linda said. "Jill is on marriage number three. Maybe she could make a tutorial. Or a Power-Point presentation?"

Well, that was an interesting fact to file away for later.

"Ha ha." Jill sipped her champagne, seemingly unbothered by the comment. She turned back to the dress Linda wore, a hideous, strapless gown with a neckline that was far too low. "Can we agree that isn't the dress for you and move this show along?"

Linda tugged at the top of the dress. "Amber, what do you think?"

I think I'm going to need at least two pints of gelato and six episodes after this.

Amber had to think about what she would say if Linda were any other client. "If you're pulling on it now, you're going to be doing that on the big day. It's a sign that you're uncomfortable, and that's the last thing you want to be."

"You're right. Thank you. I don't know what I was thinking." Linda smiled, looking relieved as she moved to the dressing room.

"I don't know what she was thinking either," Jill muttered.

Up close, Jill was even more beautiful and intimidating than she'd been from a distance. She eyed Amber with an assessing gaze. Her sharp blue eyes didn't seem to miss anything as they scanned over Amber.

"You're adorable. Too bad about the whole wedding thing, or I'd want to set you up with Nicky."

Amber practically choked. *Nicky?*

Hopefully her face didn't give away all the things that went through her head at Jill's statement. She wanted to laugh at the nickname and cry hearing Jill's statement about it being too bad. Was it really so awful if she and Nick dated? The idea at first was horrifying, but they were both adults. It only sounded bad on paper. In reality, the more time she spent around Nick, the more she wanted to. And not just as friends.

Jill, however, didn't need to know *any* of that. Amber

chose to do the sensible thing and steer the conversation away. Far, far away.

"How long will you be in town?" Amber asked.

"As long as my sister needs me." She paused. "I may stay a few weeks. I need something of a break."

Amber was still trying to make sense of the fact that they were sisters. Jill clearly could read the question on her face—hopefully, *only* that—and smirked.

"I know. We look and act nothing alike. Dye job," she said, pointing to her hair. "And we're fifteen years apart. I'm closer by six months to Nicky's age than I am to Linda's."

"Stop bringing that up! It's weird!" Linda shouted from behind the dressing room door.

Jill only rolled her eyes. "Yes, big sister."

Evie appeared at that moment with a bridesmaid's dress in one hand and an empty glass in the other. "Special delivery," Evie said, handing Amber the dress.

Jill plucked the glass from Evie and poured orange juice and a generous helping of champagne into the glass for Amber.

"Have you already picked a dress for the wedding?" Jill asked, handing her the glass. She then filled her empty glass with straight champagne.

"No. I'm the maid of honor in a friend's wedding in December," Amber explained.

"Do you need anything else?" Evie asked. "Any more dresses to try?"

"We're good for now, thanks." Jill tilted her head at Evie. "You're cute too. Are you single?"

Amber's heart dropped, and Evie's eyes went wide.

"Yes? But I, um—"

Linda interrupted, calling out from the dressing area.

"Want to help me with this one, Jilly? It has too many buttons."

"Duty calls," Jilly said drily, setting her champagne down before disappearing into the dressing room.

Amber took another, longer swallow of her mimosa, and Evie grinned. "Want another?"

"No. But do you have an escape hatch?"

"Unfortunately, no." Evie glanced toward the dressing room, where Linda and Jill were arguing about corsets and shapewear. "I'm sorry."

"It's fine." Amber shooed her toward the door, trying to tell herself that it wasn't because Jill wanted to set Evie up with Nick. "Go, while you still can!"

"Let me know if you need anything!" Evie giggled and headed back out to the front of the boutique.

The next few dresses Linda tried didn't work either. Amber didn't want to say that it was because the styles were all much too youthful, but Jill never minced words. Jill reminded Amber a lot of Emily, abrasive and honest, maybe to a fault. Watching the sisters bicker, Amber had so many questions about their family life and about Nick.

How did he usually get along with his mom? With Jill? It made her realize how little she knew about him, even though she felt so connected to him already.

"Are you going to try that on?" Jill asked, tipping her chin toward the bridesmaid dress that Amber had left hanging on a rack behind the sofa.

"I'm … not in the mood." The last thing she wanted was to have Jill's honesty directed her way.

"This isn't easy for you, is it?"

The softness in Jill's tone surprised Amber, which is maybe why she answered honestly. "No. It's … difficult."

Jill sighed. "I think it's hard on Nick too."

Amber had thought they were talking about this particular moment in the boutique, not the wedding itself. It was true either way—all of it was painfully difficult.

"He's a good guy, you know. Nicky."

Amber did know. A lot more than she wanted to let on to Nick's aunt. And she couldn't wait to call him Nicky the next time she saw him.

Jill continued. "And my sister is a sweetheart. If they manage to make it down the aisle, she'll make your father very happy."

If *they make it down the aisle?*

Amber was reeling from that statement but Jill had already pivoted the conversation.

"What do you know about that Ava girl? Would she be good for Nicky? I mean, I know you barely know him."

I know him better than you think, Amber wanted to say. The idea of Evie dating Nick made Amber's fingers curl into her palms, the nails digging in painfully.

"Evie is great. But I'm not sure what Nick is looking for."

Jill rolled her eyes. "Not another swimsuit model. That's for sure."

A swimsuit model? Amber wanted a sinkhole to open in the middle of the floor. What were the chances that Nick dated *swimsuit models?* Wasn't it enough to lose Jimmy to a supermodel? Granted, after talking to Emily, Amber saw her in a completely different light. Still. The idea made her squirm. Was her whole life some kind of cosmic joke, with all these coincidences and unfortunate connections?

Maybe she needed a new type of guy. Or a new career.

Also, there had been a definite tone in Jill's words when she said *swimsuit model*. What had the model done to Nick? Fierce protectiveness and jealousy warred within her chest.

Neither was as strong as her intense curiosity to know more *now*.

"What happened with the model?" Amber asked, going for a casual tone. The way she dribbled mimosa down her chin as she asked totally negated that. Thankfully, Jill didn't seem to notice.

"She was the worst. Lied, cheated, and generally was just a pill. Everything she had going was on the surface. It was a great surface, but that's all."

Amber absolutely hated the idea of Nick with someone else. Anyone else. Especially a swimsuit model with a *great surface*.

You have no claim over him, she reminded herself. Even if they'd had a great time the night before. It had definitely felt like a date, all the way up until he dropped her off at the curb at the end of the night. He hadn't even turned off the engine, like he was a rideshare driver or something. Amber wouldn't lie—she'd been disappointed. All night, the vibes were there between them. At least, she felt them. He seemed to as well.

You're the one who said you wanted to be just friends, she reminded herself. Amber had no one to blame but herself if she was now stuck in the friend zone, watching while Nick's aunt set him up with other women. Like Evie.

Amber wanted to pound her chest and yell, *MINE!* Clearly, she needed to get it together. Or, talk to Nick. They'd dismissed the idea of dating, or *she* had, but maybe they shouldn't have.

"Okay, I think this is it."

Linda stepped out of the dressing room and Amber drew in a gasp. She looked classic and beautiful in a cream lace gown that was fitted at the waist with a sweetheart neckline and three-quarter-length sheer lace sleeves.

"Wow," Amber said.

Linda beamed. "You like it?"

Amber swallowed, remembering again that this was his father's future bride. What would her mother say about Amber being here for this moment? Guilt felt like a tight vise, squeezing her chest.

"It's beautiful," she managed to say through strangled breaths.

Jill got to her feet and walked over, examining Linda while circling her like a lioness. Amber was thankful that for the moment, both of them took their attention away from her. She sat on her hands to keep them from shaking.

"How does it feel?" Jill demanded.

Linda walked—no, she glided—over to the full-length mirror. She turned to the side, tilted her head, and bit her lip, which did nothing to hold back her bright smile. Amber had seen this dozens of times, the moment a woman found THE dress. It made her choke up every time, even though now the emotions were tangled in her chest.

The guilt continued to clutch Amber with its cold fingers, leaving her frozen as Jill and Linda continued to admire the dress. She felt like the worst kind of traitor, as though just watching this was a betrayal.

I'm sorry, Mom. I'm so, so sorry.

"I think this is the one," Linda said.

Amber was glad that Linda didn't turn and ask for an opinion. There was no way she could have responded without bursting into tears. Thankfully, with a few more deep breaths, Amber managed to shove all the big feelings down and even out her features.

Jill wrapped an arm around her sister's waist. "You look gorgeous. Hank would have loved it."

Linda gave a little gasp. "Jilly!"

"What? He's gone now. But he'd want you to be happy. And I know he'd approve. That's all."

But Linda recoiled, and almost ran back to the dressing room, slamming the door on Jill, who sighed heavily and stood just outside, rapping with her knuckles. Amber watched, feeling like she was intruding on a private moment. In a way, she felt better knowing this wasn't easy for Linda either.

Then, why marry my father? Doesn't he deserve someone who isn't thinking about her late husband? Why are they both rushing this?

Jill continued knocking on the door, her voice soft. It didn't suit her. "Linds, don't be mad. I'm sorry. It seemed like an okay thing to say. I guess I can see why it isn't."

Amber could have sworn that she heard a sob from inside the room. Jill leaned her head on the closed door. "Linds, please. Let me in. I'm sorry."

"How could you bring him up? Here, of all places!"

Amber slipped out of the room, feeling like she might explode at any moment. Her chest felt tight, and she wasn't sure if it was compassion for Linda, grief for her own loss, or if she was still feeling territorial about her father.

Or, in a completely different way, territorial about Nick. Maybe all of the above.

"Are you okay?" Evie asked when Amber made it to the desk out front. She held out a tissue, and Amber took it, though her eyes were dry. For now.

Amber leaned over, putting her head on her hands. "No. Yes. I don't know."

Evie sighed and patted her back. "I'm sorry. I know this must be hard for you. Why didn't you pass this off to Ripley?"

"Linda wanted me," Amber groaned. "God knows why."

Literally, Amber believed God did know why. She wished

he would enlighten her on some of the last week's events, which all seemed like the kinds of things you'd expect on a rigged reality show. Did he have a sense of humor? Was he punishing her for something?

Or maybe his perfect plan for her simply wasn't a smooth path. It was an unpaved road, filled with potholes and gravel that kept getting stuck in her shoes.

"What's your new stepbrother like?"

Amber flinched at the term. She would never get used to that. "He's … great." The words came out flat, even though Amber meant them.

Evie might be exactly Nick's type with her blonde curls, big blue eyes, and extra-long legs. Evie was sweet and thoughtful, patient even through the worst bridezillas that Amber brought in. She would never lie or cheat. And she probably had perfectly working ovaries, and not even a hint of cancer.

Amber didn't need to wonder why the thought of Evie and Nick together sliced through her like a blade. She knew exactly why. The feral part of her shouting *Mine!* in her mind had made itself incredibly clear.

As though summoned by her thoughts, Jill appeared. Amber straightened up and cleared her throat, tucking the tissue into her purse.

"We've said yes to the dress." Jill slid a black credit card across the counter. "And how would you feel about being set up, Ava?"

Evie, Amber thought.

"Me?" Evie blinked.

Jill plucked one of the business cards from the desk. "Put your number here. I'm giving it to my nephew, Nick. Amber knows him. She can vouch for him. Isn't Nick attractive?" Her eyes were piercing.

Amber swallowed. "Very."

"And a nice guy too, right?"

"The best," she practically whispered.

Jill's eyes narrowed, and for a few seconds, Amber thought she had been caught, flying her feelings like a big flag above her head. Then, Jill blinked and turned back to Evie. "Well? Ring us up for the dress and give me your number. Chop, chop. I've got places to be."

"Yes, ma'am." Evie jotted down her number, ran the credit card, then excused herself to the back to help Linda with the dress.

Jill leaned on the tall desk and turned to Amber, giving her a narrow-eyed stare. "I like you, wedding planner. Again, too bad about the circumstances. Otherwise, I'd be setting you up with Nick in a heartbeat. You're just what he needs."

Amber tried to keep her face even, not showing how much she really, really wanted that to be true. But as she watched Jill tuck the card with Evie's phone number into her purse, desperation and jealousy tore through her like a summer storm.

While kissing Nick had been the most spontaneous decision of her life, telling him they should just be friends had been the dumbest.

CHAPTER TEN

For the second night in a row, Nick stood outside Amber's door with sweaty palms. Yesterday, he'd been telling himself to take it slow, to ease into a conversation about dating.

And he'd taken it so slow that he hadn't even walked Amber to her front door. He would have done that for any other woman, any friend. But he had been afraid that all thoughts of being slow would have flown out the window if he walked her up. He already knew what it felt like to kiss her, and he wanted to do it again.

He had sat there like an idiot, gripping the steering wheel with tight fists to keep from chasing after her, watching her walk away in the dark. Alone. It felt wrong on every level.

As he'd driven home afterward, he decided that he didn't want to hold back, to be slow. In some deep way, Amber already felt like *his*.

Which brought him to her doorstep with a mixed bouquet of flowers and a bottle of white wine, since that's what she had been drinking in the bar the night they met.

As he stood in the store, staring at flowers and then wine, he hated that he didn't know what she loved. White or red wine? Dry or sweet? Or did she prefer beer? Carnations or roses? Lilies?

Despite how little he knew *about* her, in the last few days he'd started to feel eerily like he *knew* her. And there was a difference.

One meant having a knowledge of likes and dislikes, some history, and any factual details. Basic things like her birthday or the kind of wine and flowers that would elicit the brightest smile. Deeper things like her passions and fears and goals.

Knowing someone had more to do with a soul-level connection. Nick didn't think of himself as particularly new agey or woo-woo, but he and Amber had that deeper knowing. He could feel it, and he suspected she did too. Tonight, he intended to be bold. He wanted to be honest, *completely* honest, and if Amber felt the same way, then soon enough, he could fill in the gaps of what he didn't know about her.

Taking a steadying breath, he knocked on Amber's door. The television that had been blaring on the other side stopped.

"Just a minute," Amber called. He heard her shuffling behind the door, probably looking through the peephole. Then she swung open the door, her eyes wide. "Nick?"

Nick couldn't help smiling. Amber looked ... adorable. Her hair was falling out of a messy bun, her pajamas had a chocolate stain on the front matching the smudge on her chin, and she wore glasses with black plastic frames.

Glasses! Why were the glasses the shove pushing Nick over the edge? He didn't have a thing for girls in glasses, not that he was against them or anything. But *Amber* in glasses ... wow.

"You have no idea how beautiful you are," he said, his voice rough with the truth of his words.

Yep. I just said that. But the confession felt *good.*

Amber's eyes went even wider, making her look almost owlish behind the glasses. One hand flew to her hair.

"I—*what?*"

Nick grinned, and shouldered his way past her into the apartment. He had jumped from the plane, pulled the parachute cord, and now just had to see how he landed this thing. No going back to slow now. Oddly, the thought didn't scare so much as excite him.

His eyes took in Amber's apartment greedily, feeling like it was a secret decoder to the things he didn't know about her. It was bright and clean, with photographs and art prints framed on the wall, a potted plant with big green leaves in the corner. He could see vacuum lines in the rug.

But the couch and coffee table told a different story. Crumpled-up tissues and two empty cartons of ice cream were spread over the coffee table. A soft blanket and a bed pillow had been tossed on the couch, like Amber intended to sleep there. Or *had been* sleeping there.

When he took in the television, Nick chuckled. Amber fumbled with the remote in one hand while picking up her mess with the other. Whatever she was watching had paused right as a man—or vampire?—had his sharp teeth in someone's wrist. Blood was everywhere. Never in a million years would he have pegged Amber as a horror movie buff.

"You like horror movies?"

"No, um, it's a show. *The Vampire Diaries.*" She clicked off the TV, holding all her trash in the other arm. A tissue fell to the ground, but she didn't notice.

"Huh. Isn't that one of those teenage shows?"

Amber's cheeks flushed. "It's based on young adult

novels, though they aren't nearly as good as the show." She finally managed to get the television off and scurried to the kitchen with her trash.

"Do you like to read, then? About vampires?" Nick asked, wandering around the room glancing at the framed photographs and art prints. Most of the photos were of Amber and a woman Nick knew on sight must be her mother. They looked exactly alike, even down to the dimples. Something about seeing the woman his mother would replace—not the right word, though he didn't have a better one—made his heart lurch sideways in his chest.

Nick loved his mom, and he could even understand her loneliness. But to slide right into a space so recently occupied? To dive into the middle of someone else's fresh grief?

Honestly, it made him angry. It felt like a violation.

"Are those for me?"

Nick spun around at the sound of Amber's voice. He had almost forgotten the flowers and wine, despite the fact that they were still in his hands. He held both out.

"They are. I didn't know what you liked, so I guessed. I should have gotten ice cream and vampire books, I guess."

Amber laughed, slapping him playfully on the arm before taking the flowers and wine. She buried her nose in the bouquet, taking a long breath. Then immediately sneezed, losing her glasses.

Nick grinned, retrieving them from the floor. He placed them gently back on her face, tucking back a lock of hair as he did so. His thumbs grazed her cheeks as he pushed the glasses up to the top of her nose.

Their eyes met, and the air between them had all the uncontrolled energy of a live wire. For a long moment, they simply stood, gazes locked.

Amber blinked and stepped back, out of reach, then

turned and spun away, disappearing into the small kitchen. Nick wanted to stalk after her like a wolf, corner her, and refuse to release her until he'd kissed her as senseless as he felt.

"The wine is perfect. Would you like a glass?" Amber called.

"Sure. Thanks."

"No, thank *you*. This really is a surprise."

"Do you like surprises?" he asked.

There was a pause, and Nick heard the sound of the cork popping. "Not usually."

Nick filed this away in his growing list of things he knew about Amber. She wore glasses (sometimes), liked at least one teenage vampire show, and didn't like surprises.

"I can go," Nick said, having no intention of doing so.

"Nope." Amber stood behind him, holding out a glass. "Tonight, surprises are okay."

Nick took the glass, making sure his fingers brushed hers, feeling that touch like a jolt. They sat on the couch, and he didn't miss that Amber scooted to the furthest edge, pulling her feet up between them as though she needed a barrier.

"So," Amber asked. "What brings you by?"

"You."

Her cheeks bloomed pink, and Amber stared down into her glass. A small smile twitched on her lips. "Oh?"

"I also needed to escape. My aunt, Jilly, is in town. She and my mom together are …" Nick shook his head.

"I don't see how they're related. They're so different."

It took Nick a moment to remember that Amber had gone with them dress shopping earlier. He had been avoiding the house all day, spending some time at the station, just hanging out with the guys, and exploring the island.

"Right—dress shopping. How was *that*?"

Amber shook her head. "Interesting."

"Way too vague," Nick chided. "More details, please."

Amber set her glass down on the table and began reworking her hair. Nick watched her arms and fingers as they moved gracefully through the long strands. He took another sip of wine.

Amber smiled, and her eyes gleamed. "So, should I start calling you Nicky?"

Nick groaned. "Nope. No. Absolutely not. I have not ever answered to that name and never will."

Amber laughed, and he threw a throw pillow at her. She caught it, hugging it to her chest. "I thought it was cute, *Nicky*."

He wouldn't answer to Nicky, but did like the idea of Amber thinking he was cute.

"Do you have any embarrassing nicknames?"

Amber shook her head. "Not even any non-embarrassing ones."

"We should fix that. Just to level the playing field. Let's see … Amby? Bambi!"

She tossed the pillow at him. "Don't you dare."

"Amberoni? Ambience?"

Amber groaned. "I'm out of pillows to throw."

"Here." He tossed the pillow back, and then returned it again after she'd thrown it at his face.

"Bramber? Bram?"

"That's not terrible. I'll think about it."

"I kind of like it. Bram. Anyway, dress shopping with my mom and aunt. They didn't tell embarrassing stories about me?"

"Darn! I didn't think to ask." Amber picked up her glass again, swirled it around for a moment, then took a sip. "They did try to set you up with someone."

Nick's mouth went dry, and he studied Amber's face for a clue as to how she felt about that. He couldn't read her expression, which was like a closed door.

"Yeah, they try that sometimes."

Amber's eyes flicked up to his. "Evie's really nice. She's the one they … you know." She cleared her throat. "She's beautiful too. Your aunt said you'd dated a swimsuit model. Evie would probably be your type."

None of this was good. Nick dragged his hand down his face. Kim. They had brought up *Kim* to Amber? And tried to fix him up with someone in front of her? He was going to yell at them both the minute he got home.

"I thought you said they didn't tell any embarrassing stories about me." He tried to make his voice sound playful, but it was difficult with his chest so tight.

Amber shrugged. "It's hardly embarrassing. Dating a model. Emily was a model too."

The last sentence was spoken quietly, almost into her wine, which Amber finished in a quick swallow. She set the glass on the table.

It took a moment for the significance of her words to sink in. Amber had dated Jimmy, and he chose a model over her. Nick had also dated a model. That was an unfortunate coincidence.

Amber pushed her glasses up her nose, smoothing a hand over her hair again. Self-consciousness practically radiated off her. She really didn't know how beautiful she was and probably didn't feel all that beautiful now, comparing herself to the ghost of a swimsuit model.

Nick reached out and touched her knee. "Just so we're clear, I don't usually date models. That was a one-time thing, and it is embarrassing how blind I was to see how little we had in common and what a terrible person she was."

Amber's face didn't change. Probably because his explanation sucked. He made it sound like he'd been blinded by Kim's beauty or her body. *Partly true*, Nick had to admit to himself. They had chemistry, but it had been all physical.

But Amber was far more beautiful in this moment than Kim had been even all made up. And the chemistry between Nick and Amber ran far deeper than the physical, in ways he couldn't even explain. Physical attraction? Oh yeah. But there was so much more. He felt a tug of something on a level he never had before.

And you know what? It's time to stop hesitating and do something about it.

He moved closer to Amber, scooping her feet into his lap. "I'm not interested in being set up with anyone."

Amber watched his hands as Nick began to lightly massage her feet through the fuzzy unicorn socks she wore. "No?"

"No." Nick kept his eyes trained on her face, waiting for her to look up. When she finally did, their eyes locked. Something shifted in her gaze, the nervous, self-consciousness from a moment ago disappearing.

"Any particular reason you don't want to be set up?" she asked, not looking away.

"I'm already interested in someone. It's not official or anything. But I'm hoping to win her over. To woo her. To make sure she knows how worth it she is. I thought we could just be friends at first but ... I think we both feel more."

Amber's mouth spread into a slow grin, one she tried at first to hide, giving up to let it take over her face, those dimples winking at Nick.

"How do you think it's going so far? The wooing, I mean."

He squeezed her feet, letting his thumbs glide up her

arches. "I think okay. I'm not sure I've done a good enough job telling her how beautiful she is. No matter what she's wearing. Even if there's a little chocolate on her chin."

Amber's eyes went wide, and her hand flew to her chin. "What? Where?"

Nick grinned. "I've got this."

Before she could protest or stop him, he curled one hand around the back of her neck, leaning in. Her eyes fluttered closed as his mouth found just the right spot. Nick tasted the chocolate on his tongue, kissing it away before he let her go and leaned back, massaging her feet again.

Amber didn't move. Her eyes were still closed, lips slightly parted, and her whole body still.

Too much? They'd already kissed, but that had been totally different. It was unexpected for them both, really. Nick didn't pick up women in bars, and the more he knew Amber, the more out of character he could see it had been for her.

His thoughts paused there, as though tripping over that realization. Why had Amber asked him to kiss her? What had been the news she got that day if it hadn't been her father getting married?

While debating if this was something he could ask about, Amber's eyes opened. "Can we ... do this? I mean, our parents ..."

Nick sighed. "Really unfortunate, right?"

She nodded. "But it's not like we're actually related."

Nick shuddered. "I'm thankful for that. And we're both adults. It shouldn't matter if I ask you out."

Amber's lips twitched, and she raised one eyebrow. "Are you going to ask me out?"

Nick flashed her a smile. "Oh, did I forget that part?"

She nodded, and he paused dramatically, as though deeply considering. At least until she poked him in the chest. He let go of her feet to grab her hand, placing a gentle kiss on her knuckles. He kept her hand, holding it loosely between his palms, unwilling to let go.

Clearing his throat, Nick met and held her gaze. "Amber—*Bram*." Her smile widened. "Will you go on a date with me?"

Amber bit her lip, and started to nod. Then, her expression changed in a way that made Nick's stomach plummet. Worry and hesitation crossed her features.

"What is it?" he asked.

"Our parents."

"I thought we decided not to worry about that."

"And I do think it's fine," Amber said. "But we have to *tell* them. I'm not sure about you, but that's not a conversation I'm excited about having."

Oh. *Oh*. Nick sighed and squeezed her hands. He hadn't thought through the actuality of announcing to his mother that he was going to date his soon-to-be stepsister. He had a feeling she wouldn't mind after the initial shock. But Amber's father? He hadn't walked away from dinner with the best impression of Nick. He could still remember Tom's hard stare. The man probably wouldn't approve of Nick even without him being a future stepson.

Nick traced her knuckles. "Right. Your dad is not my biggest fan. I still owe him an apology."

Her eyes flashed. "And he owes you one."

"Even if he doesn't give me one, I'll make it right. That will help." But he wasn't going to apologize and then ask to date Amber in the same breath.

"Jill all but told me today it couldn't work between us."

"She said that?"

"She said a lot of things."

"I'll bet," Nick muttered. "Look, what do you want to do?

There are complications. But I don't want to walk away. I don't want to be just friends. I think we're on the same page."

"We are. But I also don't want to lie or hide a relationship."

The way they did. She didn't have to say the words. He understood.

"What if," Nick said, "we wait until there's something concrete to tell them?"

What he felt already was concrete enough. *But,* he told himself, officially, we're just going on a date. There isn't a label. Yet.

"That makes sense. I mean, I don't tell my dad about every first date I go on."

Nick's hand tightened on hers. "You go on a lot of dates?"

Amber smirked. "Wouldn't you like to know."

He would, actually. And also … he wouldn't. Because he hated the idea. "How do we decide when to say something? I mean, after how many dates or is there some official marker?"

Amber grinned, those dimples making him lose his reason. "Hey, hot stuff. Feeling a little cocky? How about you get through a first date with me, and then we'll see."

He pulled her hand to his lips again, giving her a slower, sweeter kiss this time. "Oh, I plan on passing through date one with flying colors."

CHAPTER ELEVEN

Going on a first date turned out to be a challenge. Between Nick's long and irregular shifts that sometimes kept him at the station for days or at weird hours and Amber's schedule that included several night events, a few days passed without them even seeing each other, despite near-constant texts throughout the day and night.

What couldn't wait was the start of Amber's treatment. The morning after Nick brought her wine and flowers, she had arrived bright and early at the hospital for the first cycle of what Dr. Espana called an aggressive course of treatment. She had been weighed, poked, prodded, and then poisoned.

One treatment down ... a whole bunch left to go, Amber thought, walking out of the hospital. She paused to lift her chin, letting the late October sun slant over her face. She thought she would feel something, or feel different after her first chemo session.

I feel fine, she thought, getting behind the wheel. *Like nothing happened at all.*

Except the poison she knew was now inside her body,

along with the invasive cells. How strange to feel nothing, but know there was a silent war being waged on a cellular level.

Honestly, she thought the whole thing would be different. She had imagined sitting in a dark room hooked up to something or with a machine humming ominously nearby. Alone (since she still hadn't told anyone yet), scared, and in pain.

She hadn't expected a bright, turquoise room, looking out over the ocean, filled with what looked more like her father's favorite recliner than a hospital table. There were half a dozen other women of varying ages, all with their own IVs or PICC lines. They chatted and gossiped throughout the treatment. The whole thing had a barbershop vibe to it. Well, except for the fact that at least half the women in the room had no hair.

It's funny—that was the one big side effect everyone associated with chemo. But a few of the women still had full heads of hair, even after months of treatment.

The women had practically pounced on Amber because it was her first time and she was the youngest of the group. And when they found out that her mother had died not three months before? Forget it. Amber now had six new women, vying for the position of adoptive mom, big sister, or honorary aunt.

The love and care had reduced Amber to a mess of tears, before they made her laugh again, sharing way too much information (that she definitely didn't need or want) about things like sex during cancer.

Amber's phone was now filled with these women's emails, phone numbers, and also resources and links for things she might want or need from wigs to sources for medicinal marijuana, even though she hoped she wouldn't get to a point where she would need or want most of the things she offered. The surprising love and care made Amber feel less alone, especially considering this was still her secret.

Or, it had been. She was on her way to the office now to talk to Deondra. There was no way to plan the treatments around work hours. And even if Amber felt fine now, there was no guarantee she would continue feeling that way. Hopefully, Deondra could keep it between them. She still didn't want to tell Ripley or Nick or anyone else, until she'd told her dad.

That conversation seemed harder with every hour she waited. Which gave her an unwelcome sense of understanding for her dad and why he kept Linda from her. He should really be the first to know, but Deondra had to know, since this would impact Amber's work.

This will be practice, she thought, when Deondra waved Amber into the office. *A warm-up for telling my dad.*

I can't lose you too, he'd said during their breakfast last week. The words hung over her like a ghostly refrain. Now, she also had another confession to make at some point, one about her and Nick. Assuming things went well on their date.

Who was she kidding? Amber was practically ready to skip ahead six months in their relationship. Nothing felt new or uncertain with Nick. He felt like the surest thing in her life right now, aside from God. She better start preparing to tell him everything as well.

Hey, Dad. I'm dating the son of the woman you're about to marry. But before you freak out! I also have cancer.

Oh, Nick—by the way, while we're getting started, I have cancer and I won't be able to have kids. Still want to date me?

Yeah, none of that would work.

"What did you want to speak with me about?" Deondra asked with a smile.

She closed her laptop, giving Amber her full attention. Amber kind of wished she had *less* attention. She picked at a hangnail until it started to bleed.

"Recently, I got some news," Amber started.

That sounded more like she found out a long-lost uncle had died or something. Deondra waited, her expression attentive and a little concerned. Clearly, she was getting the nervous vibes Amber was putting out.

Amber picked at the hangnail again. *Just rip the dang thing off.*

"I got a diagnosis. Ovarian cancer. I started treatment today."

Deondra sat back in her chair, mouth open. She blinked several times before speaking, and Amber could see the control her boss was famous for slipping. "Amber, I don't know what to say."

"You don't need to say anything. I mean, cancer sucks. We all know that. It is what it is."

Amber wanted to smack herself. Of all the dumb phrases she hated, *it is what it is* was one of the worst.

Deondra leaned forward again, her dark brows knitting. "It does suck."

Amber almost jumped. She had never heard her boss use such an uncouth word before.

"I am so sorry that you're going through this. What do you need? How can I help support you?"

The kindness sent a tremor through Amber, and she clasped her hands in her lap, squeezing. "I don't know. I started my first cycle today."

"This morning?" Deondra's eyes widened. "And then you came to work?"

"I want—I *need*—normalcy. As long as I can, I don't want this to affect me."

"Sweetie, you can't stop it from affecting you. Even if you feel fine. How *do* you feel?"

Amber shrugged. "Totally normal. Which is weird, right?"

Deondra smiled. "There is no normal or weird when it comes to cancer or treatment. Breast cancer survivor, here." She pointed to herself, fingers grazing the buttons of her white dress shirt.

"Really?" Amber shouldn't have been surprised. She was living proof that you had no idea how many people were going through or had been through some version of this nightmare at any time.

"It was almost ten years ago. And I'm still here. Still fighting." She smiled. "So, again—what do you need?"

What Amber needed was to talk. And without meaning to, she told Deondra everything—at least related to her treatment. Tears sliding down her face but voice steady, her words spilled out to Deondra until Amber felt pleasantly empty, and yet somehow more whole than she had walking in.

CHAPTER TWELVE

"This will be better than the dress shopping," Amber said out loud as she pulled into the bakery parking lot. "Because there's cake."

She was meeting Nick's mom and aunt for the cake tasting. Perfect timing, because she was starving after her third chemo treatment. Worried about nerves and nausea, she couldn't bring herself to eat before the treatments. So far, so good.

And today, cake sounded amazing. Hanging out with Nick's mom and aunt? Not ideal. But they could just focus on the food. Cake covered over a multitude of sins. She needed to buy a sign with that phrase for her kitchen.

Before walking in, she adjusted her sweater, pulling it down over her arms to hide the small bandage hiding her IV. A bruise bloomed blue underneath on the inside of each elbow. Despite how well it went telling Deondra, Amber hadn't managed to tell her father or anyone else. Yet.

The scent of sugar and coffee filled her nose instantly. Amber spotted Linda and Jill at a table in the corner, but her greeting caught in her throat as she saw Nick. He hadn't told her he was coming, and his wicked grin told her that he was enjoying the look on her face.

Hope he enjoys payback. Because I'm going to get him back for this.

Not that it wasn't good to see him for the first time since the other night. It was. He looked even more handsome than she remembered, and that was saying something. And therein was the problem—how could she hide her feelings from Jill and Linda with Nick sitting right there?

Recovering herself, Amber crossed the room with a smile, focusing on Linda. "You didn't start without me, did you?"

"Of course not!" Linda said. "Hope you don't mind that Nick tagged along. He insisted."

"I don't mind. Good to see you again, Nick. Or should I call you Nicky?"

Jill laughed, and Nick shot her a look. "Nick is fine."

Yes, he is.

Amber shot him a sideways glance as she sat down at the four-person table. He occupied the chair on her left, Linda on her right, and Jill sat directly across from her. Amber's stomach rumbled loudly.

"And that," Nick said, patting his flat stomach, "is exactly why I decided to come today."

"Is it?" Jill said.

Amber snapped her eyes across the table, noting that Nick did the same. Jill only grinned, raising her eyebrows at Nick as though in challenge. Had Jill already figured them out? How? Amber chose to ignore the questions. For now.

A teenage girl in an apron with the bakery logo reached their table, providing a much-needed break in that tension. Amber had called earlier in the week, putting in Linda's requests so all the cake samples would be ready. It was going to be a lot, as Linda couldn't narrow it down between thirteen flavors.

"My name is Mindy, and I'll be helping you today. I'll have the cakes out in a minute, Mrs. Blair."

Amber froze, her vision swimming in black for a moment. Her *mother* had been Mrs. Blair. Not her. These moments when the grief hit her suddenly were the absolute worst.

"It's just Amber."

"Could you bring us a few waters?" Jill asked. "And a coffee for me."

"One for me as well," Nick said. "Amber?"

He seemed to sense her disquiet, and his knee touched hers under the table.

"I'll take a coffee as well," Amber said quietly.

"Sure thing, Mrs. Blair."

This time, Amber flinched.

"It's Amber," Nick reminded Mindy, who gave a quick apology and scurried away.

Nick's leg pressed harder against Amber's, and by the look she stole at him, he seemed to understand exactly what was bothering her.

It's fine, she told herself. *You're fine.* But she had learned that grief took different forms. Sometimes it was like a fog, settling over her for days. Other times, like now, it knocked her over like the sharp slap of a wave.

She wanted to appreciate Nick's touch, to think of his strong thigh nudging her knee, his handsome face watching her with concern. But her mind was spinning out, and her hands felt shaky. All she could do was lean slightly closer, letting his steady presence anchor her until the pain dulled enough for Amber to rejoin the conversation.

Jill steepled her fingers on the table, turning her attention to her sister. "I hadn't realized—you're going to be Linda Blair."

Linda rolled her eyes. "If I take his last name." Her gaze darted to Amber. "Which I'm sure I will. So, yes. I'll be Linda Blair."

"What's wrong with that name?" Nick asked.

Jill laughed, her dark hair glinting like raven feathers under the lights. "I forget how young you are, Nicky. Linda Blair is an actress, best known for vomiting up pea soup in *The Exorcist.*"

Gross. Amber's stomach did a barrel roll to the left at the thought. Thankfully, Mindy returned, not calling Amber Mrs. Blair even once. The tiny tasting plates practically took up the whole table after adding in the drinks. Apparently, this was just round one of flavors.

"Before you start," Amber said, pulling out her notebook. "I want to make sure I get your impressions. Normally, I'd say we should all try the same ones at the same time but ..."

She glanced around and almost laughed. Jilly's fork was suspended halfway to her mouth with chocolate cake on the tines. Nick had already cut into what looked like the cinnamon molasses cake and Linda covered her mouth as though to hide the fact she had already taken a bite of something. There was no point.

"Just have at it. Let me know what you like and don't like," Amber finished.

Linda dropped her hand and smiled while chewing, her eyes sparkling with warmth. Nick's mom really did have a joy about her. *That is something Dad needs,* she thought. The idea was still difficult to wrap her head around, even at a tasting for their wedding cake.

Ten minutes later, Amber's mouth felt soft from all the sugar, almost like it had been coated in sweetness. Nothing tasted right today, though she seemed to be the only one with that issue. With a jolt, she realized that it might be the chemo. There were so many side effects she'd read about that they were all a big blur. Clearing her throat, she took a sip of coffee as Mindy cleared the second set of plates.

"What are the frontrunners?" Amber asked.

"Chocolate buttercream," Jill said. "No question."

Linda shook her head. "I want white. The lemon-lavender was divine. Or maybe the almond."

Jill made a face. "Lavender belongs in body soap, not cake."

Amber agreed. Even on other days, lavender wasn't a flavor she'd ever gotten behind in food. As a scent, it was refreshing. But she didn't want to *eat* refreshing. Her stomach twisted, and Amber wished she hadn't tried so many of the flavors in one sitting.

"Nick?" she asked. "What were your favorites?"

Amber had tried to be purposeful in not talking to him too much, but not ignoring him either. Meanwhile, under the table, he alternated between nudging her with his leg, poking her with his foot, or grabbing for her hand in brief moments when they could get away with it.

Linda was none the wiser, but Jill seemed to have been onto them from the start. Amber couldn't even meet her gaze, and hoped she wouldn't spill the beans to Linda before anything had even happened.

"I'm with Jilly for once, Mom. Chocolate buttercream."

He and Jill high-fived, and Linda sighed, turning to Amber. "How do I decide?"

"Ultimately, it's your choice. Your wedding." She tapped her pen on the notebook. "You could also ask my dad what he likes."

Again, as with everything so far, her father seemed to be

an afterthought. Maybe she was being too hard on Nick's mom. Linda smiled at the idea, like it was a novel idea to ask her fiancé what he liked.

"I'll send him a text. Or—do you know what his preference would be?"

"Probably the chocolate buttercream," Amber said.

"And chocolate buttercream has the popular vote," Jill cheered.

Linda frowned. "But we're not doing my wedding by democracy. I want your opinions, but ultimately, I'm going to choose. Were there any other cakes we all liked?"

Amber felt the weight of all their gazes on her. She let her eyes travel over the notes she had written, as the beginning of a headache was making the words seem to swim and blur.

As though he could see her struggle, Nick grabbed the notebook and scanned the page. Grateful, she dropped her hand and squeezed his knee under the table. He didn't give any sign that he'd felt the touch.

"Your favorites were the lemon-lavender, the almond, and the vanilla bean," Nick said. "We all liked the almond and vanilla bean, even though they were distant seconds and thirds to chocolate."

"Can we just veto lavender?" Jill asked.

"No. You don't have veto power," Linda said.

As the two of them began bickering, Nick shot Amber a look before sliding her notebook back across the table. His fingers brushed hers slowly, eliciting an eruption of goose bumps up her arm. He gave her a quick smile before he pulled back his chair and stood.

"Well, this has been delicious, but I'm meeting Jackson to look at houses," he said, standing.

Jackson? Amber shouldn't have been surprised. That

group had a way of folding people in, just as they'd brought Amber back in as though she'd never left.

"I wanted to go with you," his mom said.

So do I, Amber thought. But looking at houses together was probably much too intimate for a first date, which they would be having that night.

"I promise I'll show you any final contenders before I make a decision," Nick said. "Unless I make a decision today."

He walked behind the table, dropping a hand on Jill's shoulder and a kiss on his mother's head. Amber found herself wishing that they didn't have to hide things. Would he squeeze my hand? Give me a kiss on the cheek?

He winked at Amber over their heads, mouthing, *See you tonight*. She tried to keep her cheeks from flushing, but it was no use. Instead she took a long swallow of coffee, calling out a goodbye just before the door shut behind him. Jill shot her a knowing smirk that Amber ignored. Suddenly, she was feeling exhausted from trying to keep her feelings hidden for the last half hour.

"Back to cakes," Amber said. "Do you want to go with your top choice, the lemon-lavender? Or do you want to wait and consider?"

"I won't forgive you if you have a wedding cake that tastes like soap," Jill said, crossing her arms.

"Your second wedding cake had bourbon buttercream!" Linda said.

Jill rolled her eyes. "So? What wedding couldn't use a little more bourbon?"

Amber pressed her fingers to her temples briefly, trying to dredge up the energy for this conversation. She reached for the coffee again, then pushed it away as the smell filled her nostrils, bitter and acrid.

"I'm not sure," Linda said.

"We don't have to decide today. You can think about it and let me know."

Suddenly, Amber became acutely aware that the rolling of her stomach had moved into something more urgent. It wasn't an overload of sugar, but actual nausea, likely an effect of the treatment she had all but forgotten about. "Excuse me," she said, aiming for polite control but instead sounding panicked and shaky as she darted toward the bathroom.

"Amber!"

Linda's voice followed her to the narrow hallway, and Amber collapsed to her knees, barely getting her head over the toilet bowl in time.

Moments later, Amber finished, wiping her eyes, nose, and mouth with a wad of toilet paper.

"Are you okay?"

Her head jerked up to see Linda and Jill in the doorway. She had been in too much of a hurry to lock the door. There was no point in pretending. Not when she still practically hugged the rim of the toilet.

"I know that look," Jill said. "Pregnant?"

Linda gasped. "Jilly! You can't just—"

Amber's laughter interrupted whatever Linda was saying. It had an edge of hysteria to it. She dropped her head on her arms, trying not to think about how gross this was. Sweat dripped down her back, but she didn't want to remove her sweater in case they saw the bandage on the inside of her elbow.

"I'm definitely not pregnant," Amber said. *Just the opposite, really. I'm killing any chance I could ever get pregnant.* Which reminded her again that she should probably slow things down with Nick. Or at least be up front about her treatment and its consequences.

"I'll call your father," Linda said, pulling her phone from her purse.

"No! Please don't. He'll just worry. I'm fine. Just a … bug. I'll let him know later."

Amber got to her feet, knowing she had to prove herself or else have her father alerted. Today, she did not have the energy, physically, emotionally, or otherwise. At least Nick missed the big show. How embarrassing *that* would have been.

Nick … their date tonight. She groaned again. There's no way they could go out now. Disappointment rolled through her. Or was that more nausea? Amber needed to get home. Now.

Her legs wobbled, but Amber managed to splash water on her face and locate a small smile.

"I'm going to go home and climb into bed. I'll tell my father. Think about the cakes and let me know by the end of the week so we can place your order. I'd personally recommend going with the vanilla bean or almond. Chocolate makes for messy photos and too many people don't like lavender."

Even mentioning flavors made her stomach lurch again, but Amber forced herself to push past Linda and Jill, who for once, looked alike with their matching expressions of concern. She made it safely back to her apartment before losing the contents of her stomach again in the privacy of her own bathroom, knees pressed into the pink memory foam bath mat.

CHAPTER THIRTEEN

"What do you think?" Jackson glanced at Nick as he locked the front door of the cottage rental. "I know you were unsure about your budget, but do you see any potential?"

Nick hesitated as they moved down the stairs to the parking area and Jackson's Jeep Wrangler. Jackson seemed low-key and casual. Not the kind of guy who was a billionaire, or close to it, like Amber had said. The guy drove an older model Jeep with the doors off, not a Tesla or Bentley. Still, talking finances with Jackson made Nick self-conscious.

"I like the place," Nick hedged.

"But?"

He struggled for words. Sure, he saw potential in every place they looked at today. There were no bad views on the island. Some of the places needed a lot of fixing up, but he didn't mind doing labor. It was more the finances and commitment that made his stomach tighten into more of a knot.

The prices weren't a surprise, but it was still disappointing how much even the rentals would stretch his budget. Renting felt like dropping money into a dark hole, never to be seen again. And after having been here a week, did he want to even consider buying?

Amber's face flashed into Nick's mind. He could see her brown eyes lit by the fire on the beach in front of Jackson's. He thought of Beau and Jimmy, who already felt like fast friends, real friends. The sense of belonging washed over him again, the sense that this island was more than a temporary stop. That Amber would be more than a temporary girl.

It was probably too soon to even consider that, as their first official date was tonight, but that's how Nick felt. They had been texting almost constantly the past few days while he was working shifts at the station. She stayed on his mind constantly, as though she'd always been there.

He hadn't been able to resist going to the cake tasting, though he knew she didn't like surprises. He *had* to see her. His heart thudded a new beat in his chest when she walked through the bakery door. It was all he could do to keep his feelings under wraps, their touches brief and under the table. Jill seemed to see right through them both, and he could only hope she wouldn't tell his mother before he had a chance to.

They reached the Jeep and Jackson leaned against the side of it. "Is it the prices? Location? Or something else?"

"Honestly, I'm not sure. I usually go with logic, but something doesn't *feel* right."

Or maybe part of me is just afraid. Maybe his hesitation was about more than being conservative about his money. After Kim, and maybe even more after everything with his father, Nick had grown conservative with his hope. Especially with the idea of love and a family, a future.

But Sandover and its people had ripped right through the barriers that kept him thinking about those things for himself. Now, he wanted them. Badly. But the prospect of planning out a future, of allowing himself to hope, was terrifying.

"I'm sure that sounds stupid," Nick said.

"Not at all. I make decisions based on my gut all the time. Well, gut or what might be a God thing," Jackson said. He grinned. "Or indigestion. Sometimes it's hard to tell."

Nick laughed as they climbed into the Jeep. Jackson put the key in the ignition, then turned to give Nick his full attention.

"So, it's more of a gut thing than a budget thing?"

Technically, Nick *could* afford any of the places they looked at today. His fireman's salary wouldn't have been enough on its own, but he had saved over the years, multiplying his income through stocks and investments. A few of the other guys at the Charlotte station had introduced him to a day-trading app, and it turned out that Nick had an eye for stocks.

But he had always saved. Spending was risky. So was committing, even to this island that was so warmly welcoming him.

"Maybe it's just that I haven't bought property before," Nick said. "I have the money, but it's hard to think about actually spending it. I tend to be pretty conservative. That's at least a part of it, I think."

"Believe it or not, I understand the feeling," Jackson said. "But I'll also tell you that you'll more than get your investment back on any of these properties. Whether we On Islanders like it or not, the rest of the world has discovered Sandover."

Nick knew that was true, and it did make him feel better. The island was in a transition, and as much as it probably did bother the people who grew up in what had been a sleepy beach town, there was a buzz of excitement and growth that spoke to a healthy economy and booming real estate market.

Jackson grinned at Nick. "Let's think about this a different way. What would you feel comfortable with spending? Not what budget you have, but what budget would make you feel *safe*."

Nick blew out a breath and gave Jackson an amended budget, one that was probably too low for any property on Sandover. Jackson thought for a moment, the Jeep's engine idling. Then, he popped his sunglasses down and smiled, reversing out of the driveway and began driving toward the sound side of the island, to an area Nick hadn't yet explored.

"I have a few ideas. We'll see how your gut feels about those."

"Okay," Nick said, wishing he had been able to plan this around Amber's schedule. He hadn't wanted his mom to tag along, but would have loved to get Amber's perspective, to know what kinds of places spoke to her and felt like home.

Yeah, you're totally sunk, he told himself.

"I've got a feeling about you, Nick," Jackson said. "You seem like the kind of guy who's going to stick around. And I think I have a few places that might make the perfect island home for you."

Nick nodded, but knew that as he looked at the homes, he wouldn't just be imagining himself inside them.

———

If today hadn't already packed enough in, Nick had scheduled one more stop before the date. He parked his car outside Tom's small private law practice, staring at the door for a moment or two before telling himself to stop being such a baby. Even if they weren't announcing it to their parents yet, he couldn't go on a date with Amber without first apologizing to her father. He knew it would be like a splinter, a tiny edge of worry and concern the whole time.

As Tom's administrative assistant ushered Nick into the office, he took another long look at his mother's fiancé. He still had the bookish look about him, tall and lean with glasses and a pinched expression, even before he glanced up to see Nick.

His mom really wanted to marry this guy?

He had nothing of Amber's brightness and easygoing nature. Everything about him seemed ironed, tucked in, and buttoned up from his glasses to the stiff collar of his shirt. Tom looked nothing like Nick's father, who had been handsome, with the same square jaw and broad shoulders Nick and his brothers all shared. A booming laugh and the ability to charm a room.

Which was part of the problem, Nick thought bitterly as Tom set down his pen and gestured to the chair in front of his desk.

Maybe Mom realized she needed someone completely different. Or maybe I'm just not seeing the side of him she does. I need to give the guy another chance. If not for my mom, for Amber.

"Hello, Nick," Tom said coolly.

"It's good to see you, sir."

"Is it?"

Nick wanted to bristle at the comment, and the look in Tom's eyes, which was nothing short of disapproving. Nick knew it was his own fault for being such a jerk the night they met. Even with the shock, Nick should have handled himself better.

This is for Amber, he reminded himself.

"I deserve that. I know that I didn't make a good first—or any—impression the other night."

Tom leaned back in his chair. "We can agree on that."

Nick again pushed past his irritation, hoping it didn't show on his face. "The last year hasn't been easy." The last few years, honestly, but Nick wasn't about to get into that with Tom. "Out of all my brothers, I've been sort of the unofficial protector of my mother. It's why I relocated here. We thought she could use support."

Tom's face thawed, but only a few degrees. "That's admirable of you."

"She and I have a good relationship. I'd like to keep it that way, which means I want to have a good relationship with you as well. I'll admit I didn't handle the news well. I hope you can understand how much of a shock this was for me and Amber."

Tom's face iced right back over at the mention of Amber. "Don't presume to speak for my daughter."

Nick clenched his jaw, debating his next words. He felt like he was walking through a room with weak floorboards, just waiting for them to give way beneath his feet.

"Sir, I'm sorry for the way I behaved the other night. For my anger, and how I took it out on everyone else."

"Including the man you assaulted? Personally, I think you should have been arrested."

Nick's shoulders tensed. "I think you might have responded in a similar way if you'd heard what he said to your daughter. I was only protecting her."

"Amber doesn't need your protection," Tom spat.

Nick stood slowly, disappointment curdling in his belly. He wasn't going to be scared away from Amber by Tom. But he also knew that Amber had a good relationship with her father. Nick needed Tom's approval, and at the moment, earning it seemed impossible.

"Sir, I didn't come by for more conflict. I wanted to

humbly apologize, and I'd like to ask your forgiveness for my rash and emotional behavior. Will you please forgive me?"

Asking forgiveness rather than simply apologizing took more humility. It stung more to ask for it, especially with how Tom was treating Nick. But it was something his mother had ingrained in the boys from an early age. *Anyone can say they're sorry,* she had said. *Godly men ask for forgiveness.*

Nick also knew it was harder to give forgiveness. It really did require letting go of anger and hurt, or at least, owning up to it.

As he watched Tom struggle, Nick felt sorry for the man. *He lost his wife just a few months ago,* Nick reminded himself. *He's still grieving.* The angry stage of grief lasted a long time for Nick, though he had different reasons for his anger, not all having to do with his father's death.

"Yes," Tom said, pursing his lips as though the word tasted bitter. It didn't sound like forgiveness at all.

Nick held out his hand across the desk, though it was honestly the last thing he wanted to do right now. "I'm looking forward to getting to know you better, sir."

Tom shook his hand quickly, but said nothing more. And as Nick left the office, he couldn't push down the worry tightening his chest, not only for his relationship with Amber, but for his mom. The concern grew when his phone buzzed with a text.

Jill: Just a heads-up. Your girlfriend started puking after you left. So, in case you had any plans with her, they might change.

Nick shook his head, wondering how Jilly always seemed to read him so easily. He didn't respond but sent a text to Amber.

Nick: Heard you aren't feeling well. I'm on my way with supplies.

Amber: I'm sorry about our date. You don't need to come!

Nick: You can't stop me.

Amber: Please stay away. I feel awful.

Nick: That's why I'm coming.

Amber: No.

Nick: Yes.

Amber: NO!

Nick: Sorry. Can't text and drive. See you in half an hour.

Amber: I hate you. Also, um, if you're getting supplies, I need toilet paper.

CHAPTER FOURTEEN

"Amber!"

Nick pounded on the door with a little more force. When he pressed his ear to the door, he could hear the television. Maybe she fell asleep watching a movie? Too bad he didn't have a key. He didn't want to have to use brute force … even if he *could* get through the door if needed.

Knowing Amber was sick on the other side had Nick feeling all kinds of desperate. "Amber! It's Nick. Open up."

He was about to move into plan B, which he hadn't quite worked out yet, when he heard the deadbolt slide. The door didn't open, but a weary voice said, "Come in before the neighbors call the cops, you stalker."

Nick grinned and opened the door, balancing the bags he carried in one hand as he locked the door behind him. The blinds were all closed, washing the room with pale gray late-afternoon light.

Amber was hardly visible in a heap of blankets on the sofa, a mixing bowl on the coffee table and a small trash can on the floor. Her face looked haggard, eyes puffy as though she'd been crying, and her hair fell limply from a ponytail. She hardly looked like the same vibrant woman he'd seen a few hours ago.

"Hey," Nick said. "I've got toilet paper, as asked. And a few other things."

"You really didn't need to do this." She tried to smile, but it was a weak attempt and made Nick's throat feel tight.

"I wanted to do this. Now, stop arguing and let me pamper you. I brought crackers, ginger beer, and chicken and stars soup, which is far superior to chicken noodle. Plus, some kind of essential oil for upset stomachs. I can't vouch for this one, but figured why not. Oh! And candied ginger. I tried it and it's not so bad."

She sniffed. "Nick, it's too much."

"It's nothing. Does anything sound good?"

When she shook her head, Nick stepped into the kitchen and set the bags down, pulling out the candied ginger and a bottle of ginger beer, which he poured into two glasses. He carried the bag of candied ginger between his teeth and set the glasses down on the table, dropping the bag to the table.

"Scoot over," he said, moving the mixing bowl which was, thankfully, empty and clean. "And before you protest, I'm not worried about getting sick. In fact, I've read that relationships that start with a couple puking together have a higher chance of lasting."

Amber laughed, though it only lasted a moment and then she groaned and put a hand to her head. "Ow. No more jokes."

"I wasn't joking. Well, I did make up the statistic. But I'm sure it's true. Do you have a headache too?"

"Yes. But I keep puking up the medicine."

Nick settled closer to Amber on the couch, pulling the blanket over his lap. "When's the last time you threw up?"

"Maybe two hours ago?"

Nick reached for a glass and pressed it into her hand. "Just a sip. Ginger beer is stronger than ginger ale. It's room temperature, which I think is better."

Amber took the glass with an unsteady hand, and Nick covered her fingers lightly with his own. Her eyes stayed steady on his while she took a small sip, then a longer swallow. Nick took the glass when she looked like she would drink more.

"Baby steps," he said. "Though I highly recommend the candied ginger. A little goes a long way. Want to try a piece?"

She nodded, and Nick tore open the bag, getting himself a piece as well before handing one to Amber. She stared at it in her palm.

"Doesn't look like much, but it's good. Very gingery. You've been warned."

The crystallized sugar melted on Nick's tongue before the tang of ginger filled his mouth. He watched Amber chew. She nodded to him.

"It's good. Thank you. But really. You didn't need to do this, and you shouldn't be here."

Nick shifted, slinging his arm over Amber's shoulders and drawing her into his chest. She didn't fight him, and contentment spread like warm honey through him as she settled against him. He debated telling her the truth—that he would rather be here with her, even while she was sick, than anywhere else in the world.

"That's better," he said. "Now, what are we watching? Vampires again?"

"We can watch something else."

"Nope. Time for you to convince me that this is a show worth my time."

"Do you even like vampires?"

"Nope." He dropped a quick kiss to her temple. "But I like you."

Amber tilted her head to look up at him. "We'll have to start from the beginning. You need the full story."

Nick smiled and brushed the hair back from her face with his free hand. "Fine by me."

"And no judgment!"

"Do I seem like a judgey guy?"

"You seem like a really nice guy. Too nice."

Nick groaned. "Oh no! A nice guy. That's the kiss of death."

Amber giggled, digging through the blanket to find the remote. "Not in my book," she said. "Nice guys finish first."

And with that, she started season one, episode one of *The Vampire Diaries* curled up close where Nick's heart thudded against her cheek. It wasn't exactly a first date, or romantic, but that didn't matter to Nick at all. He was exactly where he wanted to be.

CHAPTER FIFTEEN

When Amber woke, it was with the realization that she wasn't in her bed. The warm, firm chest beneath her cheek was not anything like her pillow.

"Hey, Sleeping Beauty."

She jerked her head up to see Nick smiling down at her. The quick head movement reminded her of how badly she felt, and how much worse she probably looked. She would have ducked back down but couldn't risk any more movement.

In contrast, Nick smiled down at her, so handsome with a day's worth of golden stubble on his jaw. His pale blue eyes softened as he watched her.

"How long was I out?" she asked, trying to assess how she felt. Her voice sounded raspy, and it hurt to talk. Probably from all the vomiting.

"A few hours," Nick said. "Want me to carry you to bed?"

The idea of Nick in her bedroom was way too much. Her cheeks burned. "Um, no."

Nick's laugh rumbled against her. "I mean that in the most innocent way possible, Bram."

The nickname he'd given her made a tiny ripple in her stomach. Which triggered a larger ripple, which meant—

"Trash can," Amber said, struggling with the blanket.

Nick yanked the blanket off her and grabbed the trash can just in time for her to humiliate herself yet again. And yep—Nick was holding back her hair.

Cancer, you suck, she thought while emptying her already empty stomach. *You're taking my babies, you're probably going to make me bald, and now you're making me puke in front of a guy I really want to like me.*

He *did* already like her though. Amber had no doubt of that, even if they had traded in their official first date for this. It was a sorry trade, and one Amber really didn't want him making for her. A guy like Nick shouldn't be walking into a relationship like this. He needed more.

I am not enough.

The thought shook Amber, and she shoved it to the furthest recesses of her mind.

"You're okay," Nick said soothingly, only making her humiliation more acute. "I've got you."

When she was finally done, Amber kept her head angled down, preferring to look at what was inside the trash can rather than having to face Nick. Seeing him would only make her like him more. But Nick definitely didn't need to see her face right now. She couldn't imagine how she looked, with tear tracks and who knew what else.

"Finished?" Nick asked. The kindness in his voice made her hands shake.

"I think so. For now."

Nick gently removed the trash can, brushing a hand over

her back as he did so. Amber kept her chin tipped down, heavy with humiliation. A moment later, he returned. The couch cushions shifted as he sat down.

"Amber? I've got a warm washcloth. Can I … help you clean up?"

Amber squeezed her eyes closed and held out her hand, which shook. Whether from the sickness or embarrassment, she didn't know. Nick was just too good.

"Thank you. I'll do it."

"Amber," Nick said, "let me help you. Please."

She told herself that it was because she felt so terrible that she agreed, not because she secretly longed for Nick's touch. Amber nodded.

With incredible gentleness, Nick ran the washcloth over the back of her neck, then tipped her back on the couch, wiping her forehead, her cheeks, and around her mouth. His other hand cupped her cheek and she held back a groan at how good it felt to have his gentle touch on her skin, which felt hungry for it. Starved, really.

Nick cleaned her face, then massaged her temples. "What else can I do?"

Amber didn't answer, and realized she was starting to drift into sleep again. But she wanted to stay awake. She was desperate for this time with Nick, despite feeling weak and horrible and embarrassed by her state.

"Your phone's been ringing," Nick said. "Liz said, 'The first ones can be the worst. Call if you need me.' The first what?"

Amber was suddenly very awake. Liz was one of the women she'd met at treatment, a firecracker with purple hair and a penchant for tattoos. She must have meant the first week of chemo.

"Thanks."

Snatching her phone from Nick's hands, she scrolled through the messages without fully reading them. There were at least a dozen from the women she'd spent time with this week in treatment, plus a few from her father and one from Linda, just checking in. She dropped the phone to her lap and pushed the heels of her hands to her eyes.

"The first what?" Nick asked again.

She should tell him everything. The truth about her cancer, her treatment, the fact that she might not be able to have children. Wasn't that the sort of thing you should say up front in a relationship? Or was it too soon to assume Nick even wanted kids? She remembered him holding Patty with such ease.

Amber squeezed her eyes closed. It wasn't fair not to tell him. But it also didn't feel fair to tell him. A nice guy like Nick would never walk away because of cancer and infertility. Or maybe he *would*. She didn't know which possibility scared her more.

"Bram?"

Amber wanted to smile again at the nickname. But she was too concerned with her response.

Tell him.

Don't tell him.

Give him a choice.

Telling him won't let him have a choice.

Let him decide.

But what if he decides to walk away?

"The first … migraine," she said. "I haven't had them before."

"I thought you mentioned not wanting me to catch it. Migraines aren't contagious."

Oh, right. She *had* said that. "I mean, the sickness caused the migraine which caused the vomiting."

Amber hated lying. The words felt unnatural on her tongue. But she couldn't tell Nick about her cancer before her father.

This is just the beginning, she thought. *Today I'm barfing in a trash can; tomorrow I'll lose my hair. Am I going to ask Nick to see me through this? To hold back my hair and see me through whatever side effects I might go through? Not to mention kids. I can't even ask if he wants kids. Because we're barely dating. Oh, and our parents are getting married.* Everything seemed suddenly overwhelming.

Amber couldn't let Nick go. And even if it was the right thing to do, she didn't want to give him the choice. She didn't want to question if he was with her because he truly wanted to be or because he felt like he couldn't leave. The last thing she wanted was to be an obligation. Which meant keeping this from Nick. For now.

She would tell him. She *would.*

Amber's phone buzzed again with a text from her dad. She sighed. "I asked your mom not to tell him for this exact reason. If I don't answer, he'll probably bang down the door just like you did."

"Would he?" Nick cocked a brow.

He had an edge to his voice. What was that about? "Wouldn't your mom do the same for you?" she shot back.

"Of course." Nick grimaced and ran a hand through his hair.

"I know you guys didn't hit it off when you met, but he's a good guy. Did you talk to him yet?" If her voice held a note of accusation, she told herself it was because of how she felt.

"I did," Nick said quietly. He wouldn't look at her.

"And?"

Sighing, he took her hand. "Let's just say that I'm going

to have to work a bit harder to rid him of his first impression of me."

Amber blinked. That surprised her. Usually, her dad was generous with grace and forgiveness. He was one of the kindest men she knew. It didn't track that he wouldn't have been that way with Nick. Then again, he was extremely overprotective of Amber. And Nick had come across like a guy with a temper at dinner. Amber might not have had the best opinion of him had she not seen all the other sides to him.

"I already told him he needed to apologize. Did he?"

"Not in so many words," Nick hedged. "Or … in any words."

"I'll talk to him," Amber said.

"Please don't. I feel like it might make things worse. I just need to find a way to get on his good side before we tell him about this." He squeezed her hand.

The touch set off a chain reaction, the contact zooming through her body, and for the first time since the bakery, Amber felt something other than nauseated. She met and held Nick's gaze.

"You still want to try this? Even after I bailed on our first date?"

"Oh, make no mistake," Nick said. "This is still a first date. And you know what? It's not the worst I've been on."

Amber couldn't help it. She laughed. And suddenly, behind her headache, she was starving.

"For our second date, I have somewhere I want to take you. Maybe in two days when I'm off again?"

"Maybe we should get through this not-the-worst first date and then ask."

Nick groaned. "Playing hard to get always works on me. Fine."

"It's a maybe date," Amber said. "Now, how about for the

second portion of our date, we dine on chicken and stars soup while you tell me your first-date disasters?"

Nick grinned, then leaned close to press a quick kiss to her cheek. "Sounds perfect. This is shaping up to be my best first date ever."

Amber watched him head to the kitchen, thinking that she wouldn't mind if this was her last first date ever.

CHAPTER SIXTEEN

Nick couldn't help but smile at the sight of the petite octogenarian clinging to Beau, her white hair slung over one shoulder as she squeezed his middle. "Thank you so much, young man! I'll make sure Rhett Butler knows what he did wrong."

Nick covered his mouth to hide his laughter, and a slow smile crept across Beau's face.

"Well, now, don't feel like you need to chastise Mr. Butler on my account," Beau said.

Nick glanced at the window of the small cottage, where Mr. Butler watched them. The oversized orange cat looked bored, his narrowed, yellow eyes fixed on them as he licked one paw. Clearly, Rhett Butler didn't feel the slightest bit guilty for needing to be rescued from a tree.

"We should get back to the station," Beau said, clearing his throat and trying to take a step back.

The woman clung tighter, her voice turning almost feline as she purred at Beau, "Oh, must you go? You're welcome to come inside. Alone or with your friends."

She gave Nick the eye, and he took a step back. Beau tried to pry the woman loose, but she had now barnacled herself to his body, and it took some effort. Nick slid his phone out and took a quick picture. He had a feeling that it would come in handy at some point.

Beau managed to unclasp the woman's arms and lightly shove her toward the front door. "My coworkers and I need to return to the station in case there are any life-threatening emergencies. Have a good day, Mrs. Wilson."

Freed, Beau practically bowled Nick over as they made their way down the steps.

"Call me Aliza!" the woman shouted. "And there's a key under the mat. Just in case you're lonely!"

"You should really tell her that it's not safe to leave a key under the mat," Nick teased. "It's your civic duty."

They reached the sidewalk, and Beau slugged Nick in the shoulder. "I'd fear for the safety of anyone entering her home, not the other way around. And I'm not just talking about the cat."

Nick chuckled as they climbed up in the truck, where Jimmy waited behind the wheel. Beau climbed into the front seat and Nick took the back.

Jimmy pointed to Beau's neck. "Looks like you got a little something right there."

"Just a few cat scratches," Beau said. "I'll clean them at the station."

"Nope. Lipstick."

Nick laughed long and hard, reaching up to high-five Jimmy. Beau tried to angle the rearview mirror so he could see his neck, where Aliza had indeed stolen a kiss. He was still rubbing at the spot when they got back to the station and Jimmy pulled the truck into the bay.

As they geared down, Nick turned to Beau. "So, is this

about par for the course on Sandover? The stereotype of pulling a cat out of a tree?"

"I bet the pace is a little different than Charlotte," Jimmy said.

Nick pulled off one boot, then the other. "Just a little. Though we had pretty routine and ridiculous calls too. That was my first cat out of a tree."

Beau chuckled. "It won't be your last. But what we get depends on the time of year. We get a lot of the odd calls during the off-season, but summer we've got an uptick in fires. Mostly tourists not being careful enough with grills. No one cares for a rental the way they do their own home. And a lot of the homes are older, which means faulty wires, things not being brought up to code the way they should. Speaking of, have you found a place yet?"

Nick groaned. "No, and my aunt is here, indefinitely, it seems, so I *need* to get out. Jackson showed me a bunch of places. There are a few places that I'm seriously considering."

The second half of his time with Jackson had proved much better, and Nick found two places he really liked. One was surprising: a rambling ranch in a neighborhood along the sound side of the island. The only hint you were on an island at all was the sea breeze, carrying that beach scent, and the slight glimmer of the sound visible through the pine trees.

"This is where Jenna grew up," Jackson had said, a smile playing on his lips. "Her house was just around the corner."

Nick wouldn't have thought a ranch home in a neighborhood would have impressed him, but the price comparative to the size of the place spoke volumes. It had a big yard, and Jackson said you could reach a shallow beach by the sound in just a few minutes. A thickly wooded natural preserve was also within walking distance. Nick could see settling here, raising kids who would run wild through the piney forest.

The other was the complete opposite: a beach cottage on stilts near the narrow, southernmost tip of the island and only six blocks from the beach. A little smaller than the others with only two bedrooms, it was in need of a little TLC. Okay, a *lot* of TLC.

Still, something in it called to Nick the way the whole island seemed to, the way Amber called to him. The whole face of the cottage, which was the same gray, weathered wood most of the original homes shared, seemed to smile. And not just because the porch had a slight sag to it.

The windows were like bright eyes, reflecting the sky and sun and sea in the distance. The porch wrapped almost all the way around the house, and the main living area had a vaulted ceiling that made it seem much larger than the 1200 square feet Jackson told him it was. Tiny, and with a bathroom and kitchen that needed an overhaul, but still—the charm was undeniable.

Nick could imagine starting to build a life in either one. As to which ... well, he hoped that Amber would help him with that on their second date. Which she had finally agreed to after he plied her with soup from a can and more candied ginger. She was an easy woman to please, at least when she was feeling awful. Hopefully, her migraine would be gone. Or ... whatever it was. He got the distinct impression that it wasn't just a migraine.

Maybe her period? Women didn't tend to be open about that with guys. She knew Nick had grown up in a house full of brothers, but she didn't know that his mother had made every one of them go out to buy tampons and pads, just to prepare them for future wives.

Honestly, the experience had been so horrifying as teenage boys that Nick suspected it's why all his brothers were still single.

But it would have made him a total creeper to ask Amber if she had her period. Later on, he could impress her with how chill he was about it. Not yet. They'd already jumped over so many lines, and this wasn't going to be another one.

Beau gave Nick a friendly grin. "Want to fill us in on you and Amber?"

Nick glanced at Jimmy, who was still gearing down. "It's really nothing," Nick said.

Jimmy held up both hands. "Don't hold back on my account."

"We're good?" Nick asked. Even though Jimmy was now married, and things seemed to get cleared up the other night, he really didn't want to have any weirdness between them.

"I didn't do right by Amber back then and always felt bad. Once Emily arrived here …"

"He was a goner," Beau said. "I knew it. We all knew it. Took them a bit to figure it out."

"Not like you did any better with Mercer," Jimmy said.

Beau laughed and looked to Nick. "Whatever you do, don't take relationship advice from us. We're lucky any of our women would have us."

"Now, that's the truth," Jimmy said. "So, Amber?"

Nick was about to answer when Beau's phone began ringing. He didn't mind the interruption. Despite things being aired out and cleared up as far as Jimmy went, Nick wasn't quite ready to talk out what was going on with Amber. It felt too new, too fragile.

"Hold that thought," Beau said, looking at the screen. "Hey, Jax. What's up?"

His face changed while he listened, and he exchanged a glance with Jimmy before sighing deeply. "Yeah, we're down. We get finished at eleven though. Is that too late? Okay, then."

When he hung up the phone, he looked at Jimmy. "Jax needs us. You up for Bible and Breakfast after our shift?" Jimmy nodded.

Nick tried to decipher the message. Jax was a nickname people used for Jackson. But what they'd be doing with Bibles he didn't know. And breakfast? Their shift tonight ended at eleven.

Beau shifted his gaze to Nick. "Want to join us?"

Nick still had no idea what he would be agreeing to. "I'll be there."

————

Whatever else Bible and Breakfast usually was, tonight it looked mostly like guys crammed into a small booth inhaling a late-night indulgence. Jackson was clearly in a mood. His eyes were red, and so were his knuckles. Nick remembered seeing a punching bag under the beach house and would have put money on visiting it before he arrived.

Nick felt like they were waiting for something, tension heavy over the table, but at least the food was good. There was just something about eating eggs and waffles close to midnight that was extremely satisfying.

Cash strode in, still in uniform, and pulled a chair up to the booth that they commandeered at the back. Nick realized that normally, all four of the guys would fit in the booth. His presence meant someone got stuck in a chair. Maybe he should go? But Cash didn't seem to mind or seem surprised that Nick was there.

The waitress brought Cash a mug of black coffee without being asked. "Looks like we're going to need to build a bigger booth," she said with a smile.

Beau studied the table crammed with plates and the

booth seats practically spilling over with four big men. And now Cash.

"We could probably do that," Beau said. "You think, Jax?"

"It's a good idea," Jackson said, though he looked as distracted and disheveled as when he walked in. "We probably need a bigger table or two."

Wait? Was the diner going to allow them to simply add on another custom booth? Or … did Jackson *own* the diner?

"I might as well get to it," Jackson said, after he'd handed his half-full plate to the waitress. He dragged a hand through his hair once, then again. "It's late."

"We're here, brother," Beau said. "The time is hardly a concern."

Jackson nodded. When he looked up again, his eyes were red and gleaming. "I found out today that my father has been having affairs. Multiple." His words were spoken slowly and carefully, like a person picking their way barefoot through a parking lot littered with broken glass.

Nick missed whatever Beau said in response because the ringing in his ears was so loud. He realized that he was clutching his fork like a weapon and set it down gingerly on the plate in front of him.

This wasn't about him. It wasn't about his father. Nick was here for Jackson. But like grief, Nick's anger often hit him out of nowhere, leaving him unsettled and unsteady.

"I don't know how many," Jackson said, apparently answering a question someone had asked. "And it's been a while … apparently things have changed between my parents for the better. They've worked through it." He sounded bitter, not relieved.

"That's still a lot to swallow," Beau said.

"He's the man I admire—admired?—most in the world," Jackson said quietly. "Maybe it's not my business, as they've made their peace. But I can't help feeling it." He pounded a fist against the center of his chest, then slumped back in the booth.

Nick's mind swirled like a dirty, unwanted tornado of thoughts. He suddenly wanted to be anywhere else. But he was on the inside of the booth, practically stuck to the glass window next to Jimmy's big body.

"What do I do? I feel like my mind is poisoned with this, and I haven't struggled with my anger this way since I was a hormone-fueled teenager. I don't know what to do with it or how to get rid of it."

Nick could relate. He wanted to punch walls or run miles or do something reckless and stupid, just to try and shed the feelings that often raged within him.

"Cash?" Beau said. "I don't know if this is something you could speak to, or if you'd want to."

Cash looked every bit the cop he had when he had arrived at the restaurant. His eyes were serious, his jaw tight. He seemed to hesitate, wrestling with an answer, before he nodded.

"Most of y'all know my story." He swallowed. "My daddy married the girl I had been dating. And yes, he also dated her at the same time."

Nick's pulse was like a hammer, pounding into his temples. He was furious. For himself, for Jackson, and now, especially, for Cash. How messed up could people be? Could anyone really be trusted?

He thought of Amber, letting him hold back her hair as she was sick, of her dimples when she smiled the night they met.

Can I trust her not to hurt me?

And then, a worse thought: *Can I trust myself not to hurt her?*

"The pain is acute," Cash said. "I thought it broke something in me. Maybe it did. They say time heals, but that alone isn't enough. They say God is a healer, but we have to let go if we want peace. That does take time and work to let go. It's not simple. I never thought I'd get there, because it also takes trust. After being hurt so bad, could I even trust a God who didn't stop it from happening? Or worse, because he knew, or even had a hand in the plans."

Nick wondered when the last time Cash had said so many words in a row. Based on the halting way he spoke, and how he gripped his mug, taking intentional breaths when he finished, it wasn't often.

The table was quiet. Nick wished he could slow the thudding of his heart, or cool his temperature, which seemed to be rising. He wasn't ready for this level of depth. Not about this topic. Not even with these guys, who had invited him into their circle. He appreciated their honesty and their vulnerability. No one was offering platitudes or quick fixes, but still. It was too much. He was boiling over.

"If y'all will excuse me," Nick said. He managed to vault himself over the back of the booth, sliding a twenty from his wallet and tossing it on the counter near the register.

"I'm sorry," he said, meeting Jackson's eyes and then Cash's. "More than you know."

CHAPTER SEVENTEEN

By the end of the week, Amber had stopped counting which day of treatment she was on. She wanted to forget. She wanted them to blur together until it was just routine, just another thing she was doing, no big deal. Cancer didn't deserve that much thought.

To be honest? She looked forward to the fellowship of the other women, gathering in a room full of people who understood perfectly and didn't need her to say a thing. Before clearing things with Emily and Jimmy the week before, Amber only had Ripley and her dad. The babies in the nursery on Sundays. That was it. She hadn't realized until now how empty things had been, how lonely she was.

"Morning, beautiful!" Liz called, waving a magazine with the tattooed arm that didn't have an IV.

"Who, me?" Amber said, settling on her chair with a smile.

"Don't go all humble on us, now." That was Lucy, a tall woman who looked like she had been a serious athlete back in the day with her broad shoulders and graceful posture. She winked at Amber.

"How are you feeling?" Liz asked, distracting Amber from the pinch at her elbow as the needle slid in.

Other than the intense nausea the day of the cake tasting, Amber hadn't thrown up. She had felt nauseated off and on but forced herself to hydrate and eat little bites. Nick's ginger was a lifesaver. The only real symptom was exhaustion.

"Mostly good," she said. "So far, anyway."

Several women knocked on anything nearby resembling wood. When the door opened behind her, Amber didn't even look, instead letting her eyes drift closed. People were always coming and going, whether patients or family members and friends who sometimes came along for support.

It wasn't until she heard Deondra's voice that Amber's eyes flew open.

"I hope you don't mind that I came," Deondra said, standing in front of Amber in the same kind of suit she wore every day to work. She had a smile on her face and a tote bag tucked under one arm.

"I—no. But what are you doing here?" Amber asked.

"Who's your friend?" Liz called.

"This is my—this is Deondra," Amber said. "She owns Sandover Events, so you've probably all been to a party or wedding that she's helped with."

The women oohed and aahed over this. "I wish you'd done my grandson's wedding," Liz said. "The fool did a Disney destination wedding. They all seemed surprised I showed up, and then they made me wear mouse ears."

Amber couldn't hold back a giggle, picturing the feisty, tattooed woman in mouse ears. Deondra pulled up a chair next to Amber's, setting the tote bag in her lap.

"To each his—or her—own," Deondra said with a smile. "But I'll confess that's not my favorite kind of wedding."

Amber could actually see the appeal. Lighthearted, filled with childlike wonder and lots of smiles. Not what she would personally choose for a wedding. Amber didn't think much about her own wedding, despite having them in front of her face constantly. It was the curse of the single wedding planner—having to be involved in wedding after wedding for other people. She'd grown kind of numb to the longing for her own walk down the aisle.

Though, if she was thinking about her ideal wedding, the aisle would be sand. Not that she let herself plan or consider specifics, but what she had always pictured was a simple, intimate beach wedding.

One with her mother present, smiling from the front row. The loss swept over Amber and she took a steadying breath, realizing she had been drifting off in her head while Deondra sat beside her.

"I'm sorry," Amber said, giving her head a little shake.

"No." Deondra touched her free arm. "No need for that. I do hope it's okay I came. You can nap, since that's what you looked like you were about to do when I arrived. I brought a project."

She held up a small cross-stitch hoop. It took her a moment to realize what it depicted, and then Amber laughed long and loud, until tears leaked from her eyes. It was a horse-drawn cart, full to overflowing with what looked like a yard sale. Above it, Deondra was finishing out the words, *Junk in the Trunk*.

"You approve?" Deondra asked. "Because I brought you one, just in case you need something to pass the time. I found this little place called Steotch that sells patterns. Some are funny and irreverent." She dropped her voice a little. "Some are a bit naughty."

Deondra handed Amber her phone, and for the next few minutes, she scrolled happily through image after image. Some she didn't get, which let her know that her sense of pop culture was growing rusty.

"I love them," she said, handing the phone back. "But I've never done this before. Can I just pick it up?"

"It's shockingly simple," Deondra said. "Here are a few that I've got on hand."

Deondra's tote bag turned out to be like a magical Mary Poppins kind of thing, with more hoops of varying shapes, thread, and printouts. Amber picked one that had waves at the bottom and two pelicans and read, *My My My You're Like Pelican Fly*. It was silly and ridiculous, and she already knew where she would hang it.

A few minutes later, she had done her first few stitches, surprised at the simplicity and how soothing the rhythmic motions were.

"I picked this up when I did my time here," Deondra said. "Then, I couldn't stop. I don't even like needlepoint. I've got a whole closet full of these. One day, my children will inherit everything and come face to face with all of them." She chuckled. "I only hope I can be watching."

Amber hadn't spent any time outside of work with her boss, and today had been nothing short of shocking. It made her ache to think about the fact that it should have been— would have been—her mother here beside her. Amber knew that once she told her father, he would probably be here daily, even if he was the only man in the room.

So would Nick.

I need to tell them, she thought. Amber knew that it was wrong to keep it from them. They would want to know. And still, somehow, she hated breaking the status quo. She didn't want them to have the same line in their life, clearly marking the time before and after knowing she had cancer. If only she could let them enjoy a little more of the before ...

"Thank you for coming," she said, after a bit of time had passed. The ocean was really starting to come along at the bottom. "It's nice not to feel so alone."

Deondra didn't look up from her own needlework, but she smiled. "I'm glad to be here," Deondra said. "And remember—you're never alone."

———

"Where are you taking me?" Amber asked, peering out the front windshield of the truck. Technically, she knew where they were—one of the old neighborhoods on the sound side of the island—but she didn't know why.

"So, you like vampire shows and patience isn't one of your strong suits. I'm learning all the little things about you, Bram."

Amber poked him in the ribs, close to his side, and he jumped. "I'm being very patient. Just curious. And it's just the one vampire show."

"Are you going to tell me if you prefer Damon or Stefan yet?" he asked.

"Wouldn't you like to know? Wait—where are we? Who lives here?" Amber asked as Nick pulled into the driveway of a cute ranch house.

The sun was beginning its late afternoon descent, and though she trusted Nick, she also needed to eat. It was Saturday, which meant a break from chemo, but she had run point for a charity luncheon, which meant being on her feet most of the time. Deondra had given her a careful look, but Amber insisted she wanted to keep things as normal as possible. Now, she was regretting it. Her feet throbbed, her head ached, and she needed food.

"Just come on," Nick said, spinning keys around one finger. With his other hand, he grabbed hers, walking her up to the front door.

When he grinned and put one of the keys into the lock, Amber stepped back, dropping his hand with a gasp.

"Did you buy a house?" she knew she was practically squealing but couldn't stop.

"Not yet," Nick said. "I have some decisions to make and I need an On Islander's expert opinion."

The sore feet were all but forgotten as she bounced on her toes. "You had Jackson with you. Doesn't get more On Island than that. What did he say?"

The front door was open now, just enough to make Amber good and curious, but she still held back. When not watching *The Vampire Diaries*, Amber was glued to home improvement shows or scrolling through property listings on the computer. Nick stepped closer, slipping an arm around her waist. She leaned into his warmth and the steadiness of his big body next to hers.

"I don't care about Jackson. I want *your* particular On Island opinion," he said, his lips tickling her hair as he spoke. "Will you come in with me?"

"Yes!" Like a hound set free after a scent, Amber hurtled ahead of him through the front door as Nick chuckled behind her.

She called over her shoulder, "You know if I was a vampire, you just gave me permission to come and go as I please. Rookie move."

Nick only laughed.

CHAPTER EIGHTEEN

An hour later, Amber had looked inside every cabinet and opened every door. Nick had followed, studying her more than he paid attention to whatever she pointed out about the home. He listened, of course, but his focus was on Amber first.

She lit up when she spoke about things she loved, and apparently, she loved houses. He wondered why she was doing event planning rather than real estate. It's like she had suddenly replaced a 60-watt with a 100-watt bulb.

At the end of her perusal, he didn't feel more sure or less sure about the house, only certain of one thing: he wanted Amber in his life. Long term. Permanently.

Those kinds of thoughts had been running through his mind, but he'd been doing his best to stifle them. Who really knew that after only a few weeks? How well could you know someone in that amount of time?

But he'd grown weary of arguing with himself inside his head, of pushing away big thoughts and big feelings. It was exhausting, and when he was with Amber, he wanted nothing more than to enjoy, to let go.

Let go. Cash's words from a few nights before whispered in the back of his mind. *We have to let go if we want peace.*

That whole conversation was definitely not something Nick wanted to be thinking about right now, not when Amber was practically skipping back to the car. One of the things he liked when he was with her was forgetting about those other things. She made him only think about the now, about her.

"Are we going to see more houses? What did you like about this one? Oh, look! You can see the sound through the trees."

Amber stopped abruptly, then snaked a hand around his waist and pulled him close, resting her face on his chest.

Nick loved the smell of the ocean mixed with the scent of her shampoo, which was something tropical. Perfectly suited for the island. Perfectly suited for him.

"That's a lot of questions. We're going to see one more house, and I'm not sure how I feel about this one, though I do like a lot about it."

Amber swung around in front of him, putting her other arm around him. Nick brushed her hair back, letting his palms rest on her shoulders before smoothing them down her arms and back up.

"Why don't you tell me what you like and don't like about it? Then, when we see the next place, I'll have that in mind."

"Okay." Nick thought, letting his eyes drift over Amber's face, her deep chocolate eyes, the dimples that were currently hidden, the pink bow of her mouth. The last thing he was thinking about right now was houses. But he was thinking about a future.

"I like that this house looks like a home. It looks like

forever. I could see growing old, or at least older, in this house. There's space. It's quiet and still has a tiny sliver of water in view." He lifted his hands to cup her cheeks. She melted into his touch, and Nick decided to listen to those two little words that had been ringing in his head. *Let go.*

"I could see being married here. Building a life with the woman I love for the rest of my days. Raising a bunch of kids who would run wild in the woods and play soccer in the yard."

At first, Amber's eyes had sparkled, as though she knew he meant her, that he saw these things here with her. But then she seemed to tense and droop slightly, losing that look of magic in her eyes.

I pushed too far. Of course, she's not ready to think about marrying me and having kids, settling down in this house with me. And I just put so much pressure on her opening my big mouth.

Smiling, Nick gave her a quick kiss on the forehead before stepping away to open the door of his truck. "We better get a move on if we want to see the next one before dark. I think I heard someone's stomach growling, though I won't name names. Could we grab something from a drive-thru?"

Amber smiled, though it wasn't in full force, and hopped into the truck. "I could eat my left arm."

"Let's hope it doesn't come to that," he said.

The words were teasing, and she smiled a little brighter, but Nick felt like he had flipped a switch on their date, taking it from fun and free to something heavier. He wished that he could take back his words, at least for now.

But when he climbed behind the wheel, Amber seemed to have followed suit and shifted into a lighter mood.

"If you want me to keep helping you, I'm going to require payment by way of something deep fried and delicious."

"Hm," Nick said, pulling out of the driveway. "Something like french fries? Onion rings?"

"Hushpuppies," Amber said decidedly.

"I'm not sure I know what that is," Nick said.

Amber only laughed. "We'll stop by one of my favorite fast-food places and you'll see."

———

Full of hushpuppies, fried shrimp, and fried fish, Nick drove toward the beach cottage, hoping he wouldn't suffer indigestion for the amount of grease in his belly later. His fingertips left shiny prints on the wheel, despite using about fifteen napkins. But Amber had been correct—the food at the Fish Shack was delicious.

"What's this one like?" Amber asked, not for the first time. "Please? Just a few details."

"We're almost there, and you'll see."

"Please, Nicky."

He gave her a mean side eye. "You think that's going to help you?"

She grabbed his arm, leaning all the way across to put her head to his shoulder and stare up at him with puppy-dog eyes. "Please, Nicky?"

Okay, so his nickname didn't actually sound all that bad coming off her lips. Not when she was so close and looking at him that way, even if he knew she was exaggerating the look a bit.

"Fine. I would say that this place is more of what you'd expect from Sandover. How's that?"

"Not nearly enough." Amber moved back to her side of the car, faking a pout.

Nick turned onto the final street and pointed up ahead

where the house was just coming into view. "How about I just show you?"

Amber's head whipped to the front and she leaned toward the dashboard, staring. Even though there was no For Sale sign in front of the house, she seemed to know exactly which one. He heard her draw in a breath, but for the first time all afternoon, Amber was silent. He didn't know if that was good or bad.

Seeing the house for the second time, especially after just visiting the ranch, Nick's reaction shifted into something more like nervous excitement. He could feel his lower back warming, almost sweating, and his fingertips tingled. His heart sped up, not unlike the way it did whenever he knew he was going to see Amber.

This is the house, he thought. *But will Amber like it?*

When he pulled up in front of the house, she craned her neck further to look up at it, still not speaking. Nick turned off the engine, and the ticking as it cooled covered the silence in the car. Distantly, he could hear the sound of the waves hitting the beach.

"Do you want to go inside and look?" he asked finally.

Amber was already climbing out before he'd finished the question. So, the silence was good, then? She really liked the cottage?

Nick trailed behind her, much as he had in the first house. Only, now he was trying to decipher her silent cues, not trying to follow the train of her thoughts that came straight out of her mouth. It was like two different sides of Amber, and he found them both equally fascinating.

Before heading up the stairs, she explored underneath the house. It was dark and could really use some lights hooked up underneath. She pried open a creaking, wooden door that revealed an outdoor shower long ago claimed by spiders and insects. Amber only sniffed, shutting the door firmly again.

She stopped before a small, shed-like area Nick hadn't looked at with Jackson. It was in the very middle along the back wall, just tucked under the house.

"Do you have a key?" she asked.

The one for the front door also opened this one, and Nick unlocked it and stepped aside. Amber opened the door and flipped the light switch a few times. Nothing happened. She pulled her phone from her purse and flashed it around the small room.

It looked to be kind of a utility room and had washer and dryer hookups. That would be annoying—having to carry laundry up and down the stairs. Nick doubted it would have central air, so probably hot to boot. Amber didn't remark, but waited while he locked up again.

"Careful on the stairs," he said as they started up. Nick took her elbow and steered her around a few places where the wood looked a little warped and where nails were sprouting up like buds in springtime.

Still, she said nothing. *Was she afraid of how much work it would take?* As much as his heart yearned toward the place, it looked much worse now, seeing it alongside Amber. Was it even livable really? He had a feeling the first inspector to pull up would slap a condemned sticker on the place.

Before going to the front door, Amber walked the porch that wrapped around the house, from one side to the other, staring out at the views. Her gaze was soft, but otherwise, there was nothing Nick could read in her face. Something in him said to simply wait, so he did.

But by the time he'd watched Amber float through the living area, staring up at the vaulted ceiling, and the two bedrooms, nerves churned in his gut. He flinched when she turned on the bathroom light. There was no master bedroom with an en suite here. Just one tiny hall bathroom. The two of them couldn't even fit inside.

Nick opened his mouth to say something about it, or about how he and Jackson discussed how easy it would be to expand it a little into the larger of the two bedrooms. But he said nothing, just watching as her brown eyes took in the dingy mirror, the water-stained shower, and the peeling linoleum floors.

Amber flicked off the light and went back to the kitchen. Nick knew that bathrooms and kitchens were usually the biggest money suck for a home, and also the biggest draw for women. That and master bedrooms or closets. This house had charm, but was essentially a gut job. Great bones and a great view, but that was about it.

He watched her open a cabinet, only to have the door come loose from the hinges. Nick barely caught it before the corner of it struck her cheek.

"I'm so sorry," he said, but when she turned, she was smiling.

Not just smiling; she was beaming. Nick stared, caught off guard by her beauty and the display of emotion after she had been so quiet and hard to read.

"This place ..." Amber trailed off and shook her head, then grabbed Nick and squeezed him into a tight hug. "Tell me you like this place better. Or, maybe, don't tell me if you don't. I know it's so much work but—"

"I love this place."

Amber pulled back. He didn't think it was possible for her to smile wider, but she did. "Really?"

He nodded. "I've been terrified for this last half hour, watching you look at the place. You were so quiet! And the last house, you wouldn't stop talking about everything. I didn't know what to think."

"The last house is great. It is. I liked it a lot. But this?" She flung her arms out, doing a little spin right there in the kitchen. "I can see what it *could* be." She stopped and grabbed Nick by the shirt, her hands fisting the fabric. "It could be amazing."

Nick's heart pounded as his eyes dropped to Amber's lips. The tension in the air practically shimmered between them. Her smile faded, and when he glanced up, her eyes were half-closed, the excitement replaced with desire.

He had never wanted to kiss someone so badly, and yet, even as he toyed with the idea of doing just that, he remembered what they had agreed: they didn't need to tell their parents until there was something to tell them.

Right now, they walked a thin edge. They could pretend that there wasn't something here. Because, really, what were they doing? Looking at homes together. He hadn't said out loud that he was imagining a future with her together in these spaces, hearing the echoes of their children.

But the moment he let his lips land on hers, they couldn't pretend. This would be something concrete that would demand explanation. And Nick didn't want to break the spell yet. Especially considering how much Amber's father seemed to dislike him. He hadn't gotten a chance to do anything to change that opinion.

Then there was the dark cloud hanging over him since the night at the diner. Questions and doubts about his ability to be faithful, about what it would take to actually place his trust in another person. Even Amber, who seemed so sweet, so guileless.

The moment passed when he would have kissed her, and instead, Nick pulled her flush against him, letting his lips land near her ear. They swayed for a moment, holding each other as though the world would fall apart otherwise.

"Is it me? Did I do something?" she asked, her voice hardly more than a whisper.

"No." Nick kissed her hair, then let his lips fall close to her ear. "It's not you at all. I just … once we cross that line—again—we'll have something to tell them. We can't keep this a secret forever."

"Right," she said, sounding miserable. "Our parents."

"Yeah, them." He chuckled.

"I had forgotten. At least for a little bit."

"Me too." She paused, but Nick could almost hear the question hanging in the air before she said it aloud. "Do you think this is how it was for them? I mean … how fast things moved?" She gave a little laugh. "I judged them both so hard-core, yet here I am …"

The words trailed off, but Nick didn't need her to finish them. It's how he felt too. He felt things he shouldn't, wanted things he shouldn't—at least, not yet. And somehow, it only felt right.

"Was it too forward to take you house hunting on our second date?" he asked.

Amber laughed. "Probably. But it's perfect. Though … maybe we need to start moving quicker on the dates. They've got a ways to go to match up with how I feel."

He knew exactly what she meant. And he didn't mind the idea of more dates, not at all. Though between their two schedules, that might be difficult unless they started counting text messages.

Amber sighed, then pulled away and looked up at him. She lifted a hand to trace over his cheek, and Nick found his breath coming heavier. "So, you like this place? You could see yourself here?"

He nodded. "I could see myself here." He paused, not wanting to make the same mistake as before when he went too far. But things felt different here in this kitchen. Everything between them felt different.

Nick met and held her gaze, hoping she would hear everything he did and didn't say. "I see everything I want, and it's right here. I see my future."

Amber smiled, dimples winking from her cheeks. But Nick swore a shadow passed behind her eyes, a worry she wouldn't voice, one she wanted to hide from him. Whatever he thought he saw, it was gone almost instantly, and he hoped that it had been nothing more than imagination.

CHAPTER NINETEEN

When Amber finished Monday morning's treatment and made it into the office, Ripley intercepted her before she sat down. She drew Amber into a hug, shaking her a little, like she was no more than a limp doll.

It's honestly how she felt. Maybe it was the treatment or the late-night texts with Nick or a combination, but Amber felt weary and thin, like an ancient piece of parchment liable to turn to dust at any time.

"Don't break me," Amber said.

Ripley squeezed harder, shook her once more, then released. "You'd deserve it if I did. Where have you been? I haven't even seen you! Not since the cookout."

"I've been at work every day," Amber said.

Ripley rolled her eyes. "Yes, but you've been coming late, and I've been out at events a lot. We're ships passing in the night."

"Such a cliché."

"Clichés are only clichés because they're true," Ripley said. "How about lunch? Coffee? Dinner? A movie?"

Amber wanted to say yes to one or all, but exhaustion wore her like she was a raggedy sweater. "I want to but I'm so busy."

Ripley put her hands on her hips and narrowed her eyes. *Uh-oh. I know that look.* Amber realized with sudden clarity that it was better to take the upper hand here, to go out with Ripley and share some, if not all, of what was going on. Otherwise, Ripley might start to dig, and who knew what she'd find.

"I need you both to check out a restaurant for me," Deondra said, appearing suddenly at Amber's desk. "It's an old favorite, but with a new chef. I need to know if it's still up to par for rehearsal dinners and catering. I just made a reservation."

Ripley clapped her hands, then recovered her control, smoothing back her ponytail. "Wonderful. When?"

"Now," Deondra said.

She winked at Amber, as though communicating exactly what Amber feared: that as soon as people knew what she was going through, they would start making concessions for her. They would see her as weak, someone who needed help and caretaking.

But there was no way to argue, and Amber was hungry. She let Ripley lead her to the car, and they drove together to the little restaurant near the pier. Amber chewed a piece of ginger in the car as Ripley drove, chatting about wedding details and arguments her mother and grandmother were having about alcohol at the reception. Amber hummed responses but was almost asleep by the time Ripley located a parking space outside the restaurant.

Coffee while waiting for their sandwiches helped wake her up. Also, Ripley's intensity turned up a few notches as she leaned her elbows on the table and stared at Amber.

"I need to know everything. And I know nothing! Usually you tell me things before they happen. I feel like your life had moved on without me. So, spill! You came to the cookout with Nick. Are y'all dating? What happened? Where have you been for the last week?"

Okay, Amber was officially exhausted again. She took a sip of her coffee, wondering which truths to tell and how exactly her life had become so full of secrets.

"Nick and I are dating. More accurately, we have been on dates and are going on dates."

Ripley gave her a look. "That explanation sounds oddly clinical and robotic. Especially for you."

"We haven't told our parents. And until something is official, we aren't telling them."

"How official is official?"

"We didn't exactly define it," Amber hedged.

"Okayyyy. So, you're playing around some invisible line, trying not to cross it while also building a relationship?" Ripley wrinkled her nose. "That sounds … healthy."

"We don't want to tell them, but we also don't want to do to them what they did to us. You know, the whole secret-relationship thing."

Ripley looked like she would argue, but then bit her lip, nodding.

Amber swallowed. Before she could second-guess herself, she let the other big secret spill out. "I also have ovarian cancer. I'm doing chemo in the mornings. It's why I haven't been in the office."

Understanding passed over Ripley in stages. First, she froze. A little tremor passed through her before tears began dripping down her cheeks as though someone had turned on a faucet. Ripley threw her hands to her cheeks, a little sob escaping her.

And this, Amber thought, feeling tears prick at her own eyes, *is why I prefer people not knowing. This, right here.*

Somehow, watching her friend process her new reality made it just that: reality. Cancer was so much more real when you had to talk about it. Like Voldemort, it should be the sickness who should not be named.

Ripley grabbed for her hand just as the waitress brought their plates. Things were good and awkward for a moment while the waitress pretended Amber and Ripley weren't crying. She disappeared as though someone had lit a fire under her.

"I'm so sorry," Ripley said. "Why didn't you tell me? I mean, I just would have been—I would have done—I don't know. I just hate that I haven't been there for you!"

Amber shook her head. "It's fine. Honestly, chemo hasn't been so bad. I was really sick one day but Nick came over and —" She stopped when she saw the hurt on Ripley's face.

"Nick knows, but you didn't tell me?"

Amber stared down at the chicken salad sandwich, which suddenly had lost its appeal. "He doesn't know. I told him it was from a migraine."

"Okay, back the bus up," Ripley said. "Who *does* know?"

"You and Deondra."

Ripley's eyes couldn't have gone wider. "No one else? Not your boyfriend?"

"He's not my boyfriend ... exactly."

"Not your *dad*?"

There wasn't a good answer for that one. The wrongness of it really hit Amber then. The full weight of it. He had to know. She had to tell him. The sooner the better. At least about the cancer, if not about Nick. She didn't know how exactly to separate the two big things going on in her life he didn't know about. But she also didn't want to hit him with two blows at once.

"I was trying to figure this out," Amber muttered, twisting the napkin in her hands. "I was planning to tell him about the cancer the night that he and Linda sprung their big announcement on us."

Ripley sank back in her chair. "You found out that day. The kiss with Nick … it all makes so much sense now."

"How do I fix this?"

Ripley shrugged. "You just tell the truth. To everyone. About everything. As soon as possible."

"That sounds so simple."

"Because it is. You can't have the people in your life who love you NOT know about your diagnosis. I mean, I'm still in shock and need to know everything. We all want to know. We need to know. Is this because you don't want to accept help? I just don't understand."

"It started as not wanting to bust up my dad's happiness, even though I'm not thrilled about the wedding. Then, he said something about not wanting to lose me …" Her tongue fused to the roof of her mouth, and Amber couldn't finish.

"Oh, sweetie." Ripley squeezed her hand. "This year is just so … hard. I wish I could take some of it away."

"Thanks," Amber said. "I know you would."

"But at least you have support," Ripley said, squeezing her hand harder. "You've got me and you've got Nick and your dad—once you tell them. And you're going to tell them, right? About everything?"

Amber nodded, even as she was starting a whole list of justifications in her head for reasons to put it off. "Of course I am."

Ripley narrowed her eyes. "Soon. Promise?"

Amber nodded, but she considered crossing her fingers under the table. "Soon."

CHAPTER TWENTY

Nick woke to a quiet house and found Jill in the kitchen. She sat at the island with her laptop, somehow managing to look both completely innocent and as though she were a predator, lying in wait.

She gave him a knowing smile as he grabbed a glass of water. "Good morning, Nicky. Long time no see. What have you been up to?"

"Work, mostly."

Work and time with Amber and working through the details to purchase the beach cottage. He was exhausted, truly exhausted. He yawned, stretching his arms above his head.

"There's coffee. You look like you need it."

"Thanks, Jilly."

"It's a little early for sarcasm, isn't it?"

Nick poured himself a mug and added a splash of cream, more to cool it down than for the taste. "It wasn't too early for an insult. Sarcasm seems like an appropriate response."

Jill grinned. "Touché. How is house hunting? I think your

mom mentioned that you found a place, but neither of us have been invited on a tour. Has anyone else seen it?"

She asked innocently, so innocently that it was clear she was baiting him. Nick took another sip of coffee. "Someone may have seen it already."

Jill closed her laptop with a quick snap and rested her chin on her hands. "Shall we play a guessing game? Or do you want to just shoot straight with me?"

Nick settled in, leaning his hips against the counter. He didn't answer, simply giving Jill a long stare, as though this might scare her off. It didn't.

"I like games. How about I get three yes-or-no questions to figure it out? First question. Is it a she?"

"Yes." Nick didn't know why he was rising to the occasion, but he decided to indulge his aunt. It's not like Jill didn't already know the answer.

"Blonde hair?"

"Yep."

"Dimples?"

"Also yes."

"Got it!" Jill slapped her hand down on the counter theatrically. "It's your future stepsister."

Nick choked on his coffee. Setting the mug down on the counter, he covered his mouth and coughed until he felt like he could breathe again.

"I see I hit a nerve there," Jill said.

"Could we refer to her as Amber, please?"

"You probably would rather forget the whole awkward sibling thing."

"*Step*sibling," Nick said. "And it's not like it really counts. We're adults. We aren't going to be living together—"

"But you showed her your new house," Jill pointed out. "You weren't planning to share that roof with her?"

"I meant with our parents. We aren't going to be actual stepsiblings who, like, share a house with our parents or something weird like that."

"Ah. Right. The technicalities."

Nick blew out a long breath, wishing he'd stayed in bed. "Jill, could we just … not? It's too early for this. If you want to talk, we can talk, but I don't want any more games. If you want to say something, just say it."

"When are you going to tell your mom?"

Nick shifted his weight. Maybe direct wasn't the right choice either. Or maybe he just needed to own up to everything, since he'd painted himself into this corner, which was beginning to feel smaller and smaller.

"We want to tell our parents when we're more sure. Things are early. We've only been on a handful of dates. It's new."

Jill studied him. She always seemed to have the ability to stare right through him. "Have you kissed her?"

"Yes, but not since we started dating." When Jill raised her eyebrows, Nick groaned and ran his hands through his hair. "Look, we met the night Mom and Tom announced their impending plans. We kissed at the bar and then … found out."

For the first time that morning, Jill looked shocked. "Seriously? Talk about luck or timing."

Nick had thought the same thing. That maybe God was punishing him, a thought he'd had many times over the past few years with his father and with Kim.

But the more things had moved forward with Amber, the more Nick felt grateful that they'd met first, before they found out about their parents. Otherwise, he might have written her off, acknowledging attraction but missing out on the real connection they shared that went so much deeper.

He definitely wouldn't have considered dating her. Meeting Amber, even that night, wasn't a punishment but a gift.

Now, he didn't want to consider his life without her.

"Honestly? That's what I thought too. I was so angry that night. But then … things just unfolded." Nick shrugged, feeling a smile tug at his lips. "She's really amazing."

Jill beamed at him, a real smile. They were so rare with her. Usually she kept herself locked up and hidden behind a wall of sarcasm and dry humor. It was hard to gauge how she really felt about most things, but Nick could feel her approval.

"Nick! I'm so happy for you. I really like her. I mean, when she's not vomiting. Is she feeling better?"

"Yeah. It was just a migraine."

"Those can be bad," Jill said. "At least, from what I've heard. Anyway, so … telling your mom. How can I help?"

Despite what Nick and Amber kept saying about not needing to tell their parents until things were official, he knew the truth. They were doing the same thing his mom and Tom had done. Except worse, because it had already been done to them.

"Can you just … be on my side?"

"On your side for what?"

Nick had heard people refer to shivers running down their spine, and he always took it as a cliched exaggeration. But when his mother's voice startled him at that moment, he actually felt it—as though an icy finger was tracing a path down the center of his back. He shivered. Jill cast him a sympathetic look.

"What are you doing home, sis?"

Linda set down her bag and lifted the coffee pot, which was empty. She made a face. "My boss offered me the morning off when I told him that my sister was still in town and my boy had the morning off."

Nick shifted on his feet. He wasn't scheduled to be at the station today, but he had plans with Amber to look at a potential venue for their parents' wedding a little later. Hopefully, his mom wouldn't try to join them now that she wasn't at work. He might have to send Jill a secret text to take her shopping. It was odd, for once, feeling like he and Jilly were on the same team rather than biting at each other.

But first … he needed to tell his mom about Amber. For a brief moment, he wondered if he should send Amber a warning text, giving her a heads-up. But there was no time.

"Mom," Nick said, swallowing hard when she seemed to sense the shift in conversation. "Can we talk?"

She clutched the counter. "If you were a daughter, this would be the moment where you tell me you're pregnant. Did you get someone pregnant?"

Jill snorted and then held up both hands in apology when both Nick and his mom glared.

"Not even close."

"Well, sort of close," Jill said. "I mean, in the ballpark, since it involves a girl."

His mom clutched his arm. "You've met a girl?"

"You've met her too," Jill said.

Nick wanted to throw something at his aunt. "You are not helping," he practically growled.

"Nick," his mom said, shaking his arm. "Tell me about the girl!"

This was it. The moment of truth, as it happened. Nick watched his mother's face carefully as he spoke.

"Mom, the night you and Tom announced you were getting married, I met someone. Just before, in the bar."

"Nick," his mother breathed. "You really like her. I see it in your face."

"I do."

"He loves her," Jill whispered, cupping her hands around her mouth like she was telling a secret.

Nick stared at her until his frustration dissolved into understanding. One that really, he already knew on some level. He *did* love Amber. There wasn't even a question in his mind, no matter how quickly it had happened.

"That's so fast," his mother said, her brow furrowed slightly. "Is it true?"

"The woman is Amber."

He let the words settle over her, watching the way confusion bloomed before his mother dropped his arm and took a step back. "Oh," she said. "Oh."

Nick waited, not sure what his mother felt or how to respond without a sense of what she was thinking. He caught Jill's eye, but she only shrugged.

"I really like Amber," Jilly said. "Don't you? Sweet girl. Perfect for our Nicky."

"Yes," his mom said, speaking as though dazed. "Sweet."

Her eyes were unfocused, or focused on something beyond Nick's head. He glanced back. The wall? The cabinet? When she smiled, it didn't feel like a relief so much as a thread of fear.

"I'm going to go lie down. Maybe after a nap we could ..." She trailed off, searching for whatever she wanted to say next. "Later, maybe we could go to the beach? Or ... to lunch."

His mom started to turn, and Nick grasped her sleeve. "Mom?"

She smiled, yet again, it seemed too bright and her eyes

were off somewhere behind him. "I'm so happy for you," she said, touching his face.

Then she left, and Nick heard the quiet closing of her bedroom door.

"That went well, I thought." Jill's cheerful words startled Nick back into the room from whatever restless place his mind had gone.

"Did you think so? She seemed—"

"Startled." Jill waved a hand. "It's fine. I know my sister. She'll be supportive. She'll be fine. Aren't you planning to meet Amber soon?"

Nick didn't know how Jill always seemed to be a step ahead of him. He could only hope she was also right about his mother's response.

CHAPTER TWENTY-ONE

"Well," Amber asked, "what do you think?" Before he could even answer, she continued. "It reminds me of your cottage."

Nick eyed the house as they got out of the car, and it did indeed remind him of the cottage he'd just signed a contract on that week. This was in much better shape, of course, and a little bigger, but the same kind of charm. The weathered shingles had been painted a bright, sky blue with white trim. It gave him ideas for fixing up his own.

"And this is a wedding venue?" Nick asked, glancing around. It hardly seemed large enough, and very unassuming. He immediately liked it, though he wasn't sure his mother would.

He tried, as much as he could considering the current task at hand, to put his mother out of his mind. At least until he told Amber that he had finally confessed. Nick thought he might feel relieved, but instead, a deep and heavy concern had sunk low in his belly.

Amber's eyes sparkled, drawing him back into the

moment, a place he would rather be. "It's a new space, just opened. I guess we'll see. Race you to the top!"

She didn't wait for him, bolting up the stairs. Nick caught and passed her about halfway up, taking the steps two at a time, even as she squealed in protest. At the top, he leaned against a post and grinned down at her like he had all the time in the world.

His grin faded when she stumbled a little. Her face paled and she clutched at the railing. He realized her breathing was so labored she was practically panting. Another migraine?

Nick met her a few steps down, taking her elbow and walking her up the rest of the way.

"You okay?"

"Fine," she said through gasping breaths. "I'm sorry."

"Let's sit for a moment." Nick led her to a wooden bench on the wide porch.

He tucked her under his arm, pulling her to his side and smoothing his palm up and down her arm. The tightness in his chest began to loosen as her breaths evened out. Now, he was aware only of the warmth of her body next to his and the scent of her.

The cottage had beautiful views of water on both sides. It was located almost at the Northern end of the island, past a large marina. Erosion from storms had clearly wiped out much of the island, which was only a few football fields wide here. Posts stuck up through the sand on the beach and beyond the waves, and Nick realized that they were probably all that was left from older homes washed away.

The crashing of waves filled his ears, the salt smell stronger than usual. A breeze brushed Amber's hair over his forearm, making goose bumps rise on his skin.

Amber gazed out over the sound, its water gentler than

the ocean side, the shore edged by wild marsh grass. A tall, white bird stood in the shallow water, hunting.

"What kind of bird is that?" he asked.

"A snowy egret."

Another, larger gray-blue bird flew in, landing close enough that the egret took off. This one was almost double the size, almost majestic as it stalked through the water on spindly legs.

"What about that one?"

"A great blue heron," Amber said. She turned to him, eyes narrowed and lips curved up in a smile. "Why? Interested in ornithology?"

"I don't know what that is. I was just curious. But now I want to know if there's a mandatory class on shore birds in the public schools here."

Amber laughed. "No. You just kind of pick up on these things growing up On Island. And for the record, ornithology is the study of birds."

"That would make for an interesting major. What's your degree in? And where did you go to school?"

Amber shifted a little like she was going to move away now that her breathing had settled. Nick tightened his arm, keeping her in place. She smiled, looking away again, this time toward the beach. It seemed almost silly that they were having this conversation now, when he had only an hour before realized he was in love with this woman.

"I have a degree in communications from UNC. Full of questions today, aren't you?"

He pinched her arm lightly. "I want to know it all, to know everything. Now I know you're an amateur ornithalologist—"

"*Ornithologist.*"

"Yeah, that. And you went to UNC and still chose to come back home. Which tells me you love this island."

"I do. How about you? Is there a school for firefighters?"

Nick laughed. "No. But our training is pretty intense. I went to App State—all my brothers did. We all played football there. I majored in sports medicine, but always planned to be a firefighter."

"Football, huh? I could see that."

"Why? Is it my impressive build?" he teased, flexing his arm, which brought her closer. When Amber laughed, her breath tickled his neck. Nick leaned over and kissed her forehead. Everything with her just felt so … easy.

"More like, you've got that whole stereotypical caveman, meathead thing going on," Amber teased.

Nick held back a laugh. "Why, thank you. I'm not sure I've ever received such a compliment."

"I'm here anytime you need me."

The words were spoken in that same teasing tone, but Nick felt them on a deeper level. He wanted to say, *Promise?* He wanted Amber to be there anytime. Her presence created an insatiable urge for *more*. And all their words seemed to have second or third meanings.

"And, for the record," Amber said, grinning up at him, "I *do* like your build."

That delighted some deep part of Nick, and he found himself transfixed by Amber's wide smile. And by her lips, which were so perfectly kissable …

"Well, don't you two look cozy!"

Nick practically jumped when a woman interrupted them. She had spiky, gray hair and purple glasses, smiling in a friendly way as she looked between them.

"Come on in! I'm Belinda."

Nick kept his arm around Amber as they stood. They

made quick introductions, Belinda still smiling widely. "I didn't realize you were the planner and also the bride. When is your big day?" she asked.

It took Nick a beat to realize that Belinda thought he and Amber were the engaged couple. Which made a lot more sense than the reality, that they were here for their parents' wedding. He glanced at Amber, whose cheeks had gone pink.

"Oh, um, we aren't—"

"Officially engaged yet," Nick said. "But we're skipping ahead a little bit. Just getting ideas."

Belinda's smile didn't dim. "Wonderful. Follow me."

When she turned away toward the door, Amber elbowed Nick and hissed, "What are you doing?" But she was smiling, her eyes bright.

"Nothing, honey boo. Just having a little fun." He kissed her again on the temple.

"*Honey boo?*"

"Honey bear? Sugar plum? Babycakes?"

"Maybe just stick with Bram."

Amber was laughing as they stepped through the bright pink door Belinda held open. The inside did remind him a lot of his cottage. *Their* cottage, as he preferred to think of it. Someday. Soon, but when enough time had passed that Nick didn't feel like he was rushing her.

Unless she wanted to rush as much as he did.

"This is amazing," Amber said. "Nick, look!"

Her excitement reminded him of when they had looked at the ranch together, when she had babbled on about counter space and flooring types and so many other things. Only here, he got the sense that she wasn't thinking of just the wedding venue, but his cottage.

Their cottage.

The interior was bigger than his cottage, maybe double in

size, but was one large, bright space that vaulted upwards to a slanted ceiling painted the same blue as the outside. White beams crisscrossed above their heads, probably a structural thing since most of the interior walls had been removed. A large wooden chandelier, also painted white, hung in the center of the room from what looked almost like ropes from a boat.

The floors were distressed hardwood, finished in a soft gray. Both sides of the room were lined with glass doors that could open onto more porch space beyond, showing off the ocean views. Belinda walked through the space, throwing open the doors, letting in the breeze and the sound of the ocean.

Nick could imagine a lively, intimate party here, and for a moment, he pictured the group from the beach cookout here, laughing and dancing. He could picture Amber, her head thrown back, blonde hair spilling over the straps of a white wedding gown. For a moment, the vision felt real, far too real, and he stepped away from Amber, swallowing hard.

"Wow," Amber said. "It's beautiful! All the natural light!"

"Thank you," Belinda said. "We wanted to take advantage of the views and keep the beach cottage feel. It's not a massive space, but both sides of the porch have been extended to create more outdoor space."

"I love it," Amber said. "How many people can you hold? What about seating? Where do the vendors set up for food?"

Nick could practically feel the excitement vibrating off Amber. She tilted her head up to look at the ceiling. The position was almost as he had imagined her a moment ago in a wedding dress. Desire gripped him in a hot fist, and he took another step away.

As they began to talk specs and specifics, Nick walked out to the porch on the sound side. The top of the railing had been extended so it served as a place for drinks and food. Metal stools in turquoise and white were tucked underneath. Nick pulled one out and sat down, resting his elbows on the wood.

Maybe it was the conversation with his mother and Jill, with Jill's proclamation that he was in love, but Nick couldn't shake the image of Amber as a bride. As *his* bride. Just the thought made that same hot feeling rise up again in his chest.

Nick tried to steady his breathing, watching the great blue heron that still moved slowly along the shore, its cool, dark eyes roving over the water.

"Nick, there's more downstairs," Amber said, coming up behind him and squeezing his arm. "Come on! Let's go see!"

He chuckled, letting her drag him toward a second set of stairs at the back of the porch. This one turned, and as the bottom came into view, Belinda flipped a switch upstairs, and strings of lights hanging underneath the house lit up.

"Whoa," Nick said. They stopped at the bottom of the stairs, and Amber took his hand, lacing their fingers together.

The concrete floor, which under normal cottages was a parking area, had been covered with a wooden floor. Large, potted plants were everywhere, and a garden complete with a trellis full of climbing flowering vines and a bubbling stone fountain. Clumps of the kind of beach grass that Nick had seen on dunes surrounded the area, making it more private. It had a totally different feel from the open and airy upstairs.

Music started to play, some kind of classical song with a romantic vibe. Nick squeezed Amber's hand. "Could I have this dance?"

Beaming, she smiled up at him. Nick led her out to the center of the wooden floor, curling his arms around her waist and pulling her close. She threaded her fingers through the hair at the nape of his neck. The light tug sent a shudder down the length of his spine.

And now, Nick was imagining this moment as a dance with Amber at *their* wedding. Night would be falling around them, the summer insects beginning to strike up their chorus. He would be holding Amber closer, though, and as he thought this, he pulled her against him until her face was nestled against his chest.

"This would be a perfect spot for a first dance," she said, her voice startled him out of his thoughts.

"Or the last dance," he said, letting his lips brush her cheek. "Just before leaving all the guests. A last public moment before it's just ..." Nick trailed off, realizing that he had almost said, *before it's just us.*

His hands on her waist suddenly felt heavy, and he dipped his head so he could smell her hair.

"Would you want a small or large wedding?"

Maybe Nick was imagining it, but her voice sounded like it was threaded with emotion.

"Small. Intimate. Just the size for a place like this," he said.

"I'd like to get married on the beach," Amber said. "Belinda said people have done that. The ceremony there, then everyone walks back here."

"I like the sound of that."

"Me too."

Nick nuzzled deeper into her hair, tugging her even closer. The tension between them was as strong as the pressure change before a summer storm, a charged and living thing in the air. Her fingers threaded in his hair, fingernails lightly scraping his scalp.

He could see it. He could see it all.

"It's so fast," Amber said, and though she could have been talking about their parents, he didn't think she was.

"Maybe," he said, his lips grazing her cheek. "Or maybe, it only seems that way to people outside the relationship. Inside it? The timing is simply perfect."

The song ended, and Nick didn't want to move away. He wanted to tilt Amber's face up and kiss her, pouring out everything he felt, the things he hoped and longed for into a searing, claiming kiss.

He leaned back enough to see her face, and the raw emotion he saw there was like a jolt of adrenaline to his system. Amber felt what he felt, she wanted what he wanted.

And before he could question it, Nick fused his mouth to hers.

The kiss didn't start slow and build so much as it shattered him from the start. They had kissed before in the bar, and it lit up something inside him. This felt like the natural continuation of that, as though that moment was tethered to this one, a natural outcome.

It was right. It was theirs. She was his, and he was hers.

They may not have said vows and danced their first dance, but this kiss felt like the culmination of those things, as though they had skipped ahead of a ceremony just as they had skipped over so many other things.

Her lips moved against his and her fingers moved through his hair. Gently, he cupped her cheeks, slowing and steadying their movements into something less frenzied. Something patient and sure.

Their love—for there wasn't another word that would describe this—had bloomed overnight, and yet, they didn't *need* to rush. They could still let it unfold, bit by bit in its own time. That knowledge made Nick sigh against Amber's lips, pressing a last kiss there before he pulled away, letting his forehead rest on hers.

"Well, what do you think? A potential location for your wedding?"

Belinda's voice startled them, and they jumped apart like teenagers who had been caught. Then, they both laughed.

Your wedding. He realized suddenly that this whole time, he hadn't once thought about their parents getting married in this space. In fact, he couldn't even imagine it. There was only him. And Amber.

Amber kept her gaze on Nick as she said, "Yes. I think it's perfect."

CHAPTER TWENTY-TWO

Amber floated through the rest of the afternoon at work. Her sighs and dreamy expression earned her an eye roll (but also a grin) from Ripley, who seemed to understand exactly why Amber was hovering six inches above the ground. She couldn't have put it into words even if Ripley had asked her to explain.

Kissing Nick was … nothing like Amber had remembered. That first kiss had been with a virtual stranger. It had been about escape, about living, about a desperation to embrace the moment. There had been an adrenaline rush, a giddiness and an instant connection in the bar when their lips met.

But under the cottage, in Nick's arms, the kiss had been consuming. It held a raw power that swept her up in the promise and the hope of that moment. It was a wedding day kiss, the kind that confirms the vows you've taken. And she knew Nick felt the same. That when they were talking about weddings and last dances, they hadn't been speaking of their parents.

Her phone buzzed, drawing her back into her chair and

the vendor spreadsheet Amber should have been updating before she left for an event. *Speaking of parents … Ugh. Talk about a buzzkill.* She stared at her father's name as it flashed across the screen with his call. The last person she wanted to speak to right now was her dad.

Even though the kiss had been crossing a line that took Amber and Nick past the point where they could pretend things weren't serious. They needed to tell their parents. And she still needed to tell Nick everything. *Double buzzkill.*

A text came through almost immediately, while the phone still sat in her hand.

Dad: We need to talk. Call me when you get this.

Amber's mind immediately went to worst-case scenarios … but she had already lost her mother. What was left? Maybe he and Linda called off their engagement? That filled her with a thread of hope that immediately sank into guilt. Still, it would be a relief.

Or maybe he found out about you and Nick.

That thought stopped her cold. But he couldn't have … could he? Honestly, with an island like Sandover, it was totally possible that he could have found out. They had been on a few dates. Probably all of Nick's friends knew. Jill seemed to suspect. Belinda had thought they were a couple this morning at the venue.

With unsteady hands, Amber tried to send a text that sounded casual.

Amber: Hey, Dad! I'm at work and can't talk. What's up? You okay?

The waiting made her take deep breaths, even though it wasn't long before his message popped back up.

Dad: I need to see you as soon as possible. Can you drop by the house when you're done with work?
Amber: Sure. It will be around 7. I have an event to drop by. What's this about?

She chewed the inside of her cheek, waiting for his response. Could he be sick? No. Amber couldn't begin to think of a world in which she lost her mother, got sick with cancer, and her dad suffered with health issues as well. It *had* to be Linda. The other possibilities were far less pleasant.

Dad: See you then.

———

By the time Amber unlocked her father's door, her stomach felt like it was going to slide right out of her body and onto the porch. It was heavy with worry, with guilt, and with more worry. Maybe there was a little nausea from the chemo mixed in for good measure. Just to keep things interesting.

"Dad?" Amber called, forcing cheer into her voice. Whatever she was walking into, she wanted to at least start things on a positive note.

"I'm in my office."

Forget positive notes. Historically, getting called to her father's office was not so different from being called to the principal's office at school. The same dread swirled through her every time, and even as an adult, she never left one of these meetings unscathed.

Before stepping inside, Amber shot up a quick prayer. *Let*

this be painless. Give me the words and the whatever I need to get through this.

"Hey, Daddy," she said, trying to force her features into a genuine-looking smile. "What's going on?"

He sat behind his desk, hands clasped on the white paper desk calendar he changed out every year. From her seat across from him, she could see a few dates scribbled on there, but his handwriting was illegible to see what kinds of things he had been up to this month. His face definitely had that *you're in trouble* look, not a face she had seen very often in her life, being a stereotypical good girl.

It has to be about Nick. He found out somehow. Or—this thought made her back stiffen in her chair—*he knows about my diagnosis.*

"You're scaring me, Daddy," she said lightly. "Tell me why you needed me to come."

"I know," he said simply. For a moment, the words seemed to hang suspended in the air between them.

The thing was, when you carried more than one secret at a time, when someone dropped that vague bomb, you had to play it cool. Amber shrugged her shoulders, keeping her expression neutral.

"Know what, Daddy?"

The tension underneath his calm exterior snapped in an instant, his brows pulling down tight as his eyes flashed. "I know about you and that *boy.*"

Amber had been dreading this moment, but now that it was here, it honestly wasn't so bad. Maybe it was because her father was overreacting so hard to the news that she was dating Nick, or maybe it was that he hadn't found out the other secret, but Amber didn't even flinch.

Shaking her head, she gave a small chuckle. "Nick is

hardly a boy. And we've barely been dating long enough to tell you about it. Especially considering … the situation."

Her father didn't get angry often, but he was now, and it only served to make Amber feel less bothered by keeping him in the dark.

"The situation? Which one—the one where I'm marrying his mother, making him your stepbrother, or the one where I would not give my approval or blessing to this relationship, regardless?"

"I'm not sixteen anymore, needing your approval to go out with a boy, thank you very much."

"I don't like your tone."

Young lady. It was almost like both of them could hear how much those two words wanted to come out of his mouth. Amber studied her father for a moment, trying to rein in all the emotions going haywire through her system at the moment. He wasn't a big man, not like Nick. But he was solid and firm in his support—always had been, even through his own grief.

She loved this man. Dearly. They had been through one of the hardest things you can go through as a family. He'd been her rock, and she had been his. But had he ever pushed back so hard on something? Amber couldn't remember him giving high school guys she dated this difficult of a time. It irked her, bringing up all kinds of defensiveness where Nick was concerned.

"Did *that boy* come apologize to you?" Amber asked.

"If that's what you want to call it."

Why was the man being so stubborn? "Did he or did he not apologize?"

"He did."

Amber rolled her eyes. "And how about you? Did you apologize?"

"I don't see what that has to do with—"

"Did you apologize to Nick, Daddy?" Amber crossed her arms and raised her eyebrows.

He muttered something under his breath that sounded remarkably like, *You should have gone to law school.* In a louder tone, he answered, "No. I don't see why I should."

She had been reserving one more bit of eyebrow raise just in case. She cashed it in now, staring down the man who had helped her ride her first bike and who had held her in his lap while she sobbed at the news of her mother's death. It was hard to keep him pinned down with the evil eye when the tickle started in her nose, then behind her eyes. Amber sniffed.

Her father softened. Slightly, but still. He blew out a breath and ran a hand through his thinning hair. "Maybe I was a little hard on him. I should have apologized. I will. But that doesn't change the fact that I don't want you dating him."

Amber was well into adulthood. Well, a few years into official, legal adulthood. She could date who she wanted. But she had never even thought to consider that her father wouldn't approve of her choices. And she desperately needed his approval.

"You got a bad first impression of him, Daddy. You don't know him like I do."

"In the few weeks you've known him?"

Had it only been weeks? Somehow, Amber felt like Nick moving into her life marked the start of a new chapter, one she'd been living for far longer than a few short weeks.

"Are you one to talk about getting into a serious relationship quickly?"

Her father pulled at his collar. "Right. But I have years of experience and wisdom under my belt. Nick isn't the guy for you."

Amber shook her head. "What are you even basing this on? You've only spoken to him twice! And you and Mom got married when you were younger than I am now, so don't talk to me about your years of experience."

Her father didn't argue again, but she could see that he wasn't convinced. Why didn't he like Nick? It was so odd, especially given that her dad was marrying Nick's mom. Nick was his fiancée's *son*. This was all so tangled up. More than she thought it could be when she and Nick discussed this being hard. Then, it was more about the label, about their parents' approval.

Amber hadn't ever expected or mentally prepared for her father's disapproval. Knowing Nick, it was unimaginable. But was he right? Was there something her father saw in Nick that she missed, some kind of blind spot? Or was this just him feeling like no one was good enough for his little girl?

"How did you find out?" she asked, suddenly realizing how much she needed this answer.

"Nick told Linda, and she told me. Why I didn't hear it from my daughter first, I'm not sure."

He didn't bother to hide the hurt in his voice, and the anger made more sense to Amber. Was this even about Nick, or about *her*? If she had been the one to tell her father, would things have been different?

It took a moment for the sense of betrayal to soak through her. Nick told his mom. Without asking her or telling her. No warning. How long ago? Was it before or after they danced together, hinting around the idea of their own wedding vows. Her thoughts of that moment soured with this new knowledge. It felt like he had broken vows they hadn't even taken yet.

Her father cleared his throat and leaned forward, dragging her from her painful thoughts.

"The other thing I wanted to ask you about was if you picked up that bag from Dr. Lee."

Amber stared blankly at her father. Dr. Lee had been the doctor working in the ER the night of her accident. This nudged some part of her brain, some memory, but Amber couldn't quite make sense of it.

"What?"

Her father's eyebrows twitched. "Dr. Lee? He had that bag of your mother's things. You said you were going to stop by the hospital sometime to pick it up."

Right. The bag. Amber hadn't planned to ever get the bag, which held a few things of her mother's the hospital somehow misplaced and found after her death, things like the shoes she had been wearing the night of the accident. Dr. Lee had reached out. Amber knew her dad hadn't been in the right frame of mind to get them, but neither was she. The only reason she volunteered to get them was because she thought her father would eventually forget.

"Oh. Right. I, um, haven't yet. It's on my list."

Her father frowned. "Well, what were you doing at the hospital? I saw you coming out when I was meeting a client for lunch?"

Amber's heart sank. No matter how many times she had played over this conversation in her mind, it never got easier. There was no good way to tell her father.

Taking a big breath, Amber squared her shoulders, which had started to ache. "Dad, there's something else we need to talk about."

CHAPTER TWENTY-THREE

Back at the house, his mom was nowhere to be found, but Jill was back at the counter with her laptop. Nick could almost pretend like their conversation this morning hadn't happened, the one where he told his mom about Amber and she didn't really respond. Then again, she didn't freak out, so that was at least a start.

He needed to tell Amber but hadn't wanted to ruin the moment—or the kiss—they shared. His fingers twitched on his phone in his pocket, but he paused to talk to Jill first.

"Have you even moved today?" Nick asked, smiling.

"I'll have you know that I got up and stretched half an hour ago," Jill said.

"Has Mom come out of her room?"

Jill looked anywhere but him. "We went to the beach earlier."

"That's good. And how is she? With ... everything?"

The look on his aunt's face told Nick more than her words. "She's processing."

"Processing."

Nick stuffed both hands in his pockets, touching the edge of his phone again, thinking of Amber. If his mom was reacting this poorly, he could only imagine how it would go down when she talked to her dad.

The whole thing frustrated him. He and Amber should be able to date each other without going through some big interrogation or whatever. He didn't want his mom to need to *process* the fact that he'd met the girl he suspected he would want to marry sometime down the road. She should be overjoyed and squealing about grandbabies, not processing.

"How about you?" Nick asked, leaning on the counter, needing a change in subjects. "How long are you planning to stick around?"

"I decided to stay another week or two. Thought you'd miss me."

Nick frowned. "Don't you have work?"

Jill pointed to her laptop. "Crazy thing about the internet. I can work from anywhere."

"And what about Stan?" It took Nick a moment to remember the name of Jilly's current husband. Sometimes he just thought of them as numbers. Stan was number four in a string of rich—and replaceable—husbands. Jill got bored easily. At least, that's what his mom had told him.

"We're getting divorced." Nick almost made a comment, and maybe Jill saw it coming, because she continued. "He had an affair. You know how it goes."

A heavy chill settled in Nick's chest, an icy anger. "What did you say?"

Jill didn't flinch or look away from the intensity of his stare. "You know, your dad?"

Nick could have sworn that the house rocked a little under his feet. Or maybe his feet were sliding out from under him. He grabbed the edge of the counter with both hands.

"You knew?"

Jill nodded sadly. "So did your mom."

Now, Nick really was about to lose his footing. He slid down the counter, coming to rest on the floor, knees up and elbows resting on them. He dropped his head, trying to get air to move in and out of his lungs the way it was supposed to.

His mom was never supposed to know. That was the deal. The one he and his brothers made with their father when they discovered the affair he'd been having with a young mother that only lived a few streets away. They confronted him, demanded that he finally give in to their mother's wish to retire somewhere coastal.

If they moved away, Nick and his brothers had reasoned, the temptation within walking distance would be gone. And their mom would never know.

Except that she did.

Nick barely stirred when Jill joined him on the floor, crossing her legs and leaning up against him in a rare display of physical affection. His body felt like cold stone against hers.

"You didn't know we knew?"

"No," he said, his voice a harsh whisper.

"Your mom's a lot tougher than you give her credit for. But it was a sweet thing you boys did for her, insisting they move down here."

Nick squeezed his eyes shut. "Did she know about that too?"

"I don't think so. Just me."

"How do you know everything, Jilly?"

"Keen powers of observation, kid."

Nick swallowed around what felt like a boulder lodged in his throat. "I hated him so much. When he died, I was still so angry with him. I can't even remember the last words we spoke. I still hate him."

"Me too. How'd you turn out to be such a stellar guy? Guess it must be the influence of your other family. Like your older, but still very hip and cool aunt."

"I'm pretty sure people calling themselves *hip* or *cool* by definition are neither of those things."

Returning to their default banter helped ease the tight coil of tension around Nick's chest. And strangely, knowing that his mom knew, knowing that Jilly knew and that she hated his father, made Nick's anger with the man diffuse the tiniest fraction. Which was more than it had shifted since the moment he found out that his father had been cheating on his mom.

"But what if I'm not better? What if I'm like him, and will just do what he did?"

"I can't promise you won't, Nicky. In truth, we would all do a lot of things we wouldn't think ourselves capable of in the right situation. But you've got a good head on your shoulders." She wound a hand over his shoulders and patted his chest. "And I know you've got God here. The wild thing is that your parents worked through the whole mess. Before your dad died, they were the happiest I've ever seen them. I couldn't have forgiven him. But your mother did."

Nick didn't know how to feel about that. He turned the idea over in his mind. It was one thing if his mom had moved here with his father, not knowing. It was something else altogether if she moved here with all the information in hand, ready for a fresh start despite it all.

And then he died.

Guilt started trying to worm its way up to the surface,

and Nick shoved it back down. He had processed enough. Made at least one tiny stride that felt something like making peace, or attempting to at least approach the edge of it. If only he had done so before his father died.

He thought of Cash, talking of his father, of letting go. Of Jackson, the pain raw and open like a fresh wound. He thought of Amber, losing her mother, his mother, losing her husband. One whom she'd forgiven.

"What kind of party am I missing?" his mom asked from the kitchen doorway. She stood just outside the room in the semi-dark of the hallway.

"Mom?" Nick asked. Her voice had sounded a little off. Was she still *processing*? He started to get up, but Jill put a strong hand on his arm, urging him to stay in place.

"Why don't you join us, Linds?" Jill asked.

"Any requirements for entry?" His mom was trying to keep her tone light and cool, but it sounded forced to Nick.

"Just a couple of sad sacks, lamenting our life choices," Jill said. "You'll fit right in."

"You don't know how right you are," his mom said with a bitterness that made Nick's jaw ache. When she stepped into the kitchen, her eyes were puffy and swollen, red and wet.

She slid down beside him and he hooked an arm around her, pulling her close as she shuddered. "Mom? I'm sorry. Is this because of—"

"You? No. At least, I don't think so. Honestly?" She gave a laugh that sounded more like a wheezing cough, or an old hag's attempt at humor. "I have no idea why he did it."

Jill stiffened on Nick's other side, then leaned around him to ask, "Why who did what?"

Nick's mom looked up, her chin trembling as tears poured down her face. "Tom broke up with me. Called off the engagement."

Nick felt a hard knot of anger building inside him. He hadn't liked Tom from the night he met him. The second impression at Tom's office hadn't changed a thing, and now?

Now, he vibrated with the same fury he'd felt toward his own father.

Amber. "Wait—did you tell him about me and Amber?"

His mom sniffed, and Jill managed to locate the roll of paper towels and handed her the whole thing. She tore off a piece and dabbed at her eyes.

"Yes, but he seemed … fine. Well, he wasn't happy to be honest. But *we* were fine. It has nothing to do with us, not really. He called me back a few hours later, and he was a different man. I just don't understand."

She sobbed openly now, keening in a way that made the hair stand up on Nick's arms. He'd heard her make those same sounds when his father died. Heck, maybe she was crying for him too.

Nick shifted so he could hold her tightly, rocking her without saying a word. He had no words. All he had was a hot, blinding rage toward Amber's father.

And where did that leave him and Amber?

They hadn't wanted their parents to come between them, but they had been looking at the whole thing shortsightedly, as though it would work out.

The two of them hadn't discussed what would happen if their parents *didn't* make it. If they had a messy and painful breakup like this where one of them really hurt the other.

They couldn't have imagined how this would feel, how connected and tenuous their own bond now felt. Nick couldn't have imagined just how angry he was at Tom for hurting his mother, for taking the beautiful future Nick had imagined only hours earlier with Amber and smashing it to pieces.

When his mother's sobs began to subside, Nick stood carefully, watching as Jill took his place. "I have to go," he said, keeping his voice even.

"You shouldn't," Jill said, a knowing look in her eyes.

Before he left, Nick took a last look at his mom crumpled in her sister's arms. "I have to."

CHAPTER TWENTY-FOUR

Awareness came to Amber slowly, and confusion hit her first. This wasn't her blanket or her pillow—at least, not the ones from her apartment. She was in her old bedroom, still in her clothes, lying on top of the bedspread.

Why was she here? And why did she feel like she was about to vomit?

It all came back to her, almost as fast as her last meal started coming up. She raced for the jack-and-jill bathroom and barely made it before the nausea clutched her stomach, squeezing out everything she had. Sweat poured down her face and trickled down her back.

"Oh, sweetie. I'm here. I'm here."

Her mother had always been the one to take care of her when she was sick. But her dad did his best, standing behind her, rubbing her back slowly as she emptied her stomach. It clenched and heaved, even when nothing was left and she lay shaking on the bowl.

A distant knocking and then ringing of the doorbell startled them both. Her father sighed, flushing the toilet and brushing back her hair. "I'll be right back and bring water and a towel. You okay?"

"I'll be fine," Amber croaked. The doorbell rang again and it sounded like someone was pounding at the same time. "Better get that before they beat it down."

Her father closed the bathroom and bedroom doors as he left, and Amber was able to get to her feet using the counter for leverage. She avoided her reflection, splashing water on her face and sipping a little from her cupped palm.

Nick did such a better job taking care of me, she thought. Thinking about him made her chest hurt.

Earlier, when they were dancing under the lights, even before he kissed her, Amber had known what this was. Not a crush, not attraction or infatuation. It was love, or, at least, the beginnings of it. Ready to be nurtured and fanned into something lasting and real.

But Dad hates him. They would have to find a way around that, because her dad was clearly wrong. They would have to—

Is that Nick?

Angry voices carried through the closed door, and Amber made her way out of the bathroom as quickly as possible. Which wasn't very fast, as her legs felt shaky and the nausea hadn't left her. Her stomach rolled, making her feel like she was on the deck of a ship during a storm.

The raised voices came from the front porch, and it was definitely her father and Nick. Amber threw open the door to find the two men she loved most in the world nose to nose on the porch.

"What are y'all doing?" Amber's hands went to her hips, so all three looked like some kind of matching arrangement.

Her father's face swung to hers first, looking angry—and

guilty. Nick was slower, his head moving as though he was actually some kind of animatronic version of himself.

The fury in his gaze almost knocked Amber back a few steps. Her father was there at her elbow instantly, steadying her. What had happened in the past few hours? Nick was the one who had told his mom, who told Amber's dad. If anyone had reason to be angry, it was Amber.

Her father's words pinged against her mind. *There's a side to him you're not seeing,* he had said. Amber definitely hadn't seen whatever this was.

"Nick?" Her voice trembled. She waited for one of them to answer her.

"Are you okay?" her father asked quietly.

Amber shrugged out of his grip. "Fine. What's going on?"

Nick made a scoffing noise. Amber felt like she was watching someone destroy something precious to her, like Nick was taking a baseball bat to a collection of crystal vases, watching for her reaction.

She slumped, her father taking on more of her weight as the firm line of his mouth tightened. The rage in Nick's face slipped away, but it was too late.

Amber was too tired, exhausted, really.

Physically, emotionally. She was fabric, worn bare from overuse. Her whole body felt hot and shaky.

"I need to lie down," she said, to her father, to Nick, to herself.

"Let's get you inside," her father said, and dimly, Amber considered how her helplessness was a great tool for diffusing anger.

"What's wrong?" Nick asked, taking a step closer as Amber's father led her through the door, her toe catching on the step.

Her father looped an arm around her waist, hauling her

up against him with a grunt as he half carried her inside. Amber saw only half the room, her eyelids heavy and drooping.

"Let me help." Nick's voice was a ragged plea, an apology, a demand.

"No." Her father closed the door, but before he did, she heard him say, "She doesn't need you."

"Amber?"

She wanted Nick but couldn't take the tension. She needed to rest. Right now, she needed her dad. "Just go," she said, too tired to offer him any more than that.

Moments later, the cool sheets settled around her, and Amber didn't know if she half walked or if her father carried her here. It didn't matter. Sleep called to her with its siren song, and as she dipped under, she realized she still didn't know why Nick and her father were fighting.

CHAPTER TWENTY-FIVE

Nick couldn't go home. Instead, he drove to Jackson's, unsure why. He sat in his truck, lights off but key still in the ignition. He had decided to leave when Jackson appeared under the house, walking from the back patio. His hands were taped up, and he was shirtless, gleaming with sweat.

"Hey," he said with some surprise when Nick climbed out of the truck. "How's it going?"

Nick opened and closed his mouth, then shook his head, all he could manage. Jackson nodded, as though this answer made perfect sense to him.

"Want to go a few rounds with the heavy bag? Putting your fists on something—rather than someone—can help. Then, maybe we can talk?"

How did this man Nick barely knew understand him this well? *Probably because he's been through similar things.* Nick felt a slash of guilt thinking of what Jackson was currently dealing with, but then realized that's probably why he'd been drawn here. Maybe they could somehow help each other.

Wordlessly, Nick followed Jackson out back, where a lone light lit up the area with the punching bag hanging from its chain. Jackson helped him tape up his hands, then held out an arm as though holding open a door.

"Have at it," Jackson said with a small smile.

And Nick did. He went after the heavy bag as though it were the sum of all his fears, all his frustrations. He pounded his fists into it until he couldn't feel them anymore, couldn't feel the ache in his chest, couldn't feel anything at all. Gradually, a lightness lifted him. Endorphins, he knew logically. But also maybe something else. A whisper of comfort, the kind he only knew as coming from God. A solidarity with the dark-haired man who carefully watched in silence until Nick collapsed into the bag, hugging it as his forehead rested against it.

"I think I ruined the best thing that's ever happened to me," he said, finally. "And I don't even know how."

Jackson pressed a cold bottle of water into his hands. Nick didn't know where it came from and didn't question it. For all he knew, Jackson had gone upstairs at some point while Nick battled the bag.

"Want to walk or want to sit?"

Nick's arms had taken the brunt of his rage, but his legs felt spindly and uncertain. "Sit," he grunted.

When Jackson walked out toward the beach, Nick followed. Rather than sit on one of the wooden benches built into the beach, Jackson sank down on the sand at the edge of the dunes and Nick sat beside him. The tall dune grass whispered behind them while the ocean resounded with roars and the hiss of waves pulling back to the sea.

"My father had an affair too." Nick didn't know why this is where he chose to start. Jackson, clearly not expecting this, tensed beside him, then sighed.

"Do you hate yours as much as I hate mine?"

Nick had to consider this. His emotions had been surging all day, from the desire and the sense of peace and hope he'd felt with Amber so long ago as they danced and kissed, to the rage he felt when his mom announced Tom broke up with her.

Did he still hate his father?

Had he ever?

"No," he said finally. "I'm just really, really hurt." It had taken him this long to put voice to this, to connect with the truth of it. So obvious, really, but the truth of it had been too painful to face, until now. Until Nick had lost something even more precious to him.

Amber.

He didn't know that he'd lost her, not for sure, but it sure felt like it when she told him to go. And it was his own fault for once again letting his anger direct his steps.

"I've been carrying around this anger for so long. Hurt, anger, guilt—they make a really disgusting cocktail, but one I keep coming back to drink."

Jackson laughed then, and Nick could have been angry, but instead felt a strange sort of kinship. He drank deep from the water bottle Jackson had given him, until it was an empty husk in his hand.

"I hope I'll get to where you are," Jackson said. "For now, I can taste the anger. It's that thick." He leaned back on his arms, stretching his legs in front of him. "I could use a distraction from it, honestly. I've been wallowing. Want to tell me about what you ruined?"

The last thing Nick wanted to do was to admit that he'd gone in hot to Amber's house, screamed in her father's face. Especially when she came out and saw him like that. And did she have another migraine? She had looked terrible, so unlike the vibrant vision she had been, wrapped in his arms while they danced.

Sighing, Nick started from the beginning of their story, meeting at the bar, all the way up until he watched Amber's father shut the door in his face. It hurt to recount the moments, both pleasant and unpleasant, to strip himself bare under Jackson's scrutiny.

When he finished, Nick realized that he'd crushed the water bottle in his hand, not even hearing the crunch of the plastic.

"You know," Jackson said, his voice smooth and kind, "love isn't like the movies."

Nick snorted. Then he laughed outright. "No, it isn't."

Jackson shot him a lopsided grin. "The fight isn't against a dragon or another man. It's against something harder to battle."

He tapped his own chest, and Nick's laughter died.

"Before Jenna and I got married, someone told us that we should lower our expectations. They said we needed to realize that we were simply two imperfect people, marrying those imperfections together." Jackson shook his head. "Our marriage has been a joy, but I still know exactly what they meant now. You battle *yourself*. And when you're losing the battle, when you're giving in to your own selfishness and pride, then you battle the other person. Things get ugly."

The words rolled around in Nick's head, settling there the way deep truths did, resonating as though he already knew these things. As though he already understood them and simply hadn't had the language to put them into coherent thoughts.

"But what about Amber's father? He can't stand me. I don't know how this will help me there."

"It may not," Jackson admitted. "We can't change other

people. We can only work on ourselves. Thankfully, with God's help."

"So, I need to what—work on myself and then go beg for forgiveness?"

"I'm not sure what you need to do," Jackson said. "I don't know how you win over Amber's father, or if you can. But I do know that you can't give up. Not when it's something real. Maybe take a step back. Give it some time, then come back in swinging. In the good way."

Jackson turned back toward the sea, and neither of them spoke again, sitting in silence as the moonlight glinted fiercely over the never-tiring waves and their endless struggle against the shore.

CHAPTER TWENTY-SIX

Amber didn't know which was worse—the visceral pain in her body or the pain centering around her heart. One left her weak and vomiting, but the other left her devoid of hope. Truth be told, it was the loss of hope in Nick that hurt worse. The other pain? She almost welcomed the distraction.

The day after she had shown up at her father's house, he drove her to treatment and they moved her into a private room instead. She had a fever and some kind of viral infection. Hooked up to an IV of fluids rather than chemo, she gave in to sleep and delirium, a wet, rattling cough taking over her lungs. She thought days had passed but couldn't be sure.

She didn't ask about his work, didn't ask if Nick had come back, didn't ask about her own job. The sickness that had grabbed hold of her weakened body consumed any waking, lucid thoughts, which were few.

Once, when she woke but was too weak to open her eyes, she thought she heard her father and a doctor whispering about her lowered immunity, needing to build up her strength before they could begin the treatments again. Something about fever, white blood counts, and a transfusion. Whenever she was asked any direct questions, Amber simply nodded, too weak to argue or push for more details. Her father was here. He knew what she needed.

Ripley came to visit, Deondra and Phyllis too with a massive bunch of flowers, all wearing masks to prevent infection. Clearly, the secret was out. Her father had told the whole island about her diagnosis, it seemed.

Had he told Nick? Because he was the only person who didn't call, text, or come by. Eventually, her father admitted that he called the wedding off to focus on her treatment.

"It was a mistake anyway," he'd said, and though Amber had never been excited about her father's decision to remarry, she didn't like hearing about their breakup any more. She could imagine Linda's sweet face, losing its smile.

Was that why Nick had been so angry that night? Amber regretted not telling him everything before, not telling everyone everything. She needed all the help she could get, and wasn't too proud to admit it.

Once, she swore that she saw Linda, but that had probably been a hallucination. Jenna stopped by, telling Amber how much she wanted to bring Patty, but the doctors advised against it.

"Children are a cesspool of germs," Jenna had said apologetically. "But she misses you."

The thought of children was a clanging reminder that it was probably a good thing that Nick hadn't texted or called. If she even survived this, which she honestly wondered if she would, what kind of future could they have? It would be awkward anyway, with their parents' breakup hanging between them. She tried to tell herself that she never should have let herself fall for Nick, even as another part of her knew that she never could have stopped herself from falling, especially not if she couldn't stop how she felt now.

He was the only one she really longed to see. And he was the only one on the island, it seemed, who didn't stop by her room.

In a moment that felt like clarity but might have simply been fever, Amber wondered how she could find the will to fight this when her hope was tied up with the one man who stayed away.

Not for the first time that year, Amber wondered why God had given her so much to shoulder. But she wouldn't crumble under it.

She would be just fine.

"Knock knock."

The last person Amber expected to see poking their head around the door was Emily.

"Are you decent?"

Amber snorted. "Not particularly. Don't get too close. I'm not only contagious, but I think I smell."

"Perfect." Emily stepped into the room fully, shutting the door behind her.

"Nice mask," Amber said. Emily had drawn a lipstick mouth on the blue hospital mask covering the bottom half of her face.

"Thanks. Someone's got to keep their sense of humor around here. How are you?" Emily pulled a chair closer and sat down cross-legged.

"I'm fine."

Emily cocked an eyebrow. "No, you're not."

"I mean, I'm sick. And I have cancer." *And Nick left. And my mom is dead. And I'll never have kids.* She forced herself to shrug. "But I'm fine."

"You're really good at that."

Amber was starting to regret letting Emily in the room. "Good at what?"

"Lying to yourself."

Okay, now she really regretted letting Emily in. They hardly knew each other. And now, Emily was trying to act like she could read Amber's mind? Plus, who came into someone's hospital room and accused them of lying to themself?

Oh, right. *Emily* did.

"I'm not lying. Things suck right now. But I'm *fine*. I am."

"Want to know what I think?"

"I bet you'll tell me even if I don't."

Emily dropped her feet to the floor and leaned forward. "I wouldn't be saying this if I hadn't done this myself. You look to me like you've been running through life, stuffing all the bad stuff down where you don't have to look at it or feel it, then telling yourself and everyone else that you're fine."

Amber glared. "I've dealt with things."

"Have you? Because from where I'm sitting, you have a lot of things to deal with. Need me to list them?"

"No! I think I know what I'm dealing with. Better than you, that's for sure." Amber muttered that last part, though Emily could still hear every word.

Emily was just plain wrong. Amber had grieved her mother's death. And she'd had it out with her dad in the diner about his engagement. The cancer diagnosis had been a blow, but she was dealing with that too. And Nick … well. She had no idea what she was doing there.

"Have you gotten mad at God yet?" Emily studied her nails, like the conversation was boring her.

"Why would I get mad at God?"

Emily only blinked, slowly, several times. It infuriated

Amber. She debated pushing the nurse's call button and asking them to throw Emily out. Her head was starting to hurt.

"Why would I be angry?"

"Why wouldn't you be? With all you've been through, you should be furious. Raging at everything."

Amber clutched the rough hospital sheet in her hand, wishing she could tear it in two. "That's not … healthy."

"Ha!" Emily pointed a finger. "That's where you're wrong. Have you ever read the Psalms? David—who, as a reminder, is called a man after God's own heart—totally lets loose on God. He's furious, irate, and indignant. Asking God to break people's teeth, wondering why God isn't just. He questions everything."

Emily stood, then sat down on the edge of Amber's bed. Amber resisted the urge to shove her off. She doubted she had the strength.

"And then? By the end, God has changed him. His outlook shifts because he doesn't look away. He stares at the pain straight on, standing on the railroad tracks while the train hits him, full speed. Bam!"

She clapped her hands, and Amber jolted. She found her gaze drawn to the lipstick mouth on Emily's mask. An uncomfortable feeling began to worm its way through her.

"Can you tell me that you've done that? That you've faced down the things that have happened to you, *really* faced them?"

Amber's face felt warm, and it took her a moment to realize it was because hot tears were pouring down her face. "No," she admitted quietly.

Emily cupped a hand around her ear. "What's that? Can't hear you."

"NO! I haven't been angry. I haven't yelled at God or

thought he's unfair, no matter how terrible this year has been. What is the point? I can be angry all I want, but nothing will change. This is what he gave me. I can take it or not take it. The end. What do you want me to say?"

Amber practically felt out of breath from the shouting, which was more exertion than she'd given for days. She was suddenly limp and exhausted. But also … kind of relieved.

Emily began a slow, quiet clap. "That. *That's* what I wanted you to say. The truth about how you feel. It's a start. Do you know that I spent two years pretending I wasn't in love with Jimmy? I ran off to New York and ignored my feelings, just stuffed them down inside. I was fine too. Except I wasn't. And you're right—things may not change in your situation. Being honest, being angry—that doesn't change the circumstances, but it changes *you.*"

"What's going on in here?" Amber's dad strode into the room. "Did I hear yelling?"

"We're fine," Emily said.

Amber started to laugh. "No," she said. "No, we're not fine, Dad."

He glanced between the two of them, his eyes above his mask confused.

Amber squeezed Emily's hand. "We're not fine, but we will be."

CHAPTER TWENTY-SEVEN

Nick knew that taking a week off within a month of starting a new job wasn't the best course of action. Neither was ignoring phone calls, texts, and messages from anyone on Sandover, including his mother. But Nick needed the time.

He'd told his mother he wouldn't answer her calls or texts before he set out on the long and rambling drive to Atlanta, where his oldest brother, Bryan, let him crash on the couch, no questions asked. Well, *few* questions asked.

Jackson's words echoed in his mind the whole time, and Nick wrestled with them, feeling like Jacob in the Bible, wrestling 'til dawn until he could extract a promise from God. But what did Nick *want*, exactly? He didn't know what he was wrestling for, only that he felt like he was engaged in some kind of battle that would determine the rest of his future.

Bryan, having not set foot in a church in years, listened as Nick tried to summarize, but in the end held up his hands and told him, "This is outside my wheelhouse, bro. But my couch is yours as long as you need it."

Nick knew that Jackson, or even Jimmy or Beau or Cash would have more to say to him, and he questioned leaving Sandover. But sometimes, clarity came with space and distance.

At least, it had in the past. But by day four, Nick started to get twitchy and almost checked his voicemails. Something was niggling at him, but he ignored it, chalking it up to phone addiction, and how strange it was to not have a phone in his hand every few minutes, checking in with the world at large.

I need this break, he told himself. It felt like he was shoring up reserves for a battle. And maybe he was—the battle for Amber, the battle with himself and maybe partly against Amber's father.

But on day five or six—he'd partially lost count—Bryan walked in with a deep frown etched on his face. "You need to call Mom," he said.

Nick rolled his eyes. "I told her that I needed a break this week."

"No, dude. It's about your girlfriend."

And within moments of calling his mother, chilled to the bone by words like *cancer* and *infection* and *hospital*, Nick was out the door.

Some 600 miles and one speeding ticket later, Nick arrived at Sandover's only hospital, where he discovered that it wasn't so easy to just show up and demand to see a patient you weren't related to, especially after official visiting hours were over.

"Are you her brother?" the bored woman working at the desk asked. Clearly, this wasn't her first time dealing with someone like Nick.

He almost laughed. He almost explained that she was almost his stepsister, if their parents hadn't broken off their engagement.

"No, but I know she'll want to see me." He didn't actually know this, not after the mess he left behind. Not after she had hidden this from him and told him to go.

But he *hoped* she still wanted to see him, that she hadn't given up.

"I'm sorry. You'll have to wait until tomorrow."

Nick couldn't wait another day. Not another hour or minute.

"I'm going to be her fiancé," he said, with a confidence that surprised him. Especially given the fact that he'd essentially deserted Amber at a time when she needed him most. His guilt over that and his anger with her hiding this warred within him.

"Come on back when you're official," the woman said, her expression never changing. "Otherwise, you can come back tomorrow at nine."

For a brief moment, Nick thought about storming the doors behind the desk. But he knew that he would end up in the grasp of a security guard or maybe, at worst, taking a ride in the back of Cash's cop car. Instead, he dragged his hands through his hair and plopped down in an uncomfortable chair in the farthest corner from the desk. He needed space from the woman who was keeping him from Amber.

Logically, he knew that it was hospital policy, not the specific woman who happened to be behind the desk. But he'd abandoned any remaining logic somewhere around the North Carolina state line.

"I know that look."

Nick glanced up at an older woman who was knitting

what looked like a scarf a few seats away. "That's the look of a man desperately in love."

"Guilty as charged," Nick said wearily, his exhaustion over the nonstop drive and the emotional turmoil he felt suddenly hitting him full force.

"What are you going to do about it?"

Her voice and eyes were sharp, and Nick sat up a little straighter.

"What can I do? I'm not going to get kicked out of the hospital or arrested. I'll just wait." He crossed his arms over his chest.

She clucked her tongue. "I admire your steadfastness in staying here, when I'm sure you've got a more comfortable bed somewhere. But I'm deducting points for creativity."

Nick blinked at her, drawn to the movement of her hands, wrinkled and spotted with age but moving the knitting needles nimbly.

"You—what?"

Her brown eyes were smiling as they met his. "I think someone with your tenacity could find a way in there. If you really *wanted* to."

It was a challenge, and more than that, Nick wanted to be with Amber now. He didn't want to wait until the morning. Once he was behind the doors, it was just a matter of looking confidently like he belonged and finding her room. At some point, he also knew this would mean having to talk with Tom. He would deal with that when the time came. For now: he needed to get behind those doors.

"Any ideas?" Nick asked.

"Well, now. I have several. First of all, I could create a diversion, allowing you to get through the doors. That one's a little risky. You could also ply her with coffee or other drinks, which not only gets her on your good side, but means more bathroom breaks. She gets up; you go in."

"That's not bad," he said. It definitely mitigated the risk.

"Or," she said, doing some kind of more complicated loop with her yarn, "you could head around to the ER entrance. That place is hopping. You'd be able to slip through undetected a lot more easily."

Now, that was an idea. Because his job was essentially emergency personnel, Nick had spent some time in and out of ERs. Even on a smaller island like Sandover, those places tended to be busy, especially at night when a lot of regular doctor's offices and urgent care places were closed.

"Was it true, what you said about being her fiancé soon?"

Nick swallowed. "Hopefully, yes."

"You don't think she'll say yes?"

After the way he left things, maybe not. But that wasn't his biggest problem. "I'm not sure her father approves. In fact, I know he doesn't."

She made a humming sound. "Anything else?"

"I don't have a ring. Or a plan. I hadn't … we hadn't really talked about it. Things moved fast. And now she's sick." He swallowed. "Cancer."

Oh, how he *hated* that word.

"I'm sorry. I've lost a few friends to it. Walked some through it and out the other side. Puts things into perspective, doesn't it?"

Nick's leg began bouncing. He was eager to get over to the ER and try his luck at sneaking through security without getting busted. But he didn't feel like he could just desert this woman mid-conversation.

"It does." He started to get up, but she continued, and he resisted the urge to sigh as he sank back in the seat.

"Do you have a ring?"

"I wasn't planning to propose right now."

"And why not?"

Her question left him speechless. There were so many reasons why not. Specifically, her dad. And the fact that the last time he saw her, he made a fool of himself and then he left town without so much as a text. *While she was in the hospital with a virus and also cancer.* He couldn't just show up and get down on a knee.

Could he?

The woman sighed heavily and put her needles and yarn aside. She began digging through her purse, and Nick took the opportunity to stand.

"Thanks so much for—"

"Here." She thrust her hand at him, something glittering between her first finger and thumb.

Nick stared. It was a ring. "What?"

Rolling her eyes, she shook it at him. "Take it." When he did, she leaned back and clasped her hands in her lap. "That was mine. Nothing fancy, and definitely not in style. But it's an engagement ring."

Nick's breathing had stopped as he stared down at the ring. The band was gold, the diamond small. But it was an engagement ring.

"I can't take this," he said, holding it back out.

The woman shook her head, grinning as she wiggled her fingers. He noticed for the first time how swollen her knuckles were. "I can't wear rings anymore. I'm lucky I can do my knitting. My days of romance are behind me. My two granddaughters don't want it. One is already married and the other—well, let's just say it would be a miracle if she got married. Take it. Win your woman's father, then her. Get her something different later if you want to be flashier. It isn't much."

"It's ... amazing." Nick couldn't quite wrap his mind around the gift, which felt like so much more. "I don't know what to say."

"Say you're going to get your girl. And you're not going to keep letting things like hospital policy stop you." She clucked her tongue again and picked up her knitting.

Hugging would be awkward with the woman in her hospital chair. So he leaned down and gave her shoulder a soft squeeze. "Thank you," he said, his voice rumbly with emotion. "I'm Nick, by the way. What's your name? I should know this if I'm taking your ring."

"JoAnn. Nice to meet you, Nick." She waved a hand, giving him one last crinkly eyed smile. "Don't waste another minute, tiger."

Nick didn't plan to.

———

It only took sneaking through a few doors and hiding once in a bathroom stall from a security guard, but Nick made it to the wing where Amber was staying. He'd texted his mom for info, getting a room number, though she warned him that he needed to talk to Tom first.

Amber's dad was like the dragon, guarding the treasure. And Nick was ready to face him head-on.

He hadn't planned to do so by literally running into Tom, spilling hot coffee all down the front of them both.

"For the love of—oh. It's *you.*"

"I'm so sorry, sir," Nick said, already looking around for paper towels or napkins or something to mop up the floor. Both of their shirts were soaked and pretty much hopeless.

"Why are you here? How did you get back here?"

A nurse looked up from the nearby station, narrowing her

eyes. The last thing Nick needed was to get all the way here and get thrown out. Up ahead, he could see Amber's door.

"Could we talk, sir? Maybe in private."

Tom crossed his arms, crushing the cup in the process. "Right here is just fine."

Okay, then. Here goes. All the practiced speeches for this moment, the ones Nick had thought about while driving here from Atlanta flew out of his mind. He could only see Tom's anger and think about his own foolishness. He could only hope that he was enough.

"I love your daughter, sir."

Tom looked unimpressed. "You barely know her."

"That is true. We don't know much about each other. But from the moment we met, there was something different between us. I know she felt it too. It's unlikely, and it's not traditional, but I love Amber, and I'd like your permission to marry her."

That got a response. Not the one Nick was hoping for. Tom grabbed Nick by the shirt collar and dragged him into an empty waiting room just around the corner.

As soon as they were out of sight, Tom gave Nick a small shove and stepped back, as though he were afraid of what he might do if he didn't put distance between them. His hand crushed the coffee cup. Nick waited, hoping he could somehow get through to the man, who seemed slightly unhinged.

Not unlike how I felt when I found out Amber had cancer, he thought. The realization helped him have compassion for the man who stood in front of him, probably just as frightened to lose Amber as Nick was.

"My daughter has cancer," Tom said. "She is fighting a nasty infection, and she hasn't asked about you once."

Okay, that stung. But somehow, Nick didn't doubt that Amber wanted him there. He'd thought about this a lot as well on the drive, processing his anger with her for not telling him. He couldn't know for sure, but Nick suspected that she kept it from him because she didn't want him to feel obligated.

The reasons he now stood in front of Amber's dad were the furthest from obligation he could get.

"And where have you been?" Tom continued. "Why haven't you been here?"

"She didn't tell me, sir. I came the moment I heard. I was dealing with some things and went to stay with one of my brothers."

"Dealing with some things?"

Tom seemed to be gearing up for more of a fight with every word, which only made Nick deflate more. He was almost desperate to get through to this man, but didn't know what it would take.

"I was angry with you for breaking off the engagement with my mother. She was devastated. Maybe she mentioned how my father hurt her. I'm a little bit protective. I think you and I have that in common."

Tom's shoulders slumped. Nick took this as a good sign and continued.

"I know that I haven't given you much to admire about me. Mostly, you've seen my anger get the best of me in some heated moments. I have been working on my temper and how to deal with it. I'm a work in progress. But there's a lot in me you haven't seen. Things that Amber has. I believe that she and I could make each other very happy, and I'm willing to stake my future on it. I'd like your permission to ask her to marry me. I want to be with her through this, fully be with her, as her husband."

Tom sighed so deeply that Nick could almost feel the weariness. When he looked up, his eyes were wet.

"You're willing to commit to her, right now? To walk through this battle with her?"

"I am, sir."

"It's almost a sure thing that biological children will be an impossibility. Did you know that?"

The words sunk in, and Nick's breath hitched in his throat. But it only took a moment for him to process. He was surprised at how quickly he made up his mind and how sure he was about his answer.

"I didn't know. And I want kids, but they don't need to be biological for me to love them. I don't love Amber for what she can give me, children or otherwise. I love *her*."

That had a tear escaping his own eye. Nick didn't bother brushing it away. *Let him see*, he thought. *Let him see how much I love his daughter.*

But Tom didn't give in as quickly as Nick had hoped. Instead, his face hardened a bit.

"We'll see," he said, finally. "For now, I won't have them kick you out. But you can't see Amber yet. I'd like to consider this, and while I do, you wait."

Nick could work with that. It's not like he had planned to leave. Not now that he was so close. He would stay here in this waiting room, if that's what it took to show Amber's father he was serious. He wished Amber could know that he was here. He hated thinking that she felt deserted by him.

But as he sank into an uncomfortable waiting room chair, Nick saw Tom nod, something like respect in his eyes.

I'll wear him down, Nick thought. *And then, if I have to, I'll wear Amber down too.*

The only thing he wouldn't do was give up.

CHAPTER TWENTY-EIGHT

Amber didn't know how many days she had been in the hospital. If someone hadn't coined a term like hospital fog for how she felt, there really should be. Maybe she could look into trademarks whenever she made her great escape from this hospital bed.

But when she woke this time, her fever must have dropped because her skin didn't hurt and her eyeballs didn't feel like they were melting in her face. Light streamed through the window, but the brightness felt cold to her.

It highlighted the empty chair that nine times out of ten, held her father whenever she opened her eyes. Honestly, she was glad for a moment alone, just to breathe and assess. No one was taking her blood pressure or temperature or waking her up to ask how she was feeling. There was still a little port for the IV in her arm, but at the moment, it wasn't hooked up to anything.

Does that mean I'm better? I feel better. Ish.

Amber didn't feel normal, but then, she hadn't felt fully

like herself since the very first day she got sick. The day Nick took care of her.

She swallowed at that memory. Hard. And it hurt—her throat and the memory. She took a sip from the pink plastic water cup with a handle that was within arm's reach, sucking down cold water from the straw like it was going out of style, wishing that coolness could numb the pain in her heart.

Where had Nick disappeared to? Why had he been so angry with her father? His absence felt like a sinkhole in the very middle of her life. Impossible to ignore, and potentially ready to collapse even further at any moment taking who knows what else with it.

And the thing was, she couldn't just text him. Because if he asked how she was, Amber couldn't hide the fact that she was, in fact, pretty terrible. That she was now in a hospital bed. Then he would *have* to come back, *have* to respond, and only out of guilt. Nick was way too nice not to come back for her when she was sick. It was the cancer card, and she didn't want to play it. Plus, he had to already know by now.

Even if her father had broken off his engagement, which Amber really, really hoped wasn't because of her cancer, he still talked to Linda. She had heard him talking in low tones to her on the phone when he thought Amber was asleep. Once, Amber thought she heard Linda's voice in the hallway outside. If Linda knew, Nick knew.

So, why wasn't he here?

She still hadn't been able to get the story out of her dad, only a lock-jawed, hard-eyed expression and the equivalent of, *don't worry about it*. Amber wasn't worried about it.

Worry would be the wrong word. *Obsessed* was more accurate. *Destroyed. Confused. Crushed.*

And maybe because the breakthrough when she was

talking this over with Emily, Amber was feeling all the things. She was not anywhere close to fine.

Hospitals, she decided around the time she came up with the term hospital fog, were like prisons. Way too much time to just … think. The food was probably pretty similar too. Thankfully, there were enough differences between the two, at least, as far as she imagined, that she didn't have to worry about someone sharpening a toothbrush into a shiv.

When was the last time I brushed my teeth?

Amber was running her tongue over them, noting how soft and icky they felt, when her father walked inside the room, a funny look on his face, one she could read even behind the mask he wore. Amber had gotten to the point she wanted to rip the masks off people's faces. Until today, she hadn't had the strength.

"You're awake," he said, blinking in surprise. "And you look better."

Amber shuffled in place from hip to hip, feeling a soreness in her bottom and back that only came from being confined to this bed for so long. "What day is it? Do I have a toothbrush?"

She started to swing her legs over the side of the bed. Her father was right there, arms cupping hers gently, like she was a hollowed-out egg, ready to be dyed for Easter. Amber both loved and hated that feeling. Because it meant that she was breakable, and it also meant that he cared. So much.

"Easy there. Maybe I should call a nurse."

Amber rolled her eyes. "I don't need a nurse. I've gotten up to pee dozens of times this week."

Probably not enough times, but then, dehydration had been part of the problem they were dealing with. That and some punk virus she'd caught, and finally gotten over. Also?

Most of the time, she did have a nurse helping her shuffle to the bathroom.

Her father kept her in bed with the force of his gaze. "We need to see the doctor first. Just to check on your fever."

Amber slumped back into bed while her father pressed the call button. Thirty minutes later, the doctor had said that she had passed through the danger zone. Her fever had broken, and they could hopefully release her in the next day if she stayed stable.

"Now can I shower and brush my teeth?" she asked her father when the doctor left.

He helped her to her feet. "Let me help you get there. And don't fight me like I know you want to."

"Pfft. Me? Fight off perfectly good help? Please."

Her dad snorted, and she tried to make sure that the back of her gown was closed. No need to make things take an even deeper nosedive into awful. Amber was pretty much pitching a tent in what felt like her own personal hell as it was.

"Why did you look so weird?" Amber asked. "When you came in, you had this look—*that* look!"

It passed over his eyes again, something like guilt and maybe a little bit of something else she couldn't name. Oddly, she thought it looked like sadness one moment and hope the next.

"We'll talk when you get done."

"No way." Amber braced herself on the doorframe. She had little to no strength right now, but her father let her stop their forward progress. "When I get in there, I'm taking a shower, changing out of this sweat-soaked gown, and brushing my teeth."

"That's a very good idea."

Now, her father looked amused, and also like he knew something she didn't. It was the look he had on his face the one time he and her mother tried to throw her a surprise party. Amber figured it out hours beforehand because of that face. She stabbed a finger toward the center of his nose.

"What are you hiding, old man?"

"Just take your shower. You need it."

When Amber flashed him a look of mock outrage, black dots appeared at the edge of her vision, and she gave arguing with him a second thought. If she wanted to shower, she needed to do so before she passed out.

"Can you set my pajamas just inside the door once I'm in the shower?"

"Sure." He let her go as soon as she had a firm grip on the sink. "Amber? I owe you an apology."

She waved him away, feeling her energy wane a little more every moment. That shower was calling her name. "You're forgiven."

"No, I need to say this. I was wrong about Nick and wrong to try to warn you away from him."

The last name Amber wanted to hear right now was Nick's. Every time she thought about him, it was like peeling off a scab that was still too soft, exposing the raw, unhealed wound underneath. Nick was, for reasons she still didn't understand, gone.

"It's fine, Daddy. It doesn't matter anyway." Amber leaned against the sink, blinking away the darkness until she could see her father's eyes above the mask clearly. There was that look again. What was that about?

"Well, for what it's worth, I'm sorry. And I approve."

He closed the door on her next question. "Approve of what?"

If she'd had more energy, Amber would have chased after him, but as it was, she needed a shower and then, embarrassingly, to climb right back into bed. Was it too much to hope that a nurse might change the sheets while she was in the bathroom?

Thankfully, when Amber finished showering, brushing her teeth, and had changed into the pajamas her father had placed just inside the room as asked, her bed looked like it had been stripped and changed into new linens.

But she barely had time to take note of that. Because the room was dim, lit only by a whole bunch of candles. Candles she could hardly see, as the whole room was filled with flowers. Every surface and even the floor had big bunches of hydrangeas and peonies.

She clutched the doorframe to the bathroom, muttering, "What in the actual heck?"

"I hope you don't mind. Mom couldn't cancel the order, and they already had them in stock. Rushing the order wasn't such a big deal."

"Nick?"

He really was standing there. Near the door, in shadow and wearing a stupid mask, which hid half of the handsome face she had missed so much in however long she'd been there. As Amber made her way closer to him, she stumbled over a large arrangement of flowers near the empty IV pole. Instantly, Nick's hand grasped hers, and she felt more secure than she had in … well, maybe ever.

"Hey," she said. "You're here? With all this?"

His eyes crinkled, but she couldn't see his smile. "Sorry it's a little bit much. Mom couldn't cancel a lot of the orders for the wedding, and most places were more than happy to move dates around."

Her brain connected the dots as he was speaking. These weren't just peonies and hydrangeas. They were the arrangements Linda had picked. That's when she heard the faint strains of a string quartet. Her eyebrows shot up.

"I got special permission, but not for long. Enjoy it while it lasts. I'm sure someone higher up than the hopeless romantic at the desk on this floor will kick them out."

"Nick." Amber studied his face—what she could see of it —as though she hadn't seen him in years. It felt that way, though in all likelihood, it had been just a few days. "I don't need all this. I just wanted"—she had to clear her throat to get the next word out—"you."

His face softened, and then he was pulling down the face mask, revealing those full lips that she hadn't tasted nearly enough, and the smile that she wanted to see every day. "The doctor said it was okay now to see you without the masks. I asked before I came in. Anyway, I know. I shouldn't have left."

"You actually left Sandover?"

He nodded. "Just needed to think. I went to one of my brothers' houses after the fight with your dad."

Nick sighed heavily, and Amber swayed on her feet. His hand squeezed hers and his eyes shifted to concern.

"Let me help you sit."

Amber would have loved to wrap her arms around him instead of climbing into the hospital bed, her knees shaking, but she did as he asked. She really would collapse in a moment, and she'd done enough embarrassing things like that in front of him already.

Nick tucked the sheet around her legs, then smoothed her hair back from her face. It was wet, desperately in need of conditioner, not just a tiny bottle of hospital shampoo, and a blow dryer, but right now, Amber would take any touch from Nick.

"Better?" he asked, and Amber nodded. "Are you hungry? Your dad said you might want to eat."

Her stomach clenched from being mentioned, but Amber

ignored it. "You talked to my dad?" Her father's comments from earlier suddenly made a lot more sense.

"I did." Nick sat on the edge of her bed, taking both her hands in his. "I shouldn't have come in hot like that at your dad. It just confirmed a lot of what he already thought about me. He broke things off with my mom and—"

"He was the one who broke things off?"

Nick nodded, and Amber wanted to scream and shake her father. Nick must have seen the anger in her eyes because he held up a hand.

"Actually, turns out it's a good thing. He and Mom talked. They both agreed that they didn't take enough time. Which is surprising."

"Why surprising?"

Nick stood, the bed shifting as it lost his weight. "Because they both wholeheartedly approved of this."

He dropped to his knees, still holding one of her hands in his. The other slipped into his back pocket and came out with a ring. Amber blinked, then blinked again, wondering if maybe she hadn't woken up and taken a shower at all. Maybe this was just a lovely, cruel dream that she would wake from any minute now. She bit her lip, hard, thinking this might work to wake her up.

Nope. Nick still knelt on the floor, staring up at her with a grin that she wanted to kiss right off his face.

"My dad said okay?" She'd heard her father's words earlier, how he said he'd approved. It made sense now, but she still needed to hear it. Probably because the last time Nick and her father were together, they looked like they would come to blows.

"He did. We've made a lot of progress the last few days. I've been camped out in the hospital since I got back. But I'd rather talk about you and me right now. Not our parents."

Amber nodded enthusiastically. "Yes. Enough about them."

Nick chuckled. "Amber. Bram." He drew in a breath, his eyes tracing her face, like he was cataloguing every feature. "I know that we haven't known each other long. But you and I feel *right*. I don't have doubts. Even in spite of all the reasons we shouldn't. Even if we don't have biological children."

The words hit Amber like a solid smack. He knew. Nick knew. Every time she had to think about this reality, she mourned a little bit. Talking to Emily forced her to let herself feel the things she was feeling rather than stuff them down. It hurt to process, but when she let herself feel and work through things, she really did know that she would be fine.

Especially now—now that the one person she wanted more than anything was here.

"Even though I think we have a lot of work and growing to do. I would rather do that together, now, as we're building a relationship rather than waiting."

Amber held up a hand. "I hate to interrupt you, especially because I love what you're saying. But, I'm so sorry I lied to you about this." She waved her hand around the hospital room and down her body. "I shouldn't have kept it from you. I just didn't want it to be the reason you stayed."

Nick shook his head. "I understand, and it isn't. Though, I'll admit, it's part of the reason asking you this doesn't feel as crazy."

"Asking me what?" Amber asked.

His grin widened, and Amber loved that he felt as sure as he said, not doubting the fact that this was right. She felt it too, deep in her bones, like a truth resonating.

"Amber, will you do me the great honor of being my bride?"

She was nodding before he finished and sniffing as she cried, "Yes!"

Nick practically threw himself at her, but with care, as though he knew exactly how much of a hug she could take. Amber relished in the scent of him, the feel of his warm body next to hers as she let her tears wet his shirt.

"I love you, Amber."

"I love you too."

And then the room was louder, the door open and the string quartet launching into a jaunty version of "Here Comes the Bride" before someone in the hallway started shouting for them to leave.

Amber's father was there and Linda, holding out what looked to be a small wedding cake, surrounded by a few of the nurses and familiar hospital staff. She didn't know whether she was laughing or crying when Nick surprised her with a kiss. Soft and sweet and over much too soon as he pressed his forehead to hers.

"I okayed this with him too. Had to get my temp taken and some blood drawn to check my white blood cells, but hey! You're worth it. Oh, and this?" He tapped her arm, near the vein where she still had the IV port. "The blood going around in you is partly mine," he said proudly. "We're a match. I made some directed donations. I thought maybe if you had some of me running through your veins, you would be more likely to say yes."

"There wasn't a chance I would say no," Amber said, kissing him a little less soft and sweet. He was grinning when she pulled away, touching a finger to his lips. "My answer would have always been yes."

Amber couldn't have asked for better weather, especially not in November, which could bring nor'easters or icy weather. Now, as her bare feet met the sand, she squeezed her father's arm and gave a quick prayer of thanks for a warm, almost balmy late afternoon.

Even the wind seemed subdued, a caress rather than a gusty gale. It shifted the strands of the shoulder-length, blonde wig around her bare shoulders. She didn't know if she would ever get used to the feeling of the manufactured hair on her skin. Hopefully, she wouldn't have to know for much longer. Her first round of chemo had finished earlier this week, and Dr. Espana was pleased, and Amber wanted to let herself be hopeful.

Over the roar of the waves, Amber heard the strains of Mercer's guitar and the beautiful lilt of her voice.

"Are you ready?"

Her father looked happier than Amber had seen him in months. She could only nod. The only thing missing was her mother, and Amber wished more than anything that she could be there. She spent time weeping and a little bit of time wailing about that earlier in the week. Emily had been so right—getting the emotions out and being fully honest with herself and with God, if not a few good friends, really did help. Even if it didn't change the reality.

"I miss her too. But she would be so proud. And she would have approved of Nick. Much faster than I did."

Her father pressed a kiss to her forehead, and they began to walk toward the sound of Mercer's song.

The aisle was lined with shells and candles, with a few dozen of their closest friends and family standing in front of white, wooden folding chairs. But Amber didn't look at their faces or any of the details she and Ripley had put together over the past few weeks.

Amber only saw Nick and the broad grin aimed her way, the glisten of tears in his eyes. She saw her future—however long it would be.

The walk seemed to take a year and no time at all, much like their relationship. It started with a kiss in a bar, and now they were about to recite wedding vows. And Amber's only doubts since Nick slipped the ring on her finger, one he apparently was gifted from someone in the hospital waiting room, revolved around her sickness.

"I'm a wild card," she had told Nick. "If you marry me, you don't know what you're getting."

He had silenced her with a kiss and a smile any time she brought it up. "Hey, what's that they say? Sickness and health? We're just getting some of the sickness out of the way early. It wouldn't be like us if we did things in order."

No, it wouldn't, Amber thought as she and her father reached the front of the aisle where Nick stood. But she prayed every day that 'til death do them part wouldn't come early for them, for *her*.

Her own tears started the moment her father embraced Nick. The two men had their own quick shift—from dislike and distrust to something that almost resembled a father and son. She couldn't make out what her father whispered in Nick's ear, but it probably wasn't a death threat, because Nick smiled and nodded.

Amber's heart seemed to still in her chest as her father stepped away and Nick took her hand. His cool blue eyes were warm for her. His brilliant smile was all hers. And within a few minutes, they would belong completely and officially to one another. Nick squeezed her fingers, and together, they stepped forward side by side.

————

The wedding had all but ended. Rather than have a big send-off, the way Amber and Nick had spoken about only weeks ago under this very same house and the very same lights, they had chosen to ride the night out with their closest friends, saying goodbyes to friends and family as they left little by little.

They had pulled the chairs around a small stone fire pit. The temperature had dropped a little, and Amber felt colder than she usually did. Probably another chemo side effect. Everything seemed to be a side effect. What would she blame when she was in remission?

But snuggled up in Nick's lap, his suit coat draped over her shoulders, she didn't mind the chill. It was probably time to head back to her apartment, where they'd be living as the renovations on Nick's cottage—their cottage—were finished. But Amber didn't feel quite ready to leave the circle of friends.

Ripley and Cash, Beau and Mercer, Jackson and Jenna—

they all sat around the fire together, riding out the best night of Amber's life. Emily and Jimmy had disappeared a little while ago—probably making out in a dark corner. But they said they'd be back.

Amber yawned, and Nick squeezed his arms tighter around her waist, pressing a kiss to her neck. He would probably have to carry her up the stairs, but she didn't mind. He probably didn't either.

"I've got some news," Beau said, grasping Mercer's hand in his. "We've got some news."

Amber braced herself for a pregnancy announcement. She was working through her grief over not being able to have biological children. One day it might not sting to hear about pregnancies, but for now, it did. Even if she could be happy for people as she grieved her own loss.

"We're moving."

Silence stunned the group, and Mercer leaned forward. "Temporarily. Beau is going to seminary—then, God willing, we'll be back."

"From fireman to pastor," Jackson said with a smile. "I can see that."

Amber could see it too. But it was hard to imagine Beau not being here, even for a little while. "How long will it be?"

Beau shrugged. "It depends on the degree. But probably two to three years. I'll be in Charlotte, so you'll have to come visit."

"I'll have to get you together with my brothers. Maybe you can straighten them out," Nick said. "Though I'm not sure it's possible."

"I met them earlier tonight," Beau said, grinning. "You might be right."

Emily and Jimmy reappeared, both of them laughing, both

of them wearing hats. Jimmy carried a plastic grocery bag. "We brought supplies for s'mores!"

Despite the wedding cake, s'mores sounded delicious. Cash hunted around in the bushes, coming up with a few dry sticks that they shared, passing them around until everyone had sticky fingers and hands. Nick kissed the corner of Amber's mouth, letting his lips linger, reminding her of the night he kissed chocolate off her chin.

Even the smallest touches from him elicited a fire in her. Maybe it was time to start thinking about heading home.

"And ... one more surprise," Emily said, looking at Amber with a wicked grin on her face. "We did a thing."

Jimmy shook his head, chuckling. "Yes, we did."

"Should I be scared?" Amber asked.

"Nope." Emily whipped off her ball cap, Jimmy right after.

Amber gasped. She wasn't the only one. Both Jimmy and Emily had shaved their heads.

"You—what! Why?" Amber sputtered.

Emily ran a hand over her own head. "I know you're rocking the wigs but consider this solidarity. And selfishly, I always wanted to see if I could pull off this look."

Jimmy kissed her cheek. "You can pull off any look, Em."

It was true. The lack of hair somehow just accentuated the bone structure in her face. She looked strikingly beautiful, and somehow more intense than before. Amber sighed as the depth of the gesture hit her right in the chest. Things had been awkward with Emily for eighteen months. And now ... Emily shaved her head for *her*. It was so ... much. Too much. But, she was beginning to realize, that's who Emily was. Too much, in the best way possible.

"Thank you," Amber said, trying not to cry. Emily only winked, and Jimmy gave her a friendly smile.

Nick pressed a kiss to Amber's cheek. "Want me to shave my head?" he whispered.

"Heck, no!" she whispered back, earning her another brush of his lips, this time on her mouth.

"I hate you, Em," Ripley said. "Both because you look good, and because you're going to have a shaved head in all my wedding photos."

"Oops," Emily said. "I wasn't thinking about that. Hey, Amber—can I borrow a wig?"

"Anytime. But you actually look amazing. I, on the other hand, do not like this look for me," said Amber.

"As long as Jimmy likes it," Emily said, turning to her husband.

He grinned. "You still look hot, Em. Though I'll be glad when it grows back. I like running my fingers through it," Jimmy said.

Emily glowered. "Well, now you can rub it for good luck."

Jimmy rubbed her head and pretended to make a wish. She laughed and swatted his hands. Then he picked her up and settled her in his lap with another kiss.

"You didn't need to do that, but thank you, guys. It means a lot. The rest of you are off the hook," Amber said.

They all laughed, and conversation continued easily as the stars winked overhead. The breeze picked up, and Amber shivered, yawning again.

Nick and Amber exchanged looks. "You thinking what I'm thinking?" he asked, nuzzling her neck.

"I don't know exactly what you're thinking, but I have a pretty good idea," Amber said. "And yes."

Making it feel effortless, Nick stood, holding Amber in his arms. "Well, folks, it's about that time. This has been wonderful. Thank you for coming and goodnight."

With that, he started marching away. Amber called over his shoulder, "Goodbye from me too!"

Their friends stood from their chairs, Emily standing in a chair, cheering and whooping and clapping. Nick gave a little bow as they reached the edge of the patio, dipping Amber so low to the ground that she squealed.

With a grin, he kissed the sound away. "I love you, Amber," he said against her lips. "And I'm ready to start the rest of forever with you."

"Well, let's get started on our forever," Amber said, tracing his lips with a finger.

As he walked them to his car, cradling her to his chest, Amber could only hope and pray that their forever would be a long, long time.

———

almost two and a half years later

On time is a laughable idea when you had an infant, Amber thought as she unbuckled the car seat and attempted to transfer a sleeping Olivia into her arms.

This was one of the—but not the only—big takeaways Amber had since the case worker brought Olivia to them a month before. The others related to things like sleep or the lack thereof, the ridiculous notion of letting a baby cry it out, and the well-kept secret that a baby's head is the best smell in the world.

She took a good sniff as she carefully shifted her weight, managing to get Olivia nestled on her shoulder. Almost immediately, the baby swiveled her head, which at three months was still a little wobbly, and aimed a massive, gummy smile at Amber.

"You stinker," Amber said, but she was smiling.

Through tears, of course, because everything made her cry these days. Especially the idea that she and Nick might not get to keep this perfect baby girl. But that's the choice they had made choosing to foster to adopt. And if they had to reunite Olivia with the mother who had left her so neglected … well, Amber would rage and cry and pray, for Olivia and for herself. She and Nick would be able to get through it. They had before, five times now. Each time harder than the last, and their list of children to pray for just kept growing.

"I told you to let me get her out," Nick said, but he was smiling too as Olivia yanked a fistful of Amber's hair.

"Like you would have done any better," Amber said, nuzzling her nose against Olivia's. The little girl squealed and managed to drool on Amber's chin. Nick wiped it away with his thumb and pressed a kiss to each of their cheeks.

"My girls," he said, and Amber's tears really threatened.

"Don't start," Nick warned.

"I'm trying not to!"

"I know." He wrapped an arm around them both and started to steer them toward the beach. "Let's get out there before we miss Beau and Mercer's whole welcome-home party."

Linda intercepted them before they had even passed underneath Jackson's house. Her smile was huge and she held out her arms. Nick stepped into them, hugging her, even as she swatted him away and moved toward Amber.

"Good to see you too, Mom," Nick teased.

"I see you all the time. Pass that little bundle over," she said, and with a reluctant sigh, Amber did.

Linda snuggled Olivia to her chest and started toward the

beach, Nick and Amber following behind. "Well, that's the last time we'll see her for a while," he said. "Mom is such a baby hog."

"Can you blame her? If it wasn't for Beau and Mercer, I wouldn't be here. I'd be snuggling a baby at home alone." Nick poked her side, and she giggled. "Alone with *you*, of course."

Home was not the little cottage on the end of the island, not anymore. Because of Nick's investments and the ones he managed for Jill, Jackson, and a few others, they were able to keep it, letting it pay for itself through rentals.

The house they lived in now, much more suitable for the big family they wanted and for the home assessment. It was only a street away from the ranch they had looked at a few years ago. Amber smiled every time she passed by, remembering those early days with Nick.

Her life had come full circle in so many ways. *Good ways,* she thought, watching her father kiss Olivia and then Linda on the cheek. After the drama of their broken engagement, he and Linda had become good friends, gradually easing into love—again or for the first time, Amber wasn't even sure if *they* knew.

The second time around, things had been much smoother, and it was a lot more fun to joke about being stepsiblings now. Tom and Linda's marriage (which Amber pawned off on Ripley this time around) also really did make things like holidays easier.

And both of their parents had been incredible with the fostering. Nick and Amber would take all the support offered by their little community. So far, Nick and Amber had fostered two infants, a toddler, and two pre-teens, some alone and some at the same time.

Every single child had been a blessing and a challenge.

Amber wouldn't change a thing. Except … she didn't know if she would be able to handle losing Olivia. Reuniting the children with their parents was the ultimate goal when possible, but something about this little girl had captured Amber and Nick's hearts from the moment they met her.

"There's the man of the hour," Nick said, clapping a hand on Beau's shoulder.

Beau would be finishing the rest of the seminary degree online through a satellite program here while working as the assistant pastor at their church. Apparently, he and Mercer had enough of being away from Sandover. Based on the number of people mingling on the beach in front of Jackson's, the feeling was very mutual.

Amber stepped away so they could do one of those big bro-y hugs with the back slapping. It looked like Nick and Beau were grappling to see who could lift the other off his feet first. *Just like old times.*

"Break it up you two." Jimmy appeared, and then it turned into a wrestling match of three.

"Think they'll be doing this when they're eighty?" Emily asked, appearing next to Amber. She lifted her phone and took a video.

"They'll be playing a version of bumper cars with their walkers."

Emily shorted. "I can see it. Where's my Livvie?"

"Linda has her."

Emily groaned. "No fair. I can easily force most people to hand her over by giving them the evil eye. But your mom in law has a trump card. I'll never pry her away."

"I'll make sure you get a turn. She needs to eat in a bit, and I'll hand her to you when I'm done."

Emily clapped her hands. "Thanks! If I'm not going to have kids, I need to be the best auntie ever."

Amber kept her mouth shut. Emily had somehow convinced herself that she'd be the worst mother ever, maybe because her own mom was an awful human. Amber had stopped trying to talk Emily through that ill logic. Somehow, when it came to this, the confident, unshakable Emily completely doubted herself.

"Amber!" Beau said, giving her a one-armed hug after breaking away from the guys. "It's so good to see you!"

"I'm really glad you're back for good. And congrats on the job!"

Nick slid his arm around Amber's waist. "Now that you'll be all official as an assistant pastor, does that mean you have to be stuffy and serious? No more surfing, no more fun?" he teased. "Or do you only get boring when you've officially finished with your degree and have your fancy doctor title?"

Beau crossed his arms and raised a brow, looking at Amber. "Do you care how wet he gets?"

Amber grinned, even as Nick started to back away. "Nope."

Before Nick could escape, Jimmy grabbed him from behind, and together, he and Beau tossed Nick into the ocean, fully clothed. There was a round of applause from the crowd of friends and family on the beach. It grew to cheers when Nick tackled Beau and he went under as well. Then they both came for Jimmy. Tony, Beau and Mercer's dog barked and chased the guys along the shoreline.

"Not much has changed since I've been gone," Mercer said, appearing by Amber's side.

Amber threw her arms around Mercer. They hadn't been the closest friends when Beau and Mercer left for seminary, but their friendship had budded over email and text. "I'm so happy you're back to stay!"

"Me too," Mercer said. "Though I'll admit I'm a little

nervous being a pastor's wife. That's a title with so much pressure." She made a face.

"Just be yourself. You don't need to fit into some neat box of what people think a pastor's wife should be. I think as long as you sing from time to time, it will all be forgiven."

Mercer smiled, and they watched as Beau and Nick ganged up on Jimmy, who tried to use Emily as a human shield. With an eye roll, Emily swept Jimmy's legs out from under him with some kind of kick.

"Whoa," Amber said.

"She took self defense after … after everything that happened," Mercer said, her gaze going hazy for a moment.

Amber didn't know the full details because Mercer didn't like to talk about it, but her abusive ex had followed her here years ago and attacked Emily and Mercer in their apartment.

Linda appeared by Amber's side with a grunting Olivia. "I think someone's getting hungry," Linda said. "Do you have a bottle?"

"Nick has the diaper bag. Or, he did. I'll take her."

Amber held out her hands, feeling that sense of rightness once more as she settled Olivia against her. It was moments like these that she had to remind herself of the possible outcomes. Not that she wanted to hold back any of her heart from this baby, but she had to remember that at any moment, Olivia could be gone. Their placements so far had stretched from as short as two weeks to as long as three months. But none so far has moved into a situation allowing for adoption. Amber wanted to celebrate that the children were reunited with their parents, but it was bittersweet.

"She's beautiful," Mercer said, letting Olivia wrap a chubby fist around a finger. When Olivia tried to drag that finger into her mouth, Amber and Mercer laughed.

"Guess I better find that diaper bag."

A few minutes later, Amber had settled into one of the rockers on the top balcony of the house, having made a bottle in Jackson and Jenna's kitchen. Their sink was also strewn with bottles, a handful of pacifiers, and parts of a breast pump. Jenna and Jackson's second daughter had been born a few weeks before. According to Jackson, Jenna and Laura were asleep in the master bedroom.

"Nights aren't going well," Jackson had said with a grimace as he encouraged Amber to head upstairs a few minutes ago.

Amber knew the feeling. And as zombie-like as she felt most days, she also loved the quiet moments in the middle of the night when it was just her and Olivia, and sometimes Nick, who didn't like to be left out.

For a few moments, Amber rocked, watching the activity below as the late-spring afternoon faded into evening. The only sounds were the waves, her friends and family, and the baby's noisy swallows of formula. Other than Ripley and Cash, who had gone to Asheville to celebrate his half brother's birthday in Asheville, everyone she loved most in the world was down on that beach.

These were her people. This was her place. Even growing up here, Amber had never felt the sense of home that she did now with Nick. And Olivia.

"Mind if I join you?" Jenna settled into the rocker next to Amber.

"Of course not! Also, it's your house," Amber said with a laugh. "Jackson said it would be okay. Liv can't focus on eating with all the people."

Jenna dropped her voice to a whisper. "Of course it's fine. Will I bother her?"

Amber shook her head. "Nope. She's in the zone."

"Good. I'm not ready for public consumption yet," Jenna

said, wrinkling her nose. "I need at least four hours in a row of sleep first."

Jenna did look worn out. Her hair escaped everywhere from it's messy bun and the circles under her eyes had circles.

Probably about how I look, Amber thought.

"Totally worth it though, right?" Jenna asked, taking down her hair only to tie it up again.

Amber stared down at Olivia's plump cheeks. "Totally."

Her phone began buzzing in her back pocket, and Amber shifted to slide it out. The number on the screen was the only one with the power to make her muscles seize up. Her caseworker.

She never got used to these calls. There were monthly check-ups and surprise home visits, but the calls were often about giving back whatever child she and Nick had been caring for, growing attached to, falling in love with.

Amber didn't know if she could handle that kind of call today. Her hand trembled.

"Need me to hold her?" Jenna asked.

"Would you mind?" Amber's voice came out all choked, and Jenna gave her a tight smile, as though she knew exactly what the phone call meant.

Amber didn't manage to answer the call as she shifted Olivia over to Jenna's arms. She clutched the phone as she climbed the short flight of steps up to the crow's nest room at the top of the house. Once seated, she called Becky back.

"Hey," Becky said in a careful voice that made Amber's stomach drop. "How's it going?"

Amber sighed. "Fine. Is it Olivia's mother? Just tell me. I can't—"

Amber's voice broke before she could finish her sentence.

She kept the phone to her ear but pressed a hand over her mouth, trying to hold back the sobs.

"Hey, now. You don't even know why I'm calling. It is Olivia's mom, but not how you're thinking. She relinquished her parental rights."

Those words, and all of the next ones about the sudden decision and the adoption process and all the official things Amber had only heard about up until now flew through Amber's brain as she silently wept with joy.

It would take time, and there were possibilities that it could go south, but Olivia could be *theirs*.

"I have to tell Nick," Amber said, when Becky had finished the litany of next steps.

"You do that. I'm so happy for you guys," Becky said. "I'll walk you through all of this. Hopefully, things will go smoothly, and you'll be officially her parents in a few months."

They hung up, and Amber stood for a moment in the room alone, just breathing and whispering quiet prayers of thanks. On one side, the ocean stretched out to the horizon in a deep blue-green sweep. On the other, the calmer, bluer waters of the sound reached out to the mainland miles away. Somewhere below were all the people she loved most in the world, and the baby who would soon officially be hers. Olivia would be *their daughter*.

With that thought in mind, Amber gathered up a smiling Olivia and went in search of the other person in their little, perfect, hopefully *forever* family.

———

Dearest reader,

Thank you for going on this journey with me to Sandover Island! Even though it's not a real place (I based a lot of it on memories of Nag's Head from my childhood), it FEELS real to me. So do its people.

Which makes this book a bittersweet ending of sorts.

I knew I wanted to write stories taking place in a small beach town, but really was inspired as I got stuck in an elevator in a home a lot like Jackson's. I made some good friends while we sweated in the small space, was rescued by firemen, and it just HAD to go in the story. (Jenna and Jackson's elevator incident was much more romantic ...)

I hoped you loved this installment with Nick and Amber! They were (mostly) new characters, with Amber only showing up a little bit in a few books. One of my readers mentioned not liking how Jimmy treated her in Sandover Beach Week, and I agreed. I loved having her get folded back into the group in this book. Amber was named after one of my friends from alllll the way back in middle school, and Nick was another friend from that time who passed away a few years ago. He was memorable enough to need a spot in a book.

I'd like to imagine that years in the future, fictional Nick and Amber are still together, going strong and cancer free, with a whole host of kiddos they fostered and adopted.

If you want to keep reading, you might love *Secrets Whispered from the Sea*, which is more of a women's fiction novel. It features Clementine, the granddaughter of JoAnn, the woman who gave her wedding ring to Nick. While the focus is a lot on Clementine's growth, there is a strong romantic subplot with an enemies to lovers trope going on. You'll also see more of favorite characters like Jackson and Emily.

At some point, I'd like to write the follow-up story to *Secrets Whispered from the Sea*, but I'm not sure when.

Need more books to read?

If you like humor, you might love my Love Cliches series, romcoms following five besties as they navigate the dating world.

If you want books that are a little more like Sandover, check out my Hometown Heartthrobs. *Marrying Her Dream Groom* has some plot similarities with cancer factoring in. Ever since my mom-in-law died of cancer, I've found that it creeps into my stories sometimes.

Thank you SO MUCH for being a reader! I would write even if y'all didn't read… but it's totally rewarding to know you're out there.

-e

ABOUT EMMA

Emma St. Clair is a *USA Today* bestselling author of over twenty books. She loves sweet love stories and characters with a lot of sass. Her stories range from rom-com to women's fiction and all will have humor, heart, and nothing that's going to make you need to hide your Kindle from the kids. ;)

You can find out more at:
http://emmastclair.com
Join her email list:
https://emmastclair.com/romcomemail
Or join her reader group at:
https://www.facebook.com/groups/emmastclair/

ACKNOWLEDGMENTS

A massive thank you to Jenny Proctor of Midnight Owl Editors for reading this at 85% done and giving me feedback to make it better!

Thanks to Judy of Judy's Proofreading for finding all my errors and having great suggestions.

To Evelyn of Carpe Librum Designs, your covers MADE this series.

Dude. No one has the kind of ARC readers I do. You just don't. Sorry. To my ARCs— THANK YOU!

Stephanie, this book wouldn't have the ending it does without you. For real. Huge heart eye emojis everywhere.

Emily, thanks for letting me use half the names from your family and also talking me through foster care stuff! Let's get tacos.

Thanks also to Teresa, Judy, Marsha, Ruth, Patty, Sandy, Valerie, and all of you who waited and begged and hoped for this last series.

from A Full Accounting of My Mistakes and Failures

#37 - Never try on a dress that's too tight in a dressing room by yourself.

#38 - Always carry a pair of sewing scissors in your purse. (see #37)

#39 - Don't forget to remove the scissors from your purse before flying.

#40 - If you don't remove them, do not make jokes with the TSA agents about using your sewing scissors as weapons.

#41 - Always have your lawyer's number in your phone. (see #40)

CHAPTER ONE

No one who knew me well—which was a pretty limited circle —would call me a superstitious person. But not believing in bad luck didn't stop bad things from happening to me in threes. At least, not today.

As I stumbled to the elevator, precariously balancing the box of things I just cleared off my desk and the cardboard trifold I had used for my last-ever presentation here, I heard my sister's ringtone. That could not be good. Because I'd lost my job, and my boyfriend broke up with me that morning. Before I'd even finished my first cup of coffee, which made it particularly rude.

I ignored the phone. Mostly because I had no free hands. But I also didn't want to know why Ann was calling. I really, really didn't.

So, I shoved my way into the crowded elevator, pretending I didn't hear "Ding Dong the Witch Is Dead" from the *Wizard of Oz,* Ann's personalized ringtone. I usually let my voicemail run interference when she called, which was, on average, three times a year.

"Aren't you going to get that?" asked a silver-haired man wearing a suit and Stetson.

Though I had moved to Texas for my now-former job two years ago, I still hadn't gotten used to this look, which I thought of as Business Cowboy. There were a few variations, but most included a suit paired with a cowboy hat and boots. Sometimes one of those bolos instead of a tie, and a belt with a big buckle. This guy had the full look going on, from bolo to boots.

He probably also had a concealed handgun under his jacket. Because: Texas.

I half-heartedly lifted my box and presentation board, almost dropping both in the process. "Kinda got my hands full."

"Aw, I'm glad to help." And just like that, Mr. Business Cowboy plucked the things out of my hands like they were nothing.

That's another thing that still surprised me about Texas. I grew up in North Carolina, which was definitely *southern*. There were manners. People were friendly. But they had nothing on Texas hospitality. Just like everything else in this state, it truly was bigger.

"Uh, thanks." The ringing stopped, and for a moment, I thought I was saved. Before I could grab my things, it started again.

Mr. Business Cowboy cleared his throat and nodded to my purse. "Your phone?"

"Right."

Could this elevator move any faster? It seemed to be stopping on every floor.

I managed to locate my phone and saw the picture of Ann's twin girls on the screen. I took it the last time I'd visited them, almost a year ago. I bet they were so much bigger now.

"Hello?" I tried to keep my voice low, not like I could keep the whole elevator from overhearing.

"I've been calling you," Ann said in that shrill voice that always made me want to cover my ears.

"I had a presentation." I didn't mention the fired part.

Ann was on a need-to-know basis with the details of my life. And she did *not* need to know that. She didn't understand digital marketing and thought that I spent all day scrolling through Twitter, not helping create ad campaigns for big brands.

"Nana died, Clementine."

She said it like an accusation, not a statement. As though my not answering the phone on the first ring somehow contributed to the situation. Maybe because of her tone, it took another two floors for her words to really hit me.

Nana died.

The elevator dinged. We had reached the lobby. Everyone filed off around me, while I stood there, holding the phone up to my ear.

I did not move. Not when new people got on and started pressing buttons. Not when Mr. Business Cowboy realized I hadn't gotten off and shouted "Hey!" just before the doors slid closed.

Ann continued on about the details, which I half heard: a stroke, no warning, no suffering. I gripped the phone like a lifeline, though what I really wanted to do was throw it against the wall. People got on and off at different floors as silent tears streamed down my face.

When I had ridden the elevator all the way up and then back down to the lobby again, I hung up on Ann, who was saying something about the reading of the will and the viewing.

One, two, three. Whether I believed in bad luck or not, in one morning I had lost my boyfriend, my job, and the only member of the family who ever made me feel loved.

Mr. Business Cowboy had my things near the revolving door in the lobby. Picking up the box, I tucked my failed presentation behind the nearest trash can. I stepped outside, fully expecting a piano to drop on my head.

When the only thing that hit me was the humid heat of Houston in late March, I made my way to the parking garage, ignoring my phone as it continued to ring and ring in my purse.

———

It was shockingly easy to dismantle the life I had built here for the past two years. The job and boyfriend were already taken care of. My fridge was perpetually empty, save for a shelf of mostly expired condiments and some cheese sticks. I left them, along with my cheap IKEA furniture. The apartment manager was surprised but happy to take a wad of cash to dispose of anything I left in the apartment. So happy, in fact, that I likely overpaid her.

My lazy orange cat was more than happy to move to the apartment next door. He already spent half his time there anyway. Whenever I had let him out, he made a beeline for Ms. Hill's apartment. Ollie, the big traitor, often came home smelling of tuna.

"Are you sure?" Ms. Hill asked, already hugging Ollie to her chest, his orange and white stripes contrasting with her pink floral nightdress.

"I'm sure. Family stuff, you know." I waved a hand, not willing to share any more than that.

She clucked her tongue in understanding but was already shuffling back into her apartment with Ollie, whose purr rivaled the sound of a car motor. I shouldn't have felt as rejected by my cat as I had by my boyfriend. But there it was.

"I'll miss you too," I muttered.

And then it was just me, a few rolling suitcases, and my grief.

———

Read more here! GET SECRETS WHISPERED FROM THE SEA!